A LIGHT WITHIN

Dana Alexander

For Gary. One of the kindest men I've ever known.

"In the attitude of silence the soul finds the path in a clearer light, and what is elusive and deceptive resolves itself into crystal clearness. Our life is a long and arduous quest after Truth."

Mahatma Gandhi

1

"*Bleeding hearts will never survive. Foolish girl. Faster, Sara, run!*" *a booming voice said, breaking the silence like a thunderclap. All I could hear now were the gasps of breath that escaped me and the heavy pounding of my heart thudding in my ears. I couldn't run fast enough to catch whatever I was chasing or escape from that which was close at my heels. The fact was I could see neither, but the sensation of urgency still tore through me. I tripped and fell, hitting my head.*

I blinked open my eyes and felt as though I was trying to catch my breath. A trickle of cold sweat beading on my chest and back sent a shiver through me, as I gazed out the window over the foggy landscape.

"The road is a bit bumpy. Sorry it woke you," Kevin said, glancing at me. "Are you okay? You look pale."

"Yeah. I'm fine, thanks," I said, swallowing hard. I slid a hand over the top of my head and straightened in the car seat. My heart was beginning to slow at the abrupt realization I was no longer in Ardan, another world immortals could travel to during sleep, but instead with Kevin on the mission to obtain the first key of enlightenment and, with any luck, rescue humanity. I must have dozed on the drive from the airport. I could see the faint outline of Doune Castle through the clouds at the top of the hill just a little way up the road.

"What scared you? Where were you?" Kevin asked, reading my thoughts.

"I don't know. Maybe Ardan. I didn't recognize the world I traveled to this time."

"We can wait here a few minutes if you'd like," he said, pulling to the side of the road.

"No, no. I'm fine." My head was throbbing with lack of sleep and the need for water. "Better to keep moving. Besides, we aren't going to get less tired."

After the narrow escape from the dark shadows hunting me the night before, neither of us had rested well on the nearly seven-hour flight from New York to Scotland. And now here we were, plunged into the center of our mission to find the guardian of the key, one of three that would rescue earth.

Better get used to this, Sara. There could be several sleepless nights on this journey. The gentle touch of Kevin's hand against my cheek pulled me from my thoughts. I lifted my eyes to his, deep brown with flecks of gold winking back at me, reading every thought and emotion. Through tired eyes, I dropped my gaze to his lips and back to meet his stare.

"Let's go," I said.

We left the car parked on the side of the road and climbed up the long, cobblestone path toward the main entrance of Lord's Tower, an extension of Doune Castle and a seemingly longer walk than necessary with the wind pressing against us, as though invisible hands urged us to stay away. I pulled my coat tighter around me as another gust blew fiercely past us. Kevin, undisturbed by the weather, tilted his head into the oncoming blast of cold air like a bull ready to charge his opponent. The sky was filled with shades of rain-heavy gray and white clouds, blocking out any trace of blue.

Under the shelter of the overhang, in front of two enormous wooden doors, Kevin and I glanced at each other with the knowledge of the dangerous venture that waited beyond the entrance. A few knocks upon the door produced no response until the third heavy-handed rap yielded a young woman dressed in a navy blue uniform with medium-length auburn hair and a tired look upon her face.

"I'm sorry but tours will not begin for another hour," she said in a British accent. Her eyes dropped to the floor and the door began to close. Kevin took one step forward and placed a hand on the moving door, stopping it instantly and causing the woman to meet his gaze with surprise.

"Pardon the interruption, miss. We are not here to trouble you for a tour. We are expected by Mr. Ceanag (KEN-uhk) MacCristal," Kevin said as a rather polished Scottish accent rolled off his tongue at the pronunciation of the name. "Is he available?"

"Yes, yes, of course. Do come in," replied the young woman politely. We stepped into the foyer of the castle that was even darker than the gloomy, clouded sky outside. "Who shall I say is calling?"

"Doctors Sara Forrester and Kevin Scott," I replied, smiling at her.

"Please wait here. It'll just be a moment," she said, then hurried down the hall and disappeared into a room.

Torches were lit along the dark corridor, leaving me to wonder if it was for effect or actual purpose. The castle was indeed fit for a lord, to be sure. My eyes couldn't help extending the length of the walls, taking in brick by ancient brick, and wondering what life in the castle must have been like in the late fourteenth century, during the Stewart Dynasty or later as the castle stood during the Wars of the Three Kingdoms and the Jacobite Risings in the seventeenth century. The elegance of such hardened refinement was breathtaking even from the dark foyer.

I placed a flattened palm against one of the bricks and felt an energy run from it through my hand, as if the fourteenth-century walls wanted to speak of all the goings-on. I heard the voices of what sounded like soldiers, loud voices of men, some shouting commands, a rustling of several footsteps, and a single distant scream from a woman. I pulled my hand away and returned to the silence of the small space we occupied. My extrasensory abilities had become even stronger than I'd realized over the last few weeks.

"When you spent time in Scotland, did you happen to tour this castle?" I asked Kevin. My fingers flicked over one of the brochures on a weathered wooden table against the wall. "Do you know about the rooms contained within?" I lifted my gaze and peered down the hall after the vanishing echo of footsteps.

I never visited this one, he replied in thought. Kevin had been communicating via telepathy more in the last few days in an effort, I guessed, to get me to exercise my ability. He wanted to keep our communication between us and away from curious ears, too. The practice of telepathy just wasn't that natural to me. "It's been years since I spent time in this part of the world, growing up with my father, after my mom…" He trailed off, not wanting to finish recalling the memory of his mother's murder, for which he had been a witness at the tender age of seven. His brow had a slight wrinkle. I stroked a hand down his arm. He stepped closer and wrapped an arm around my shoulder. "Are you cold?"

"I'm thawing." I tilted my head toward him and flashed a grin. The angular features of his jaw met at the center of a squared chin. His dark chestnut hair showed a few lighter waves. And the eyes, with a hint of a shadow of fatigue beneath them, pulled me into him and stared straight through me just like they had when I'd awoken in the ICU of the hospital where he had been my attending physician. Because we had bonded millennia before now, he could feel my energy from the moment I'd arrived in the ER, clasping at life's fragile hand, following an accident that had brought us together and engaged the quest for the keys. And yet I still had no memories of our previous lives together.

He squeezed my shoulder and kissed an icy cheek, his breath hot against my chilled skin. The contrast sent a warm, tingling sensation down my neck and across my shoulders. It was a feeling that made me want to curl into him and forget finding keys or those they would rescue.

"How much time do you think we have before the dark forces track us?" I asked.

Even with my growing anticipation of getting to the first key, my thoughts had never left Tarsamon, the demon that directed the evil that had recently been ordered to hunt me. I was an increasing threat to him and to his forces sucking the energy out of the humans to create an existence for the dark energy. By the time we'd fled New York, Tarsamon's shadows had accelerated their effort to consume the weaker humans who allowed fear and anger to drive them by absorbing their energy like famished vampires. Such behaviors were fuel to the dark legion—the more of it that existed, the easier the humans were to devour.

If I were to fail the quest, the Soltari—the ethereal governing order over the realms that maintained the balance of good and evil—would forever break the bond I'd shared with Kevin across lifetimes. The Soltari engaged an Alliance of immortals to carry out the details or rules of the Order. The penalty hanging over our heads would be for losing all the lives on Earth. As if the task of staying alive and finding three hidden keys wasn't complicated enough, the additional threat that faced us was, I supposed, intended as a driving force toward success.

"With your energy like a beacon to him, we don't have much time at all," Kevin answered in a hushed tone. "Where we go to find the key will be up to Mr. MacCristal. And we must rely on the guardian in order to access it. As a custodian of the key, he's spent a lifetime preparing for the possibility he would be called to lead you to it. What we need is for the rest of the team to arrive here as soon as possible to provide protection for you. Matt and Juno are on the next flight out. Elise and Aria can't…"

The clicking sound of footsteps interrupted further discussion on the matter of our team but quickly disappeared.

"Elise and Aria will be here within a day or so," said Kevin.

"Do we have that long?"

"We don't have a choice."

"But Tarsamon's ability to track us… He could find us before we can get to the key."

"We'd be safer to count on it and take any precautions we can."

I'd come a long way from the days just before I'd met Kevin. I'd learned early on never to trust anyone, with a mom who put me up for adoption at the age of eight to be with her boyfriend and a father who was nowhere to be found. I'd been betrayed by the very people that should have cared for me the most. Fortunately, I'd found a good home with my adoptive parents, Mary Ann and Robert Forrester, that helped me to ease out of my shell the tiniest bit with a good dose of love and by being taught wealth was nothing to take for granted but to share with those who helped others, through their foundation. In my short time with Kevin and our small team, I was only starting to trust those sent to protect me on this mission. And despite how normal things appeared for the moment, there was no time to waste searching for the key, not with the dark shadows close at our heels. Two days could literally determine the fate of the world.

My cell phone buzzed to indicate an incoming message. I pulled it from my coat pocket and pressed the button to see a picture of the symbol that had led us to Scotland flashing. The medallion reflected a tree, a sun, and three triskeles. Gaelic lettering was imprinted along the edge. A smaller version of the same detail had been forged into the hilt of my sword, tucked neatly in its case in the car. Though we were in the right area to find Mr. MacCristal, I believed the first key was not at Doune Castle. It couldn't be. The Professors in Ardan, who helped guide us, said the Druid priests had left the key in safe hands to be guarded until the appropriate time came to relinquish it. If that was true, and I had no reason to believe it wasn't, it wouldn't be held in a castle that had the traffic Doune has seen over centuries, including the imprisonment of government troops captured during the Battle of Falkirk. No indeed. Something so valuable would not be hidden in a place where it could accidentally be found. I would need to put my faith in Mr. MacCristal, that he would be able to lead us to the exact location. I turned as the soft sounds of footsteps from the hall interrupted my thoughts.

"What is it?" Kevin asked, referring to the message I'd received.

"A reminder to get moving."

I pressed the button again and slipped the phone into my pocket. Kevin shook his head, knowing there was little we could do to hasten our way through this mission.

The symbols, kept safely in Ardan, were believed to hold information for three different locations, one for each key—Scotland, the Yucatan Peninsula, and Egypt. Each symbol had lettering, hieroglyphs, or images that were like clues to individual puzzles and each had a guardian that we had to find first. The guardian knew the way to the gateway, a portal to the realm where the key had been hidden thousands of years earlier by the Soltari, a powerful entity that held the balance of good and evil in its governance. The Alliance of Souls, to which I belonged, handed down the order of the Soltari. And it was my mission to set the balance between light and darkness right again and push Tarsamon's evil from our world. This could only be accomplished by harnessing the power of all three keys of enlightenment.

"Good mornin' to ye. I'm so sorry to keep ye waitin'." A stout man greeted us in full kilted attire.

Costume or culture?

The man's hair was cut short around his ears, with no effort to hide the patch of baldness at the crown. It was medium brown in color with graying sprigs sneaking out beyond the darkened areas on his round head, revealing his age, I guessed, to be in his early fifties. My attention always went first to the eyes of those I spoke with, to seek the truth in their words. The blue of his were smiling at us in half-moons as he reached out a hand in welcome, first to Kevin, then to me.

"Good morning," I replied, extending my hand. He lifted my fingers gently to his lips. His thumb grazed the silver ring I wore, a symbol identifying me to others involved in our mission as the only person able to hold the keys. The ring had been set like glue on my finger since Cerys, a spiritual equal to Kevin, had placed it there a couple of months earlier.

"My name is Robert Watson, I'm the constable of the castle. I understand ye are to meet with Mr. MacCristal," he said in a thick Scottish accent.

"Yes," Kevin replied. "He should be expecting us. Is he here?"

"He'll be along directly. I've been asked to see ye to your quarters and perhaps offer some refreshment after your long journey. Might ye have baggage I could attend to?"

"Yes, in the car," Kevin said. "I'll bring it up."

"Please, sir. I'll see ye fit to your room and then attend to it directly."

"That's very kind of you. Thank you," I said, touching Kevin's arm.

As we followed the constable into the Great Hall and on into Lord's Hall, I could swear I heard faint whispering coming from all around me, as if thousands of voices were whispering at once. I couldn't make out what was being said. I glanced toward the ceiling to see carved faces in the beams above my head. *Are they there or am I imagining it? It must be the cleaning staff working nearby, preparing to open the castle to visitors, and their voices are just carrying over,* I told myself. *In whispers?* I knew better than to doubt my senses, but I couldn't help it.

Kevin leaned closer. "I hear them, too," he said into my ear.

Sound most certainly echoed from wall to wall in the great empty space. But the eyes in the faces I'd seen felt as though they were following us as we moved through the hall.

"Mr. Watson, as old as the castle is, do you have any visitors who've witnessed ghost sightings?" I asked.

"Ah, we do get the chasers of them, ye see, those that hope to find 'em. But I'm sure it's nay more than a shadow, or perhaps their own that frightens 'em." He chuckled under his breath and shook his head, dismissing the notion. "More like silly nonsense, if ye ask me. But the belief keeps them coming 'round." Kevin and I glanced at each other at the mention of *shadow*. My attention lifted once more to the ceiling.

As the door opened for us to exit, a breeze greeted us. *Hurry,* it seemed to say in a whisper that stretched from behind us as we stepped through the doorway.

We continued through Lord's Hall and outside, down a set of stairs leading to a large, grassy courtyard below. Beyond was a small stone cottage that reminded me of the French country homes I had visited a couple of times as a girl with Mary Ann and Robert, near Cumberland, Maryland, during a summer vacation. The cottage was no more than two bedrooms, with a bath in one and a sparse but adequate kitchen area consisting of the basics—an electric stove, small sink, and a refrigerator that resembled the smaller iceboxes found in the 1950s, a relic that had found its place in the quaint Scottish home. I immediately felt surrounded in comfort.

"I hope this will do?" the constable asked. I nodded and smiled, thanking him. "My wife, Mairi, tends to the guests in the house and will be up directly to see to any needs ye may have. I'll return straightaway to take ye to see Mr. MacCristal. It won't be long."

With that, the door closed with a slam, leaving Kevin and me in the peaceful company of each other. I gazed around the room as a noticeable chill sank through my coat and touched my skin. The air in the home seemed a bit stale and I wanted to open windows to clear the place. Instead, I grasped the edges of my coat and pulled it tighter in a feeble attempt to retain what little body heat I still had. We stood in silence, taking in the accommodations and feeling trapped for the moment, at least until the constable returned.

"I'll start a fire," Kevin said, echoing my thoughts. Before he could reach for the firewood stacked neatly in a large basket by the hearth, a quick knock at the door came just before it opened, letting in a fresh burst of cold air no more than the forty-two degrees the car registered on our drive to the castle. A short, plump woman entered, wearing a knee-length gray dress and white apron. Masses of white and gray curls were pinned to her head and she smiled at us as she held a basket covered in cloth over her forearm and stepped into the room. She looked rather like a sweet old grandmother straight out of a fairy tale.

"Good day to ye," she said in a pleasant voice, setting the basket on the table in the living area. "I've brought ye some fruit and baked goods from the kitchen."

"Good morning. Mairi, is it?" I asked, trying to impart the accent I had heard in the constable's voice earlier.

"Yes, lass. So pleased to meet ye." She took my hand in hers and shook it lightly.

Her eyes grew round as saucers and her mouth fell open. "Good heavens! The man forgot to light ye a fire. You're freezin', lass. Never mind," she said, patting my hand. "I'll set to it directly." She released my hand and touched my arm before she turned away.

Kevin and I watched as Mairi scurried from the fireplace to the kitchen and each bedroom. Kevin stood motionless, like one of the two wooden beams in the corners of the room, while the cheery woman mumbled dissatisfaction as she flitted around the cottage, tidying the already immaculate space. I lifted the cloth covering the basket of food and opted instead to stand by the recently stoked fire. I glanced at Kevin and couldn't help but laugh under my breath as he watched in astonishment. It was as if we were caught in a movie whose scene had been set to fast-forward. Before I could blink, the fire was stoked, a half of a ham Mairi had pulled out of the icebox was sliced and returned to the refrigerator for later, two bottles of spring water were placed next to fresh flowers at the tiny blockwood kitchen table, and two heavy woolen blankets in a green and blue tartan plaid were perfectly folded and placed on the end of each bed.

"Yes, well, that should do it," she said, rubbing her hands on the apron as she scanned the room for any chance item out of place. For the first time since realizing I was cold, she glanced at Kevin and then me. The smile I wore at seeing Kevin's astonished look remained and we both thanked her as she made her way out the door.

"You'd think she believed we were on a honeymoon or something with all the attention," I said, shutting the door behind her and giving it a forceful push as it stuck two inches from closing.

"She probably does. I wouldn't think Mr. MacCristal is sharing the details of the quest with just anyone. We'd have received quite a different reception if he was."

Kevin peeked into the basket and settled on a piece of fruit.

"You should eat something, love," he said. "Once we meet with Ceanag, I don't know when there will be another chance."

I remained by the stone hearth, where the fire was now blazing, reluctant to leave, even though my stomach was grumbling. Kevin brought the basket of goods over for my perusal, slid a hand over my hair, and kissed a temple. I smiled up at him through tired eyes and plucked a pear. My thoughts went back to our mad rush from New York and I tried not to think of the dark shadows that couldn't be too far behind us.

With no other choice, we'd had to leave Aria and Elise to face the two remaining massive hurricanes that were headed for the southeast coast of the US, and also one of Tarsamon's efforts to reduce the human population quickly. Elise and Aria were gifted in their other-worldly abilities to affect the elements of nature. The last I'd heard, three of the five hurricanes had pushed away from the coast, back into the Atlantic. Once the last two were safely contained, Elise and Aria would join the rest of the team on the quest, hopefully in a couple of days.

How long can it take to find a key? Gazing into the fire, I took a bite of fruit and patiently waited to meet with Ceanag. Finding this key was only the first step to stopping the evil that was moving faster into our world. We had a longer voyage ahead for the other two keys.

I turned to see Kevin sitting on the sofa. He reached for a magazine on the side table and flipped through the pages without directing much attention toward them. He assured me that the other members of our team were safe. So why was I feeling a sense of unrest? If C-05, someone who I was sure had left our side to join forces with Tarsamon, was on our trail, I was in potentially greater danger as the moments passed. Kevin hadn't told me that, but he didn't have to. I could feel the tension and worry from him as he explained the details of our trip to Scotland during the flight. He wasn't blocking his emotions from being felt by me now, a rare thing in the time I'd spent with him so far.

I could feel so much from everyone around me, but it struck me numb from the moment I'd met Kevin that I could not feel what he felt as an empath. It was a gift, or some might consider a curse, to feel the emotions of people around me. But it gave me insight into the truths they carried. It was most useful in my practice as a psychiatrist, while at the same time, it was a burden to carry my own feelings and to feel those of the people near me.

Tension encircled Kevin even more so now than on the plane. It had grown rather quickly since arriving in the little cottage. I could feel from him a level of impatience that he was stifling with increasing difficulty at waiting to meet with Ceanag. I took another bite of the pear and watched him. He looked like a champagne bottle that had been shaken and was ready to pop. I knew it wouldn't be much longer before he would seek out our contact himself, refusing to hold our mission up any longer under the confines of the constable and his cheery wife.

I rubbed the warmth over my arms from the heat of the fire and wandered through the cottage to get a better look at the rooms and view from the single picture window in each of the two bedrooms. Soft, handmade quilts covered the beds with a floral design, while a plaid tartan throw, of unknown clan descent, lay neatly folded over the arm of a white stuffed chair near each window, similar to the one Mairi had placed on the end of the bed. There were worse places to be held up waiting for someone. I immediately began to feel the lack of sleep catching up with me and with it a sudden desire to pull back the soft quilts and snuggle beneath for a long nap.

A knock startled me, ringing through the stillness like the thunder of a coming storm. I turned toward the door, realizing I must have been just as anxious as Kevin to get going. He was already standing on the front steps as I arrived to greet the constable, with an air of relief in his expression.

"Well now, here ye are," Mr. Watson said as he stepped past me and set the two bags and cases containing our swords inside the entry. "I was asked to give ye this, miss," he said, turning to me and reaching into his inside coat pocket. "It was just delivered this mornin', nay but five minutes ago, with special instructions that it not be left for ye but handed directly to ye." He paused and scratched his head. "Aye, the man was quite insistent," he added, handing me a small, unmarked box covered in white paper. It reminded me of the mysterious package I'd received in my office not more than a week ago that, once opened, was determined to be my sword sent from Ardan. It, too, had arrived unmarked and in a similar plain box.

"What man?" asked Kevin.

"I dinna know exactly. A delivery person, I suppose. Odd-looking fellow he was," he replied with a shrug.

I peeled back the paper and lifted the lid of an antique wood box to see all three symbols had in fact been delivered safely as the great gray wolf Karshan had promised at my last visit to Ardan. I glanced from the box to Kevin and he nodded once, acknowledging the mental image, my view, of the symbols.

The wolf was an ally I'd met in Ardan, one of many who would aid me in the mission and who'd told me the symbols would be delivered. Karshan had mentioned he had the same ability as all of us to cross the boundary of current life into the parallel world of Ardan and back if necessary. I'd learned that the immortal members of my team could do this while dreaming. But there must be another way to cross over, because in my hand were the symbols from Ardan, and the danger Tarsamon brought wouldn't wait for us to sleep.

"Thank you, sir. I've been waiting for this," I said, shifting my gaze to Mr. Watson. "Is Mr. MacCristal at home?" I felt an urgency to get the symbols to Ceanag and avoid the curiosity I sensed from our host. The small bow-tie mouth of the constable opened and shut.

"Aye, I just spoke with him on my way up," he replied. "He's asked me to bring you to his home. If you're quite ready, you can follow me."

As we headed down the path toward the constable and his car, I felt an odd sensation to take a detour. I shook off the notion as a simple distraction and kept pace with Kevin down the path from the small cottage. The wind continued to blow in mighty gusts, whipping my hair about my face. Carried high on its breeze, I heard my name. This time I stopped and turned my head away from the car.

"What is it?" Kevin asked. He stopped with me as Mr. Watson waited steps ahead of us with the door open to the large Austin Princess, a 1964, I guessed from a glance. It was a transportation car, not particularly fancy but classy enough for carting people with its resemblance to an older-style Rolls Royce.

"I can't go with you," I said to him.

"Why? What is it?" I could feel him searching for an answer in my thoughts that could not be read, not because I blocked him from his ability to do so but because I didn't know.

"I have to go there." I shifted my eyes past him. "To the River Teith just beyond those trees." I lifted a chin in the direction of the river.

"I'll go with you. We can meet Ceanag later."

"No," I replied, staring off into the distance that was calling me toward it. "I have to go alone." I turned to face him, handing him the box. "Take this to Ceanag. I'll catch up with you. Ask Mr. Watson to return for me." I pulled a few long strands of hair away that had blown across my lips and turned into the wind. "They will be safer with you, for now," I said, feeling his protest at delivering the symbols without me.

"I don't like this." He stared into my eyes knowing that he couldn't argue with the guidance to lead I'd been granted by the Alliance.

"I'll be fine."

He let out a breath. "All right," he said reluctantly. "But if you're not back within thirty minutes, it won't just be the constable who returns for you." I nodded to him as he touched my arm. He felt through my coat the silver bracelet he'd given me as a gift at his home in the Cape and seemed comforted that it would let him know the moment I was in danger by sending a signal indicating where he could find me, like a GPS device. Kevin cupped a hand along my jaw-line, stroked a thumb over my cheek, and kissed the space between my brows. "Be careful." He turned with the small box in hand and, with a few long strides, reached the car, stopping only to say a few words to Mr. Watson.

2

Kevin followed Mr. Watson up several steps to a grand home, leaving Sara to her own devices. A dangerous thing, he thought. Not because the dark shadows or C-05 posed a greater threat. He was almost certain they had a little time, some distance, too, before Tarsamon would locate her. He was counting on that small lead to have the key safely in hand and be well on their way to the Yucatan for the second. That's if there were no surprises. Of course, he expected the mission would become more perilous the deeper into it they went. That wasn't what bothered him right now. He worried because what he had come to know of Sara was that she didn't shy away from anything, determined even in the face of real danger, never fearing for her own life despite already getting a taste of what had hunted her once in Ardan and what had forced their rush from New York.

She'd come face-to-face with the flesh-colored, faceless demons, their hounds, when she'd tried to travel to the dark side of Ardan to learn what she was up against. It had nearly cost her life and their lives together for eternity. Thinking back, if he hadn't given her the bracelet that same morning, there would have been no way for her to have signaled to him the danger she'd encountered or her location, and he likely wouldn't have reached her in time. As it was, he'd caught her by only a couple of seconds before the hellhounds had consumed her energy. And that was too close.

She was much stronger in mind and body than when he had first met her, but that comforted him only slightly, and enough to leave her for thirty minutes or so. She didn't remember the parallel universe she had traveled for centuries with him as the memories of those lives and experiences had been blocked for her to function in her life on Earth. But the accident that had sent her to the world of Ardan had reintroduced her to energy, her ability to fight, and the guides that aided her. At least she remembered her skill in battle. No, that hadn't wavered. But Kevin also knew, despite her strength and ability to fight well, she didn't fully grasp the power behind the darkest forces that wanted her dead.

Tarsamon's army of shadows and creatures were cunning and manipulative, and because her memories had been hidden by the Soltari that set the rules for the mission, Sara had yet to recall the full strength of them.

With his ability to hear her thoughts, he tuned in to where she might be, walking along the banks, searching for God knows what without her sword. *Why didn't I press her to take it? It won't do her any good tucked away in the little cottage.* He reached the final step to a set of wooden double doors and glanced at his watch. *She'll be careful. She's a warrior, even if she doesn't remember it yet.* She was the primary lead in the mission, and if she was called to a task, he had to let her go.

The constable's gentle knock a second time prompted a woman of slender build in her midthirties to open one side. Her hair was tucked neatly into a white flowered scarf, tied at the base of her neck. A few wavy tendrils had come loose and were hanging over clear sky-blue eyes.

"Good day to ye, Mrs. MacCristal," said the constable. "May I introduce Dr. Scott. He has an appointment with Mr. Mac."

"Aye, of course. Come in out o' the wind," she said, stepping aside to allow both men to enter. Kevin glanced at Mr. Watson, pausing long enough to remind him of his task to return for Sara.

Mr. Watson turned to the woman and nodded. "Ye'll have to excuse me. I've got some business to attend to and will return directly," he said, nodding to Kevin. "I wanted to make sure Dr. Scott was in time to meet with Mr. Mac."

"Aye, then. Don't let me keep ye from your task."

Mr. Watson shut the door behind him.

"Dr. Scott, so pleased to finally meet ye," Ceanag said, approaching Kevin in what seemed two long strides. He extended a hand in greeting, clasping Kevin's in a hearty handshake. "I thank ye for your patience and hope ye find the cottage to your likin'?"

"Indeed, it's perfect. Please, call me Kevin."

"Aye, and I go by Mac."

He was a taller man than most Scots Kevin had met, though not quite reaching his own six foot two inches in height. Kevin noted the man was bulky, too, with longer mink-colored hair neatly cinched at his neck with a wide leather binding. It was not so much Mac's appearance but the information that Kevin had received about him that had intrigued him.

The guardian of the first key came from a very long line of Druid priests trained in the art of the ancient practices, and not only the active philosophy but also mythical beliefs of the mysterious wise ones. The Druids were said to be highly intellectual, educated people who believed the soul was immortal through reincarnation. Kevin had heard stories that sacrifice was part of the Druid practice but hoped that his current understanding regarding Neo-Druidism theology, a belief that included respect for all beings, would overshadow any such stories. The fact was the stories didn't matter to the quest. Only that he found the one man who could provide the link to the next piece of the mission and get Sara to the key. The problem, of course, was Sara wasn't here to be led but instead treading down by a river. Being here, with Mac and the symbols, was *her* business because only Sara could hold the power of the key.

"Kevin, this is my lovely wife, Aggie. And my boy is running around here someplace," Mac said, glancing to his right, then left, distracting Kevin from his thoughts.

"Beg ye pardon, Dr., er, Kevin," Aggie said, wiping her hand on her apron. "Pleased to meet ye."

"Shall we meet for a bit in the library?" Mac asked.

"Certainly." Kevin took off his coat and folded it over his arm.

"Never mind that. I'll be hangin' it for ye until you're ready," Aggie said, taking his coat and smiling. "Do you prefer brandy or whisky?"

"Whisky, thank you." *Is it already noon? Close enough, anyway.*

Kevin followed Mac down a long hallway. The wooden floor echoed their footsteps near the back end of the house. A fairly good-sized room, it contained books of all sorts stacked on several shelves, waist high all the way up to the ceiling. Kevin felt comforted to meet a man interested in reading as much as he himself was, enough to have a library of this size. He could see by the worn binding and the few that had not yet been filed, with weathered pages, that every one of the books likely had been read over many times.

"Some of them are over a hundred years old," Mac said, catching Kevin's eyes running the length of the bookcase.

"I wondered."

Mac eased into a leather seat behind a large birchwood desk, inviting Kevin to sit at one of the richly covered armchairs in front of him.

"I'm glad to see ye, but I must admit I was expecting two of ye," Mac said, smiling at Kevin. He leaned back into his chair and folded his hands across his stomach.

"Yes. Sara will be along soon." At least he hoped she would, or this meeting would be brief. It had to be almost twenty minutes that had passed since he entered the constable's car. What on earth could be keeping her? "She was called to a task just before we were to meet with you," Kevin added, feeling the gaze from Mac as he searched Kevin's eyes for a more detailed response for Sara's absence.

She was, in fact, the person Mac was meant to meet with. It was damned uncomfortable to be sitting in the room with the guardian of a key who could not release it to him. The thought reminded him of the medallions Sara had given him to deliver. Mac needed to meet with Sara to verify she was indeed the one sent to obtain the key. Confirmation of her identity could only be provided by the silver band on her finger as the symbol of her identity. That meant handing over the medallions now wouldn't matter without her here, and such an important set of items could wait a few more minutes for her to arrive.

"If I may inquire, what task could have caused her to delay for such important business?" Mac asked. Aggie arrived with the whisky, offering a glass to Kevin and Mac, for which Kevin thanked her. He took a generous sip and swallowed.

"I cannot say," Kevin paused. "I mean, I don't really know, that is. It was rather abrupt. Something about the River Teith." Mac nearly choked on the gulp of whisky he had taken at that moment. He set the glass down and reached for a handkerchief as he wiped his mouth. "It doesn't seem that she is in any danger. Not yet anyway," Kevin added, hoping to ease the worry etching across his face. "I asked the constable to return for her. I expect she'll be here soon."

Mac cleared his throat and found his voice. "Ye don't seem to understand." He leaned forward, set his glass on the desk, and patted his mouth once more with the cloth. "The Druid priests have not merely hidden the key of enlightenment. The Light Carrier will be led to the key through a passage to be opened at the river."

Kevin's thoughts raced to what possibilities could come if Sara found the passage alone with no real protection from the dark forces, save her own ability to fight without her sword. What if, by chance, C-05 or Tarsamon's shadows had arrived early? The threat to her, to obtaining the key, to their future, the billions of people on Earth who unknowingly depended upon the success of this mission grew more alarming as each second ticked by.

C-05, he thought, to save his own life after being caught in the dark world, had joined with Tarsamon under the pretense he would be able to stop Sara from obtaining the keys. Knowing the power C-05 had, Kevin was sure Sara didn't quite realize what she was up against should he try to meet up with her in Scotland. He jumped out of his seat, as did Mac.

"I've got to get to her," Kevin said. His eyes narrowed and dropped to the desk, thinking of the fastest route. To his knowledge, the constable hadn't yet returned with Sara, because he couldn't feel her presence nearby, adding to his haste and concern. "Do you have a car here?"

Sara couldn't be in immediate danger of the dark forces finding her being that the bracelet she wore had not sent a signal to him indicating danger was nearby.

"I do. But ye aren't goin' alone," replied Mac.

Kevin hadn't thought about leaving his host behind, but he'd do what he must.

"This way," Mac said. Kevin followed as they raced down the hall, slowing only to put on coats and heading to Mac's car on a fast track back to the river.

"What passage will be opened?" Kevin asked as the car bumped over the narrow road toward the tiny cottage where he'd left her.

"What?"

"You mentioned a passage. What sort of passage?"

"It is believed to be a pathway for travel to another realm. It's in that realm that the key is being kept."

"Shit," Kevin whispered, wishing the little car had more horsepower. His Audi R8 would have been there in two minutes flat.

"What?"

"She doesn't remember her travel to other realms and doesn't have her sword. The only memory she has is her ability to fight and, of course, the complete knowledge of the mission. She can't end up in a world she doesn't know without you as a guide and our team as protection."

Mac downshifted and revved the engine to maximum speed, causing the car to choke and sputter faster toward the river.

3

"Continue on." I heard the words as clear as day whispered to me on the breeze. I paused long enough to take in the sensations that guided me farther into the thicket of taller grass. I shifted direction toward the trees that swayed under the might of the powerful gusts of wind. The whisper of my name carried softly into my ear once more, drawing me down the hill and into the birch trees that stood rooted in the rich, dark soil. They lined the banks of the river like soldiers awaiting orders to move. I pushed through a narrow row of saplings, not knowing where exactly I was going but with the knowledge that I had to get there.

According to Kevin, I'd traveled to many realms in my long history with him, but those memories remained locked away. I retained the drive to defeat the darkness making its way across humanity. But while the push to fight evil ran through my veins now, strong and forceful as it ever had, I held no recollection of how Kevin and I were connected or how long we'd known each other, despite his assurance it had been lifetimes over. As I followed the force guiding me now through the trees, I couldn't help wondering what the mystery was of the forests that kept bringing me back to them. First Ardan and now Scotland.

The wind was calmer in the protection of the long, leafy branches, still covered in shades of gold and red despite the season's cooler temperatures and refusal to accept the conversion of winter. A hushed sound of *who* carried high above and mingled with the flutter of leaves in perfect harmony with an eerie silence. The scent of damp, rotting leaves that had fallen mixed with the earthiness of soil and rose up, only to be whisked away by the breeze that caught it on its current. I pressed through the tight growth of majestic birch and scattered alder and entered a small clearing with blades of grass that stood knee high. Moist soil outlined a nondescript path, and I heard my name again, beckoning me to continue. I stepped at a much slower pace, feeling sensations that prickled my skin and caused the hairs on my neck and arms to stand on end, all the while the breeze lifting my name on its wings and continuing to call.

With each step down the path, the pull to discover what beckoned grew stronger, like a child tugging at me to follow toward something desperately wanted. *What is this?* Every time I'd sensed another person's feelings, heard their thoughts, or felt the waves even of something troubling in the air, confirmation of the sensation was revealed. This was the first time I'd ever experienced a sensation of being in the right place with so much uncertainty. Beyond sight and sound, my senses were blinded by some unknown energy I couldn't tap into for information.

The path led down a set of wooden steps, through a small thicket of tall grass with a sandy bottom, to the water's edge. It was here that I still felt pulled to enter. I crouched down and touched the icy water. As my fingers plunged deeper into the river, a flash of bluish-white and yellow light connected in a stream above the water, startling me enough that I fell backward. I sat staring at the sky as if something should appear but to no avail.

It wouldn't be long before Kevin would be heading back for me. By now the constable had surely been to the cottage to find it empty. That didn't matter at the moment. I wasn't about to leave without understanding more about this connection of light and water and my place in it.

I reached again to replicate what I'd seen, plunging my right hand into the frigid water. A sudden searing sound joined with the scent of electricity in an enormous flash that raced across the sky in an abstract pattern. I held my hand in place, fighting the stinging sensation as I watched the electrical wave above me. Ringing broke through the silence, piercing my ears. The wave formed a circular pattern with flashes of light that disappeared into the circle. My hands began to twinge with pain as the cold sank beyond the layers of skin. Sharp crackles of electricity could be heard above the ringing, growing louder in my ears. And a new sensation of pain that had started at the top of my head moved to the base of my neck. I yanked my hand out of the water, unable to withstand the freezing water any longer. At the same moment, a loud growl of thunder moved across the sky. The world around me started to spin, as though I'd been caught in the sound wave of the thunderclap, followed by the sensation I was floating. Had the gray clouds of sky grown darker, too?

Mac and Kevin bolted from the car and ran toward the river. Kevin led the way as he raced in the direction he had last seen Sara headed when the car pulled away from the steps earlier. He couldn't sense where she was, no thoughts to read, nothing. It was as if he was blocked from locating her. His heart raced at the thought she might already have found the passage, or that it had found her.

"Where is this passage?" Kevin shouted, directing his voice above the wind.

"Just ahead, over here," Mac replied, pointing left and pushing past the branches that blocked immediate view of the river. Kevin turned his direction to follow on Mac's heels, calling Sara's name, but nothing was returned except the wind through the trees. They ran down the winding wooden steps.

"Sara," Kevin called again. His eyes scanned across the blades of grass. His breath was heavy with anxiety, and his eyes narrowed to focus on the river rock that lay just to the left of the field, scanning for movement.

"There. Beside the grass," Mac called to him, pointing toward the edge of the tall grass and river rock. A mass of black that looked out of place with nature was tucked into the tall green blades and extended into the water.

She was lying on her stomach, her face turned to the side as the tips of her hair waded playfully on the water's edge. In a few long, hurried strides, Kevin was beside her. Sara was unconscious but breathing. Kevin bent over her, checking her pulse, calling her name. He brushed a hand over her cheek.

"Jesus, she's freezing. What is this passage? What does it do?" he asked Mac, as he lifted her out of the grass, gently turning her over into his arms and holding her against him. *What did it do to her?*

Mac shook his head and shrugged a shoulder. "No one has opened it before. The Druids claim it's mystic, created for the Light Carrier."

Shit, Kevin thought as he stood with Sara in his arms. One more thing to figure out, putting this mission at greater risk. "We need to get her to the cottage. Need to get her warm."

This wasn't going to be a simple task of exchanging the symbols for the key. Until now, they'd been ahead of the dark shadows that had come to kill Sara in New York. Every riddle or roadblock they encountered forced a setback, nipped at the small lead they had, and allowed the danger closer as they battled against time.

Kevin carried her with ease as he raced up the hill to the cottage. He kicked at the door that stuck and placed Sara on the bed. He fought to remove the damp coat and clothing from her lifeless body before tucking her under the covers and layering her with sheet, blanket, one throw, then another.

Mac stoked the fire and searched for a towel for Kevin to wipe the dirt from her face and dry her hair.

A deep and heavy sigh escaped Kevin's chest. He smoothed his fingers over her forehead and down her cheek. She looked very much like the time she'd arrived in his hospital after the car accident. Helpless. Thankfully, her pulse was normal. Putting a hand to her head, Kevin noted her temperature warming. He looked her over to find no apparent injury from what he could tell. Had she gone through the passage or merely attempted to? She was as unresponsive now as she had been when in the Cape with him, when she had visited the dark world without protection and where the demons and shadows had intended to take her life. That little trip had knocked her out for two days. Had she run into the shadows again? They didn't have two days for her to recover.

"The gateway is a powerful force of energy," Mac said, returning. He handed Kevin the towel and took a seat in the chair in the corner of the room, while Kevin sat beside Sara. "If it detected her as the Light Carrier, which I believe it did because of that ring"—he extended an index finger in the direction of Sara's hand—"it would recognize her energy as one it should join with."

Kevin sat staring at Sara, willing her to open her eyes and speak, while taking in the information Mac was sharing with him.

"What, then, is your role regarding the passage if her energy can join with it?" Kevin asked.

"The passage can be opened by the Light Carrier, but she will not be able to enter without the symbols," Mac replied.

So she hadn't entered.

"As for my role, I am to take the passage with her."

Kevin remembered the symbols Sara had given him to deliver to Mac still tucked in his coat. "Just a minute," he said as he went to retrieve them, thankful they weren't with her. Or perhaps for sure she would have been sent to wherever that mysterious passage led and well out of his way of protecting her. He put the thought out of his head and returned to the room, handing the box to Mac. Kevin glanced again at Sara. *God, why doesn't she wake?* He needed to breathe again, to have confirmation she was all right.

"Ah, good," Mac said, lifting the lid of the box. "We'll need to take these back to the gateway," he said.

Kevin turned to look at him, eyes wide. "We aren't going back there until I'm certain what has happened to her and where that passage takes us. And I do mean *us*, you understand? I will travel with her."

"Of course. The Light Carrier opens the passage. It's understood that her companions will join her."

Both men turned at the sound of Sara sucking in a quick, deep breath and releasing it slowly, her eyes still closed. Kevin touched a hand to her forehead and stroked down the length of her hair, calling to her again. She blinked open eyes the color of jade, sprinkled with the same flecks of gold as his. The same eyes he had fallen into months ago, like a warm and inviting pool that gently washed over him. The squeeze of tension that had tightened with every minute that passed eased from his chest. Kevin glanced at Mac on the edge of the chair and felt from him a sudden sense of intrusion along with the curiosity that kept him fixed on the edge of the chair.

"Are you all right?" Kevin asked, staring into my eyes.

"Yes, quite," I said, pausing to assess. "A little foggy, but all right."

"This is Ceanag MacCristal," Kevin said, turning his head toward him and then back.

"Mac." Ceanag nodded, a smile barely crossing his lips.

"Hello. What happened? Why are we all in the bedroom?" My eyes flicked between them, searching for the answer in each of their faces. *And why in the hell am I almost naked?* It registered immediately that I was in nothing but my panties. The covers were tucked tightly across my chest and along my sides, locking me in place, as though I were a well-wrapped burrito.

A vivid image of water lapping at my hair as I lay on the ground was sent back to me. Kevin was listening to my thoughts again.

You're in your underwear because it was the only article of clothing that was untouched by water. I caught the quick lift of one of his brows, confirming the telepathy he was exercising. I just hoped Mac wasn't gifted with the same ability.

"We were hoping you could tell us what happened on your walk," said Kevin. "We'll add the part about how you arrived in the bedroom."

I began to explain about my path toward the water and the flash of light across the river that sent me toppling backward. "I was more curious to understand the cause of the electrical current over my head, so I put my hand back into the water," I explained. "I got dizzy and it seemed as though I was floating in the middle of the light. I could see the water below me, but I could not see myself. It was a strange feeling." I paused to recall. "Then everything went black. And now here I am with you and Mr. MacCristal."

Mac explained how he believed the passage worked, reiterating the need for the symbols to activate it fully and how my energy would be drawn to the gateway. I raised my eyebrows in interest. "In essence, you're saying I was kicked out?" I asked, smiling.

"I suspect because ye did not have the symbols with ye," Mac replied. I laughed. After all I had been through in Ardan and the guides directing me, only to find I was booted at the last moment.

"It's a good thing, aye, as we don't know what lies beyond the passage and we would not have wanted you to go alone," Kevin said. It seemed he was picking up a bit of the Scottish dialect since he had met with Mac, or perhaps recalling the years he had spent in Scotland some time ago.

"I think I shall leave ye to a bit o' rest, now that ye seem well and in good hands. I know we must get moving and your time is short. Perhaps, if you're feelin' well enough, you'd like to join us for dinner at our home?" Mac asked. Kevin glanced at me and I nodded.

"Of course," I replied.

"Well then." Mac placed both hands on his knees and stood from the chair. "I'll send Mr. Watson for ye 'round six this evenin'?"

"We'll look forward to it," Kevin said.

"Good then. I'll just show myself out."

Kevin walked with Mac to the doorway of the bedroom, whispering a couple of words before turning toward me.

Though I felt well enough, my head was spinning slightly and I doubted my ability to stand without losing my balance. An expression of concern washed over Kevin's face.

"We don't have to go tonight if you don't feel up to it," he said after Mac left.

"I'll be fine by this evening. I'm sure. Besides, we don't have time to waste."

I didn't know just how long I had been out but it seemed too long. We were to have exchanged the symbols for the key already. But after Mac had explained that what I had experienced was a passage trying to be opened, I understood nothing would be made simple in obtaining the key. Rightly so, I supposed. No one, especially the Soltari, would allow easy access to something so imminently important to humanity. Leaving this first key in the hands of the Druid priests was one part of the plan. Accessing it was quite another.

"You're okay for me to leave you to rest for a few moments?" Kevin asked.

"Of course. Don't worry. And please, don't fuss over me. I'm perfectly fine."

Kevin squeezed my hand. "Okay. I want to check on the status of Juno and Matt's arrival and check in with Elise and Aria."

"I can do that. I'm leading this mission. It's my resp—" I began.

"Not just now," he interrupted before I could protest further. "Rest for the moment and I will track down our team. There will be plenty of time once the gateway is opened for you to lead. We are all relying on it." He leaned over and kissed my forehead.

"I need to call Mary Ann, to let her know I had to leave and that I'm all right. She was expecting a call from me today." My adoptive mother had been like a real mother to me since I was eight and the only person I ever felt an obligation to ease any worry. The night before Kevin and I had left, she confided that she had been seeing the same wicked shadows in her dreams that the other members of our team and I had begun to see in reality. The dark shadows were latching on to several of the humans, weakening them with their negative energy as they slowly consumed them. People had started to look like the walking dead, changing their image to reveal deeply sunken eye sockets and hunched shoulders as they carried the weight of the shadows' energy upon them.

"You brought your cell phone in that rush we left in?" Kevin asked, stepping out of the doorway.

"I had tossed it in my bag on my way upstairs, before I ran into C-05. I don't know if it still has a charge."

"I'll check. If not, I'll send a note for you. Just rest for now."

"You brought your laptop in all that commotion?"

I heard him sigh. "I was coming from the hospital, remember? I'd had a bag packed for nearly a week in case we needed to bolt from New York. Sleep. You'll need it."

"I really don't think there's time. What I need is a shower or a bath." I yanked at the covers meant to keep me in place and sat up. A wave of dizziness clouded my vision and the room spun once around me.

"My love," Kevin said, reappearing in the doorway. He paused and raked a long gaze over the length of my body and met my eyes. "If you get up from that bed, you won't be getting any rest. I assure you. And I need you well rested." His lips pulled into a thin line with the corners turning upward. I wanted to protest but was effectively silenced with a single look. For the moment, all thought of the mission seemed to be set aside and it was just us. The memory of our recent night together, involving his shower, flashed in my mind and sent a delicious thrill through me. Words failing me, I curved my lips into a wry smile, tucked my feet back under the covers, and let my head drop to the pillow.

"I'll wake you in a bit so you can get ready," he said, turning to leave.

4

The constable's knock at the door rattled through the quiet dwelling as if the chimes of church bells had echoed off the walls of the tiny cottage. As I stepped toward the door, Kevin swept an arm around my waist, catching and pulling me to him, gently touching his lips to mine, and reminding me I had missed his soft touch. I smiled into the intense brown eyes, lost in one brief moment. My fingers instinctively glided over his ears and sank into the soft waves of chestnut hair.

"Mm. Later, love. I promise." He swept another light kiss over my lips and held my fingertips in his as he opened the door. A quick hello and we stepped toward the car.

The drive to Mac's home was a quick hop, no more than a few blocks from Doune castle. I marveled at the sparkle of the home, from the exterior hanging lights at the entry to the well-lit interior. A massive gray stone fireplace greeted us upon entering, contrasting with the delicate crystal chandelier visible in the nearby dining room. The living room was filled with masculine furniture—deep mahogany stained tables and a long L-shaped leather sofa. Two Highland broadswords hung decoratively on a wall over a library table opposite the fireplace. I'd discovered during my visit to Kevin's home in the Cape it would be a mistake to assume swords hung on the walls of those trained to use them would be for decorative purposes. They were instead proud representations of the art of swordsmanship, meant to convey the owner's or artist's ability in broadsword.

My eyes shifted to our hosts, Mac and his wife. She was lovely, with long, curly locks of dark brown and lighter strands highlighted under the glow of the room. She wore a beautiful shade of dusty blue that set off her eyes, the color of a cloudless sky. The silk blouse and slacks, cut to fit close, flattered her thin figure. She stood approximately three inches shorter than her husband, placing her at no disadvantage at approximately five foot nine inches.

"Sara, ye look rested. Feeling better?" Mac asked, greeting me this time with a hug.

"Much better. Thank you, Mac."

He turned to Kevin and clamped a hearty hand on his shoulder and shook his hand with the free one. Releasing his grip from Kevin's shoulder, Mac turned to me.

"Sara, this is my wife, Aggie."

I smiled and extended my hand in greeting but was met with a hand on each arm and a kiss to my cheek.

"We're so glad ye could make it tonight," Aggie said. My senses tuned in to her personality immediately. A keener sixth sense had come to life. I had not been able to tune in to the few individuals I'd met since arriving at Doune Castle. It wasn't that I hadn't tried but perhaps that I had been exhausted. Aggie's warm personality penetrated my senses and I felt an immediate closeness, as if we'd been friends a long time. The feeling eased me further into the comfortable ambience of the room.

"Please, do come in and sit," she said, gesturing to a large, buttery-soft sofa with textured accent pillows. As we stepped to the sitting area, a movement in the corner of my eye drew my attention. I glanced at Aggie and then over her shoulder to where I had seen something shift, but it was no longer visible.

"Iain, come meet our friends, lad," directed Mac, as if he had eyes on the side of his head.

A little boy I guessed to be no older than age seven peeked around the stones of the grand fireplace. He stole a glance at me and then

Kevin before seeking the sanctuary of the great wall once more. I smiled, sensing something about him, and decided to test my theory by sending him a thought.

"The lad is constantly running around the house. Never a moment's peace. And now, well, I may just have to invite ye over more often," Mac said with a laugh. "Come on, lad," he said, turning to look behind him.

Iain stepped from behind the wall with hands clasped behind him. His chin angled down but his eyes, blue like his mother's, hung on me as he came closer. He turned the corners of his mouth up into a smile and stopped in front of Aggie, tugging on a belt loop at her waist to gain her full attention. She bent down to meet him face-to-face. Iain leaned in and whispered in her ear. She angled her head toward me.

"He asked me if he could have a piece of the candy you brought," Aggie said with a look of puzzlement.

"Of course. If it's all right with you, that is," I said, glancing to Iain. Either the child had extrasensory abilities or he was familiar with small boxes of truffles wrapped in plain paper topped with a silver bow. I had set it on the table at the entry as I came in.

"Just one, mind ye, love. I don't want ye to spoil your dinner," Aggie said to Iain. "What do ye say?"

"Thank ye, miss," Iain said, eyes wide with delight at receiving approval to raid the box for his selection of one. His fingers gripped the edges of the wrapped box, ready to tear the paper away.

"What a darling boy you have," I said.

Aggie took the box from him and opened one end. "Thank ye. He's a wee bit of a handful at times. But most often quite agreeable. Dinner will be ready shortly," she added. "What can I bring ye for drink? Whisky?" she asked, turning to the men.

"Yes, my dear," Mac answered, glancing at Kevin, who nodded and thanked her.

"Sara, I've a lovely Merlot I've been waiting to share."

"Sounds like the perfect start to the evening. Can I help you?"

"Don't trouble yourself. Be comfortable. I'll be back before these men loop ye into some boring conversation," she said with a smile.

Kevin reached for my hand, redirecting my attention toward more serious matters as we settled into the sofa.

"What more can you tell us about the key? How difficult will it be to obtain once we enter the gateway?" Kevin asked, shifting slightly next to me and cutting straight to the business at hand.

"That's difficult to say, exactly," replied Mac. "The Druids wanted to be sure the symbols did not fall into the wrong hands by chance. Nor did they want the wrong person to enter the gateway under the guise of the Light Carrier."

"How would that be possible if only my energy is drawn to the gateway?" I asked.

"It doesn't mean a shapeshifter, for example, could not find the gateway, lass. It means only that, with the proper tools, they could open the same passage, bringing darkness with them."

"What tools?" Kevin asked, echoing my thought.

"That ring you wear is very powerful in identifying you as the true Light Carrier." Mac lifted his chin and dropped his eyes to my hand. "Should you have the great misfortune of having the ring removed from ye, with the symbols, a shapeshifter could open the passage."

By the stare on Mac's face, I realized it no longer mattered that the ring was a symbol of who I was. Not if it could be taken. Of course, I would have to be killed for that to happen. The darn thing hadn't budged from my finger since it was placed there. And I sure as hell wasn't letting anyone take an appendage without them losing one in return.

My thoughts shifted to the precious time between now and opening the passage. Kevin's growing anxiety wouldn't still until we entered the gateway.

"You're safe for now, but that can change, as I'm sure you're aware. We must get started soon," Mac said. "I suggest we leave tomorrow."

"What about the rest of the team?" I angled my head toward Kevin. "Will they be here in time?"

"Juno and Matt will be here in the morning. Aria and Elise, not until the following day."

"Dinna fash yirsel, lass. Once the passage is opened, your team will be allowed access," he said, turning to Aggie, who had just come into the room with drinks. "You'll show the others the way, once they arrive?"

"Yes, of course," Aggie replied.

She turned to me and handed me one of two glasses of wine she held.

"Ye see, when you open the path, it remains so, not only for your team but also for the dark forces," Mac continued. His eyes trailed toward the floor. "Assuming the entrance to the passage is found, with no help from ye, my love." His eyes lifted and he smiled at Aggie, who responded with a pat of her hand on his arm.

"She knows? About us and the quest?" I asked.

"Of course. None of our paths are an accident." He turned to Kevin, as something more than a look was exchanged between them for a split second. "I see there is still information she has not been provided."

"Yes. Some."

Aggie turned to Kevin and me. "Well now, shall we set talk of trips aside? Ye must be starved, with all that there was to worry over today."

"We're ready anytime you are," Kevin replied. "Dinner smells wonderful."

"Good. Sara can help me get the final preparations in place."

Kevin had grabbed a single biscuit inside the basket Mairi left for us and I had all but lost my appetite since waking in the bed. But the smells of roasting meat and seasoned potatoes from the kitchen reminded me how I'd neglected my appetite for too long.

Aggie took my hand in the crook of her arm, leaving Kevin and Mac to their discussion.

"Tell me what it's like in New York, the work you do. You're a psychiatrist, right?"

"Was a psychiatrist," I said. "An Ivy-League education I'd only used for a few years before having to give it up for the quest."

"And how did ye smooth that one over on the folks?"

"Ah. The folks are chalking it up to stress following the car accident that set all this into motion. They think my sabbatical is a necessary result of diving into my work too soon. They'd have me committed if they knew all the details we do about this mission."

Aggie laughed a little.

But there was a sting I felt at not being able to tell Mary Ann everything. She had loved me when no one else would, when my own mother had given me up to follow her boyfriend to God knows where. Mary Ann didn't need to know her daughter was delving into other worlds on a mission issued by a powerful spiritual order to save the human race. It even sounded a little crazy to me. The real world was not what I'd grown up believing it to be—hard work, rewards, struggle, and in my case, neglect and pain. Instead, reality meant eternal life that carried into other realms and different lifetimes again and again, with promises and duties to fulfill.

"What of the marvelous parties I hear the Forrester Foundation holding? They sound grand," Aggie said, interrupting further reflection on existence.

"There's not so much to tell." I began spooning potatoes into a large bowl.

"I should say there is. I've seen pictures in magazines of all the glitz and glitter. And who isn't captivated by all those famous faces?"

I tended to glaze over the well-known and the photographers who captured their poses at the engagements. But of course, our regular contributors were always important to each event.

"The foundation is an organization my adoptive mother set up to bring aid to charities around the world. I suppose over the years I've gotten used to seeing the same faces."

"I'll never know that feeling. Ye had one of the parties recently. Did ye not? Let's see, it was"—she put down the giant fork she'd used to transfer the roast to a platter and stared out the window as if reading the article that detailed the event through squinted eyes on the glass— "Europe. That's right, just a wee bit away. And to think ye were that close not days ago. But I can't recall what charity it was supporting."

"That particular cause was domestic abuse and neglect," I answered.

"That's right. The article said ye'd given a speech for that reason. Ye don't normally give them?"

"On occasion I will. Speeches are generally left to those who are better at giving them. Mary Ann, my adoptive mom, believes and has taught me that supporting such organizations is one of the most important acts of giving back." I tapped the spoon against the bowl to shake off a stubborn slice of potato. "Those benefits are just a lot of very wealthy people contributing and a whole lot of boring conversation. But they do indeed sparkle." My emotions took a brief and sudden dive as I was reminded of Mary Ann and the uncertainty of when or if I'd see her again, much less assist with the effort of such extravagant events.

"I'd give anything to sparkle among some of the diamonds I hear make it to those parties."

"Well, you're most welcome at the next one, and I'll introduce you to whomever you'd like should we be successful in pulling off this quest for the keys."

"I'll take ye up on it. I don't know what I find more fascinating, your evolution from your early childhood or the fact that you have remained so down-to-earth in spite of all the wealth. It's quite a rags-to-riches story, if ye don't mind me sayin' so."

"Not at all. I prefer to be low-key, avoid the press as much as possible, and leave that attention up to my father, business tycoon that he is. He handles it better."

While Robert Forrester, my adoptive father, funded several charities, Mary Ann's financial status before they'd met was nothing to scoff at. Her father had been an antiquities dealer and had left her well-off. She'd be fine without Robert's money. But wealthy people often loved lavish details and to mix with other wealthy people around tantalizing gourmet food and plenty of sparkle. And when they felt good, they tended to be more generous.

I didn't realize Aggie was so well informed of my background. But then again, it was her husband's job to know who would likely approach him for the task of finding the key. And of course, it was no surprise that *he* would share everything there was to know with his spouse.

As the wife of the man burdened with the task of escorting our team into the time warp that would lead to the Druid priests for the key, she, too, was burdened with knowing that someday her husband would leave for a time. I wondered if she feared his responsibility might not bring him back. Yet I felt nothing of the sort from her, only total acceptance and support for what had to be done.

We talked well past dinner and more wine, saying good night to little Iain after a light cake following dinner. His tummy full and eyes drooping, he'd hung around for the company and the lull of boring adult conversation until he'd curled up on the leather sofa with a few of the large cushions tucked around him for comfort. Aggie had scooped him up in her arms and hauled him off to bed.

Kevin and Mac were engaged in talk about what we might expect after passing through the gateway, while Aggie and I discussed the latest issues concerning current politics in Scotland and later about how she'd met Mac. My head was swimming in relaxation with each sip of brandy as I listened to her story, melting like smooth chocolate at the romantic points that highlighted Mac as an old-fashioned, sentimental type. I stole a glance at Kevin, who, reading my thoughts, shifted his gaze toward me and flashed a soft smile before returning to his conversation.

"So, how is it ye met that lovely?" Aggie asked as I glanced back to her. I sipped the brandy a little more slowly and smiled.

"Quite literally by accident," I replied, recalling to her my first meeting with Kevin under the most uncomfortable circumstances upon coming out of a coma and gasping for breath. I had just returned from Ardan to the realization that all I had experienced was not a dream and that I had been injured in an auto accident that sent me plunging into the parallel existence known as Ardan. I chose to withhold any mention of the details of Ardan, not certain of how much information Mac had shared with her. "He was my attending physician in the ICU," I said. I explained we had become friends and, in time, more than just partners in our mission. It wasn't until later that I learned his role was as one of the few Last Great Warriors sent to protect me from the evil seeking to interrupt my quest. Aggie smiled and glanced over my shoulder as Kevin appeared.

"Sorry to interrupt, love," said Kevin. "But we should be going. The MacCristals have had quite enough of us for a day, I should imagine."

"Nonsense," Aggie replied. "You are both quite welcome to stay as long as ye'd like."

Mac smiled and slipped an arm around her waist. "We'll need to hike back to the river tomorrow and they'll need their rest." Standing at Aggie's back with arms now fully wrapped around her, Mac playfully nipped at Aggie's neck.

Kevin and I parted with hearty thanks for dinner and good company before slipping into the rear seat of Mr. Watson's car to return to our cottage, floating high with the spirits consumed.

"When did you have time to pick up chocolates?" Kevin asked, shifting a little closer to me.

"What? Oh, that," I said, thinking of the small box in Iain's hand. "After we landed at the airport. You went for the rental car and I said I'd be just a moment. Remember?"

"I thought you went to..."

"I know. I thought they might come in handy for someone. And if they didn't"—I let out a breath and tilted my head back to rest on the seat—"I'd feed them to you." I slanted him a look and heard a faint sound escape his lips.

Arriving back at the cabin, I noticed the fire had been stoked, a couple small lamps switched on, and beds turned down. As I entered the bedroom I slipped off my shoes, placing them beside a small table next to the bed. The door of the cottage closed with a slam, to bypass the sticking of the threshold. I picked up a clear glass figurine and gazed at the angel holding a candle and was reminded that one of the keys I was to obtain was the light of understanding.

The hair on my neck brushed to one side and a soft, damp kiss on my neck drew my attention toward the tingles heading down my spine, as my body responded to Kevin's expert touch. I set the figurine down and exhaled. My eyes dropped to see Kevin's bare feet beside mine.

"Darling"—he paused and kissed behind my ear—"I've waited all evening to touch you," he whispered. His lips grazed my ear. "I need to be close to you. Inside you." The slightest moan slipped from my throat. His hand slid to my waist and up, grasping the tiny zipper on the side of my dress as he slowly pulled it down. The strap gave up its hold and fell to my arm. Kevin's breath was hot against my neck as he trailed kisses down and across my bare shoulder. I turned to face him. My hands stretched over the collar of his tailored white shirt and my fingers glided into his hair as I pulled him to me. His lips fed hungrily against mine and then suddenly stopped. His eyes held the look of passion halted too soon. I became aware of my breath, short and shallow, as it began to slow.

"I like what I do to you," he said.

"Then why stop?" I whispered.

"I want to take you slowly." His eyes blazed through mine, pinning me from looking away. Delicious thoughts of the moments we'd bonded at his home in the Cape began filling my head. And I wasn't sure if they were my own or his.

"Take me however you like but take me."

A wicked grin played across his lips. His hand lifted to my other shoulder and his thumb glided under the remaining thin black strap, causing the dress to pool on the floor at my feet. His eyes raked over me as he sucked in a breath. I ached to see him and reached for the buttons on his shirt. I was able to undo only two of them before he slid a hand over my cheek and leaned in for a slow, penetrating kiss, effectively stilling my attempts at removing his clothing. *Damn. This is too difficult. I need more of him, now.*

"Patience, love," he said against my lips, reading my thought. His hand dropped, and he pulled his shirt from his pants and over his head in one smooth stroke. My index finger lingered on the seam just below his belly button before hooking in the belt. He brought my finger to his lips and kissed it before unfastening the belt and stepping out of his pants. He lifted me to the crisp white sheets before freeing me of the remaining undergarments that blocked his touch.

"So beautiful," he whispered. My eyes locked on his intense gaze, just as they had the moment I first saw him, held by a connection I had yet to fully understand.

My hands found their mark as they pressed against his chest and slid across to his back on the search for more of him. I grazed the raised scar that extended the length of his torso and curved slightly on one side of his chest. He'd received the wound in the dark world and the area occupied by the shadows and demons under Tarsamon's command years prior when he had learned the danger that could kill us as humans but without harming us as immortal souls. He had nearly bled to death before the elves had rescued and healed him with their spells. He understood strength to survive, as did I. That connection, his desire, and the secrets of us he held tight to protect his agreement with the Soltari to be on the quest with me ignited my need for him. Right now, that need was stoked with an urge I couldn't recall having, not even when we had first made love in the Cape. All I wanted was to learn every inch of skin, to feel the length of him and the weight of his body against mine. What was fueling the increased hunger for him? Anxiety? Fear of what might happen when we entered the gateway? His fingers traced over my lips, down my neck, slowing to cup my breast before dipping lower across my stomach and abdomen and farther still to where we both knew it would be my undoing. I closed my eyes and felt him against me. I took in a deep breath, with my heart racing at his touch.

"Open your eyes, love. Feel me in more ways than one, and by God, maybe you'll remember what we are together, beyond this earthly plane, and how our spirits are connected."

I pressed my foot into the mattress and rolled us once so that I was straddling him, hoping the narrow bed could hold us. The heat exchanged between us glistened in a thin sheen across his chest.

I stared into his eyes, past the intensity and straight to his soul. My fingers locked with his on either side of his temples. "How are we connected?" It was a question I'd wanted to know the answer to since becoming aware of a bond we shared, of which he said he could not provide details. He'd given his word to the Soltari not to remind me. But I couldn't stand not knowing any longer. My need for him grew with each intimate encounter. And that had never happened with anyone, until now. I had never before allowed myself to become too close to anyone. Not only because commitment was never wanted but also because no one had ever fanned the flame of desire in the manner that Kevin did. Too much heat meant one would likely get burned.

"Through time and duty. It's all I can say."

"It's more. I know it. You know it."

"Yes. And if you like things the way they are between us, you'll accept this answer as enough."

"For now," I conceded.

Frustration bit at my neck, at the inability to know the details of the agreement for why he couldn't speak of our past together. But the attraction I felt with him at the moment was like an addict needing a fix. I released a breath and, with it, my concession to the ceiling. My eyes went to half-mast, consuming the muscular form beneath me, and then dropped to lock with the lustful stare that held me over him.

"Now, where..." he began. I leaned down and covered his mouth with mine, muffling the end of the question. I shifted slightly, feeling him harden even more beneath me, stoking my desire further. His hand pressed at my lower back and he rolled us again. "I need you this way tonight." His head slipped past my face and his lips reached my ear. "If you don't mind, darling."

I slid my fingers through the soft waves of chestnut hair and turned my face to meet his. "However you like."

He angled himself at my entrance and eased into me. His lips touched my ear again. "This time I want to feel every movement of you. Make love with me, Sara."

"I'm yours," I whispered across an exhale of breath.

He stroked slowly, while his lips captured soft moans of pleasure as they came back to mine in between the exchange of heated breaths. I pressed into each thrust, wanting even more of him. His rhythm increased and I felt myself easing toward the edge of the ecstasy that I'd only felt with him. All strength. All control. All consuming.

My chin lifted and my head fell back as he drove deeper. I gripped him harder with the need to feel every bit of him against me. Though narrowed, my eyes remained fixed with his, as sensations that ran through each nerve in my body carried me still higher, until I gasped out a name I only knew as a past love—Cerys.

"Yes, love," was Kevin's whispered reply, as he rose to his climax and held me tight against his chest.

Several moments passed as I listened to the stillness in the room. The only sound to be heard was Kevin's breath, slow and deep. Restful. The drink from earlier in the evening was still causing a slight dizzying feeling in my head, contributing to my relaxed but shocked state. Kevin nuzzled my hair as his arm came around me and looped a finger in the end of it at my shoulder. *Why isn't he angry that I called him by the name of the man I knew in another lifetime, actually a few of them? Why on earth did I do that?* I hadn't been thinking of Cerys. I had no real memories other than what Cerys had shared with me in Ardan. And those were beautiful but brief. *Cerys and Kevin.* Again and again I said the two names, trying to understand just how this connection was made, but nothing came to the forefront of my memory. Kevin's hand released the loop of hair and rested across my arm. I heard a small noise like that of a snore coming from him. It was the first time I'd ever caught him sleeping.

The small light on the table was still on. I carefully eased out of Kevin's grasp. With my elbow leaning into the pillow, I turned to face him and propped my head against my hand to watch him. The long lashes curled slightly. A peaceful expression like I'd never seen eased the hint of a line above his brow. My eyes drank in each lovely detail as they skimmed from hairline, across to his ears, his prominent but well-proportioned nose, and down as he breathed through full and slightly parted lips, until they rested on the squared chin. He was very much asleep. At last, I had full access to viewing him without the intrusion of him reading my thoughts. As I gazed over him, wondering about the puzzle he was to me, an overwhelming sensation of love and affection filled me. My body responded with heat and tingles that radiated like a live wire beneath my skin. A similar sensation to those I'd had when Cerys was present with me in Ardan. Similar to Cerys were the almond shape of the eyes and dark hair. Kevin's was cut shorter and he had a more pronounced jawline. Kevin's brows were thicker, too. I wanted to touch. But not wanting to wake him, I stared and committed to memory every line, every curve from his forehead to chin. Could there be a link between the two of them?

Before I could wonder any more about how or if the two were even connected, a sensation of fear replaced that love. The warmth left me cold and wanting for its return. I shivered once from it, pulling the tartan throw over me. If I were to show Kevin the emotions I had shared with Cerys, would he reject me? My heart knew the answer before I finished the thought. He wouldn't. My head screamed to reconsider the pain of possible rejection and to keep him at a distance. And yet I could imagine how beautiful it might be to share with Kevin the same love Cerys had reminded me of in Ardan. The thought caused tears to well in my eyes. *Cerys and Kevin.* I reached toward his cheek and Kevin's eyes blinked open, staring at me as though he'd heard every thought. I pulled my hand back, but he caught it in a lightning-quick move.

God, I forgot how fast he was.

He didn't move. He only stared at me as some deep exchange of feeling passed between us I didn't understand but still adored and feared at the same time. Realizing I was likely caught in my reverie, exposed, I flashed a quick smile and blinked, trying to shift away.

"I need some water. Would you like some?" I asked.

He squeezed my hand once and released it. "No, love."

I shifted off the bed, happy to have the distraction.

"So close, weren't we?" he said.

"Not sure what you mean." I slipped my arms through the robe, avoiding the stare I could feel boring a hole into my back. "I'll be right back." I glanced at him over my shoulder as I stepped from the room. Something crossed over his eyes. A shadow of sadness I could feel, and he knew it. Inwardly, my heart sunk with the realization I might be the cause.

5

Nestled in warmth, I stirred slightly, enough to notice Kevin was not beside me. I could only have been asleep for an hour, or so it felt. I pulled my arm back from the empty pillow and peeled my eyelids open to find my way to the living room, where a faint light glowed. He sat with legs propped on the arm of the sofa, head tilted back on one bent arm, his eyes closed. A magazine was sprawled open across his stomach.

"Are you sleeping?" I whispered, not wanting to startle him.

"No, love," he said, opening his eyes and turning to look at me. "Did I wake you?"

"No." I paused. "Well, yes. You weren't there and I wondered."

"You missed me?" His smooth, deep voice rose slightly in surprise. I shrugged a shoulder and smiled.

A sudden feeling of exposure at the precise meaning behind his question began to wash over me. He was, in fact, suggesting I was beginning to like having him close. My buried insecurities that had fought to allow anyone close, that built the wall against it, were being withered to baseless fears since Kevin had started to smooth out the rough edges. Were they no longer my fears to work out in due time? Was he aware of the internal battle I fought to allow him to be close to me? Of course, he wanted me to trust him completely. He had expressed as much just before we rushed away from New York, asking me to live with him at least until the danger had passed. I had turned him down, not wanting the commitment and not because I had other prospects. As I stood considering his question, it surprised me that, in fact, I had missed him. I also found it to be a sign of weakness on my part, a sign that my energy would need to be concentrated on someone I cared for and slightly less on the mission. That was a potential danger to the mission, at least in the eyes of the Soltari.

"It's okay. You don't have to answer," he said, moving from the sofa and reaching me in a couple of strides. He rested his hands on my shoulders and let them glide down, kissing me on the forehead. It was no surprise to find him awake. When I'd stayed with him for a week in the Cape, it was as though he never slept, always rising before the sun and waking at every shift of our bodies.

"I did miss you," I replied much too late. "Why are you out here?"

"I can't sleep, not until we are safely beyond the gateway."

"Right now is your best chance for rest. We won't know what we'll encounter once we go through the passage."

"You might be right," he said. His eyes flicked upward in consideration and returned to mine. "But I've other things occupying my mind at the moment that may help me sleep." In an instant, his eyes changed from thoughtful to smoldering.

He swept aside a few strands of hair from across my forehead with his fingertips and quickly whisked me off my feet into his arms, causing me to emit a sound that mimicked the bark of a dog. He carried me the few steps to the bedroom. My skin responded to his gentle touch as his fingers glided up the length of my arms and over my shoulders, skimming between my breasts and stopping at my stomach, which began to quiver under the anticipation of further delight of his hand.

"It's late," he said. "You need rest." He kissed the place on my stomach where his hand was and shifted to cradle me close to him.

I need you, I thought.

You have me.

"How does that help you sleep?" I asked.

"Having you rested and full of strength provides me peace of mind."

"You worry that much?"

"Sh." He pulled me against his solid form while his fingers slowly glided through my hair in a gentle repetitive stroke. I closed my eyes as my passion was replaced by his tenderness.

My thoughts drifted to the flash of sadness in his eyes that likely caused him to lie awake on the sofa. I wanted to give everything to him but I didn't have what he wanted—complete trust. Or more specifically, the ability to put myself at risk to be potentially hurt by someone I loved. How had he recovered from seeing his mother murdered at the age of seven, no older than little Iain? How had he learned to love a woman so completely again when the pain of that loss must have ripped him in two? If he could recover completely from that, I should be able to do the same. But how? Neglect had built a tough outer shell that left a vacancy inside I wasn't sure could be filled.

"Darling," Kevin said, pulling me from my critical thought. "You're not going to get any rest going over things you can't answer right now." He stopped stroking my hair and tucked a lock behind my ear. "I've not loved another as deeply as you. Ever. And I've known you across millennia. Now sleep." The repetitive stroking moved down my back in gentle sweeps, quieting the analytical mind seeking to understand.

I drifted from consciousness into the world of Ardan without much intention to do so. It was the first visit in days. The skies had changed from their usual blue-gray to a shade of evening that mirrored dark storm clouds. The outline of trees appeared black against the darkened sky. A rare breeze caught my hair and blew it to the side as I stared down an empty dirt path ahead of me. As every sound sharpened to the point of a pin, my senses indicated something was approaching. I waited patiently to see who'd summoned me.

Within moments, a faint, shadowy mist began to take shape around me that I recognized as the Soltari. I'd come to learn of the powerful collective group of spirits through a couple of visits to Ardan, discovering it to be rare that they showed themselves. In my case, however, I had already seen them twice in the past month. Three white faces formed directly in the mist in front of me, floating like small, thick puffs of fog. Beyond them were several other lingering ghostly masks.

"You have called me to you. Is that correct?" I asked.

"Indeed, we have," a single airy voice replied. No lips moved on the transparent faces that stared back at me. "Shadows have entered your path. They have traced your energy to your location. Do not be misled by the dark forces that follow." The voice spoke slowly and then paused as if a collective thought was being processed. "Follow the way of the guardian of the key, toward the magical ones. They will keep you in their protection."

"Who are the magical ones? Do you mean the priests?"

"Follow the way of the guardian," repeated the voice.

"You have come to warn me of the Dark Lord's forces. Do you know how close they are?"

A pause filled the air once more and the three faces turned to look at each other before gazing back at me.

"At your doorstep. Open the gateway that leads to the magical ones, quickly." The three misty faces blended together into one and lifted to join with the others in the enormous white fog that consumed the space where I stood. The entire lucent mass came together in a swirling funnel high above before stretching across the sky and disappearing into darkness.

I woke instantly to find Kevin dressing in the silver glow of the moonlight streaming in from the sheer window coverings. I pulled my senses together, realizing my two worlds were joining together faster by the moment.

"The shadows," I began, shoving my fatigue aside to formulate my sentences. "They're close. I was just warned."

"As was I. Let's get going. We'll need to wake Mac and head for the gateway right now. We can't—" Kevin was cut off by the sound of pounding at the door. I shot out of bed, grabbed for my clothes, and ran into the bathroom to dress as Kevin shut the bedroom door behind him.

I stepped out moments later to find some of my team congregating in the cozy living area of the tiny cottage. They were all dressed in full gear, prepared for battle as I had first seen them in Ardan, swords tucked discreetly behind the folds of each of their long coats, evidently having received the same warning.

"Matt, Juno, it's so very good to see you," I said. The last I had seen of them was as they battled Tarsamon's forces at my home, while Kevin and I had sped away, with the hope that my leaving would cause the evil to disperse.

"The dark shadows are close behind us," Juno said, shifting his gaze to the other faces in our group. "We've seen their arrival here in Scotland and don't have much time, probably no more than a few hours, before they catch up."

Matt and Juno held the unique ability to see coming events, serving them well in their roles in the military's Special Forces and now, on this mission. Matt was in the 160th Aviation Regiment known as the Night Stalkers while Juno had brought his expertise as a SEAL to our team.

"That means Elise and Aria will be arriving behind the shadows," I said. "Are they in greater danger entering the passageway behind Tarsamon's forces?"

"Dinna fash, lass," Mac replied. "Aggie will guide them to the gateway safely. The shadows may follow your energy trail, but they won't be hunting down Elise and Aria."

I turned to Kevin, concerned about our two remaining companions. "Do they know to meet with Aggie?" I asked.

"It's all arranged. There's no need to worry about them," Kevin replied. "I made contact with them before we went to dinner last night." His eyes remained set on mine with the understanding I had to trust his word they'd be in capable hands. "The safety of the team is my responsibility. You don't need to worry about them throughout the quest, okay?"

I nodded. Kevin might be handling security detail, but it didn't mean I wouldn't worry for them.

Mac stepped forward. Reaching for my hand, he placed the three symbols in my open palm and closed my fingers around them. I slid the medallions into my coat pocket and made sure my sword was in its sheath, fastened beneath my coat.

"Mac, if you'll lead the way," I said.

Though the path from the cottage down to the river might have been familiar, it was better led by someone who'd spent a lifetime studying the path we'd take through the whisper of the mystical winds to the electromagnetic fields of the passage to another realm. The extreme chill in the air bit at my cheeks as I struggled to see the trail Mac was making for us, a single flashlight in hand. We continued in silence, reserving our energy for the gateway.

As we arrived at the end of the path, the water spilled across the bank of the river's edge and I felt the pull again to enter. It was much stronger this time. Kevin instinctively moved closer to me, his hand at my back. Juno and Matt stood to my left while Kevin and Mac were flanked to my right. A picture flashed in my mind of us joined by hands in a circle, as though an unseen power detected the need for further instruction to be delivered. The other members of the team moved to form the shape, already in tune with the tele-pathic thought that had been delivered. I pulled the symbols from my pocket and held them tightly in my hand, recalling the image of the sun and the tree of life located on the front of the first symbol. My thumb skimmed over the top, confirming the accuracy of my memory, before I slid all three medallions back into my pocket. I grasped Kevin's hand.

A bright white light flashed several feet in front of us over the wa-ter like a transient electrical storm, then another, as a sound resem-bling the hum of electricity grew louder, filling the calm stillness of the evening. With the increasing noise, the formation of light held its position above and expanded across the water in the shape of a circle. Rippling waves of light filled its center. The sound grew deafening. I closed my eyes tight and ducked my head. I wanted to tear free of the hands I held to cover my ears. Instead, I clung tight out of sheer de-sire to keep contact with the familiar. The pull at my body at that mo-ment was powerful. Our grip in each other's hands tightened at the realization we were no longer touching the ground. I opened my eyes but could see no one, only a waterfall encircling me. My body was cocooned in some sort of protective bubble, moving with the flow of the water around me. Where were the others? I'd never felt my hands break free of theirs. The trail of water ahead was not visible. *Where was this going to*—The water holding me gave way as gravity pulled me down in a rushed fall. My stomach lurched from the quick descent before everything went black.

I opened my eyes to a canopy of enormous tree arms extending above me. Soft branches of flowing fernlike leaves grazed over my forehead, like the gentle stroke of feathers. In an instant, the dark evening sky at the River Teith had shifted to a fine sunny day. I blinked at the harsh light, allowing the rods and cones of my retinas to adjust to the intrusion of bright white. The air carried a cool undercurrent on its breeze.

"Kevin," I called out, pausing for a response. "Mac."

I heard movement nearby and sat up, turning my head in the direction of the sound. Juno, Matt, and Mac were lying in the same supine position, stirring to life. I moved to get a better view of my surroundings and noticed my clothing had changed.

"Holy Christ," I said, glancing down. Still sitting, I scrambled to pull the dark blue floor-length skirts up to find my pants were still in place, along with boots. My coat lay discarded a few feet away. A flash of silver from the hilt of my sword beamed from beneath a corner of leather. I scanned the area for any sign of Kevin, finding mostly brush and a thicket of trees and stopping at the base of a tree several feet away, to where he was sitting. My head was spinning, either from the journey or from rising too soon. Relieved that everyone was alive and unhurt, I tucked my head between my knees to wait out the dizziness and the nausea that accompanied it.

"Rough landing," Juno said. "Perhaps that will get better with practice."

"One could only hope," Matt replied in an equally pained voice.

"Is Kevin all right?" I asked, still holding my head down. I felt a hand on my back and lifted my head to see that it was indeed Kevin. Having the ability to feel what others felt emotionally and physically meant in addition to Kevin's and my misery from the journey, we could feel the anguish from the others. I was relieved to see that he looked all right, faring much better than some of us.

"Block your senses," he said. "It will help you to only feel your discomfort and to deal with it." Kevin was more experienced with the manipulation of the energy around us than I. I didn't block much of anything, whether they were the thoughts in my head that he could hear or the feelings coming from others. I still had to work at it. Following his instruction, I found the block relieved me of the nausea while providing the chance to focus. The dizziness still remained as I moved slowly to a standing position to gauge the scenery.

"Mac, I take it we're still in Scotland?" I asked, brushing a hand over the corset area that had cinched my breasts into a personal pillow tabletop on my chest. At least they were fully covered.

"Yes, we should be. Though I do not recognize this particular place." Mac was gazing ahead, over Matt's shoulder. "And judging by the garb, I'd say we are."

"I feel like I'm dressed for a damn costume party," I said, lifting the heavy skirt.

"Aye, but you'll need it should we encounter town folk. We wouldn't want ye to stand apart from the others."

"I suppose not."

"This will take a little getting used to," Juno said under his breath.

He was dressed in the same kilted attire as the other men. Despite the clothing, it would be hard to hide his darker features and spiky black hair that clearly defined him as anything other than of Scottish decent.

I glanced across the landscape, a lush paradise of many different species of trees and plant life.

"These trees, are they found in Scotland?" I asked. I was certain about the willow tree that I had landed under and, glancing about, others like it, while there were some I didn't recognize.

"Yes, many varieties of willows, to be sure, are found in Scotland," he replied. "As are the rowans, just ahead over there." He pointed in the direction of a large group of trees in the distance, clusters of white flowers dotting the green foliage. "The Celts believed the rowan to be a source of protective energy."

"That seems the most likely place to locate something protected," Juno said.

"Indeed," Mac replied. "The priests will not be found in this forest. We must keep moving. Sara, you should be guided as well. Your presence is detected by the energy here."

"I can feel something strong in this place. And I think Juno is right, that energy is down by there," I said, lifting a chin in the direction of the rowans.

We hiked the distance across the barrage of trees, down a bank of tall grass, until we reached a shallow stream that cut through our path. We stopped for a drink before trekking up the hillside. The view from the top revealed the rowans to be the only cluster in sight, hopefully confirming we were on the right path. I felt a distraction behind me and turned to see Matt and Juno stopped in discussion. Kevin turned back to join them.

"Keep going. We'll catch up with you and Mac," he said. I sensed his concern regarding the shadows and their proximity. Feeling his urgency, I realized we needed to get under the protection of the priests soon. I turned to continue, steps behind Mac.

The rowan trees had been well within sight during the hike. But as we headed down the embankment, they became lost in the thicker branches of trees that joined together in a ceiling over our heads. Mac and I pressed through dense groupings of velvety ferns and tall grass, with me moving in one direction while Mac veered off in another, both headed toward the same goal in front of us.

A whisper, similar to the one that had led me to the River Teith, flowed to me from the shade of the leafy branches. I stopped walking to listen and heard my name, calmly at first and then forcefully, as if it were angry I had not answered. I turned once and continued on, stumbling over something rough and falling into a large fern. *Damn dress. How the hell does anyone function in these things?* I hiked it up with both hands, debating whether to rip it off and deal with the odd looks from unknown town folk before reason took hold. Mac was right. We didn't need to draw unnecessary attention to ourselves any more than we might. I reached out to push myself up and touched a short wall. *What is this? Odd place for it.* I glanced around. There was no sign of Mac. I stood and brushed aside the tall ferns and grass to see what had diverted my path was a headstone. A few steps behind me, where I'd fallen, a single similar stone sat upright in the rich soil, pieces broken and trailing around the main stone.

I felt the sudden presence of someone. I whipped my head around to see the apparition of a man standing only feet from me. *Run or talk to him? I'm not getting any bad vibes.* His tall transparent form stood rigid. Gray hair rested in long strands against his chest and his expression was solemn as he stared at me. I shifted to regain a steadier footing in the soft dirt. He was cloaked in white, and tucked in the crook of his arm was a leather-bound book.

"Light Carrier," he said. He tilted his head slightly to one side, extended an arm, and pointed in the direction I had been headed before I'd stumbled. "Continue on."

My eyes drifted across the field.

"Sara!" Mac called back to me, shaking me out of the trance I had been in upon seeing the ghost. I shifted my attention in the direction of Mac's voice and back again to the now empty space in front of me.

"Over here. Behind you," I shouted, hoping he would follow my voice. I crouched down to try and read the writing on the marker but found it to be in Gaelic.

A hand gripped my arm firmly and lifted me up. I gasped, startled at the sudden action and never hearing the footsteps. "My God, are you trying to frighten me?" I asked, seeing Kevin, Matt, and Juno standing around me.

Kevin laughed. "Not afraid to fight a demon lord on his turf, but frightened of those who would protect you?"

I pressed my lips together in a smirk, remembering my trek to Tarsamon's world before we had escaped New York and the battle with the demons that nearly put an end to me and the quest before it had even begun. If it hadn't been for Kevin's speed and the bracelet that acted as a tracking device to help him find me, none of us would be here now.

"Ye've found the markers of the Druid Priests," Mac said, joining us. "We are close now."

"Do they say anything that would be of particular interest to us?" I asked. "I can't read Gaelic." Kevin looked at the broken stone for a moment, while Mac gazed at one that was intact.

"This one describes the name and rank of the priest who lies here," Kevin said. "But I cannot make out the rest of the writing with the damage to the stone."

"Nay. The stones wouldna have anything useful to us. The rowan trees are sacred to the Druids. They believe in their protection and divinity, choosing to plant the trees among their deceased," Mac explained. "The priests would never have wanted to prophesize the coming of the Light Carrier. Not here, anyway."

I lifted a gaze up and across the shadowed space. All my focus had been on the stones, and a ghost, and I hadn't noticed the rowans planted among us.

"There's a powerful energy surrounding this space," I said as we continued on. "Can you feel it?" I turned to glance at Kevin and the others. Matt and Juno looked at each other. "What?" I paused, trying to sense their hesitation. "What did you see back there?" I asked. "You don't need to protect me from your vision. Tell me so I can be prepared."

Matt and Juno looked at Kevin. He nodded his approval and I saw the vision. The evil shadows were swarming the early-morning landscape at Doune, seeking the gateway. We were only a couple of hours ahead of them at this point, maybe less.

"Is this a private affair or can ye share what ye see?" Mac asked, forgotten by us for the moment, a few feet away.

"Sorry, Mac," Kevin replied. "We didn't mean to exclude you. The shadows are at the hillside at Doune."

"Aggie. Is she safe?"

"Yes. There's nothing to worry over regarding your wife. She doesn't appear to be of interest to them. It's good that Aria and Elise have not yet arrived seeking her help. If they had, the shadows would have tracked their energy directly to Aggie."

Couldn't they still?

They want entrance into the realm to track you, Kevin answered, hearing my thought. *Still, we don't want any casualties because your energy can be tracked to the home, too. But we don't need to worry Mac.*

Of course not.

"It also means we have even less time than we thought to find the Druids and get the key," Matt added. "The path grows more dangerous as each moment passes."

A whisper mingled in the currents of the breeze as it picked up and settled, echoing the urgency felt by all of us. The location we were searching for couldn't be much farther. As several seconds passed, the sound of indecipherable whispers grew louder in my ears, drowning out the crunch of our footsteps against the dead leaves and grass, until the noise changed to something similar to static. I realized it was similar to our arrival at the gateway at the river but without the hum of electricity.

My head began to throb and the pressure in my ears grew uncomfortable. Kevin reached out both hands to rest on my temples, sensing my distress. I could see the mouths of the others moving but could not hear them.

It's here, isn't it? This is the place, right? He sent the thought to me.

I nodded, my forehead pressed into his chest. *Yes. Any moment. Stay close.*

He said a couple of things to Mac, causing the others to move together. As they did, a rumble beneath caused the Earth to separate. I tried to step to the side of it with Kevin beside me. But the crack extended past my feet and soil fell into the open space. Was this what had happened to some other poor soul to cause the headstone I'd stumbled over earlier to be erected? Kevin's arms tightened around my waist but the force was too strong. His grasp broke free. I reached for him but it was no use as I went spiraling into a wormhole that had opened beneath my feet, down a dark and winding tunnel at lightning speed. The dress lifted around me, cocooning me in a blanket of navy blue. I'd just begun to recover from the effects of the last portal only to face a new round of nausea and dizziness, until the fall began to slow and it was as though I was floating in a dark, warm lagoon.

Nothing but peace surrounded me. I wanted to keep my eyes closed and dwell in the comfort of it. But the quiet was being severed like a pinprick to the skin by the sound of a woman's voice, followed by a familiar male voice.

6

"You're running out of time to stop her." Tarsamon's booming voice slammed off the walls of the large cavern and into C-05's ears. "How could you have let her slip away in New York?"

"She wasn't alone, my Lord," C-05 replied. "She is guarded carefully, as you would expect." Tarsamon's glare and minute of silence had C-05 more than uneasy. He could swear his skin was crawling, trying to escape the frame that held it.

"I expect you know how to work around the technicalities. You know her team better than anyone, intimately. As she obtains each key, the opportunity to stop her will become much more difficult."

Arriving in Scotland just one evening prior, C-05 carried specific instructions leading to Doune Castle and to Sara. He had been diverted this evening to meet with the Dark Lord in the realm of Ardan where the Soltari had granted him occupation to answer to why Sara had escaped.

"The Light Carrier is closer to those who can protect her. The magical ones." Tarsamon folded his arms and curled long fingers under the dark shadow of a chin. He sucked in a constricted breath and stood motionless, glaring at C-05. "I'm doubting your ability, your desire. Maybe you would rather get back to the Alliance." He laughed under a throaty growl. "As if you could."

C-05 knew that he had given up any chance of going back to the safety of the Alliance, to rejoining the good side of this war. They would never take him back once he'd made the decision to shift sides against them. But he'd had no choice after being captured by Tarsamon's forces.

C-05's gaze darted first to the corner of the room where a demon no larger than four feet tall glared at him through yellow eyes set in blackened hollows and what appeared to be gray deteriorating skin, before directing his attention back to Tarsamon. The demon lord appeared more like the grim reaper without a scythe, he thought, and yet more menacing than any picture he'd ever seen of the reaper. Tarsamon's cloak trailed behind the shadow of the figure he was as he floated about the cave like a puppet suspended by an invisible wire, a mere foot above ground. There was a faint outline of a face. His jaw and cheekbones were only visible when he was speaking. Eyes that shifted color from yellow to red, depending on his mood, floated like the tip of a red-orange laser pointer aimed in the blackness that surrounded them. Those beams were nearly burning holes into his eyes. C-05 forced himself to hold the gaze, pressing back the fear that sought to give him away.

"She is only protected once the Druids have identified her as the Light Carrier," C-05 replied. "Until then, there is opportunity." He paused, considering his options. "She hasn't yet reached their protection. There is still time to get to her. She has a weakness for caring too much for people, especially those closest to her."

As the sole person who had been selected by the Alliance to bring Sara's team together on Earth, he knew the whereabouts of each member. And if they didn't block him, he'd be able to read their thoughts and learn the next phase of their plan, although that likelihood was slim. Without explanation, C-05's ability to tune in to Sara or a few of the other members had become hindered upon his arrival to Scotland. He wondered if that would change once he passed through the gateway. And there sure as hell wasn't any reason he could see to share the recent limitation of sight with Tarsamon. The members of Sara's team were likely blocking him since he'd been present for the attack on her in New York. By now, they were fully aware he'd switched sides to aid Tarsamon. It was also possible the supernatural strengths they carried might be altered in the presence of certain energy fields, like that of strong electromagnetic fields, those that could move people through time and space.

While Tarsamon was familiar with C-05's advanced intuitive abilities and planned on using those to get information, he'd never fully trust him. The man had shown his weakness, having turned so easily against his team by letting fear consume him. He was a traitor. And a traitor once might be a traitor again. He'd have to keep him in line. The sheer darkness of Tarsamon's soul was often too much for any other spirit to endure. Anyone who had once belonged to the Alliance, as C-05 had, possessed advanced gifts that were known in the spirit realm to find a way beyond even the most advanced supernatural strengths possessed by other immortals in Ardan. C-05 was a tool to be used carefully.

Tarsamon turned slowly away as he contemplated the outcome of Sara Forrester obtaining one of three keys of enlightenment. The thought soured his mood further. If she was successful, it would put an end to all the preparation to obtain the light on Earth to expand the evil that had already built his army. Nothing would deter him from the goal to overcome Sara's world and make the Soltari pay for striking him from the Alliance and sending him away to rot in a tiny corner of Ardan.

The humans were weak, most of them, and could easily be consumed by their own negative thoughts, greed, and narcissism, resulting in their demise. There was little he had to do but feed that hunger for more anger, stress, worry, and fear. Fear was the driving force dividing them and leaving them weak for the taking. After all, it was easier to feel bad than to rise above negativity and reach for what felt good. But waiting for the humans to be consumed by that negativity would take much longer than he was willing to allow. Tarsamon's dark forces, the shadows and demons he had called to Earth, would make quick work of the path humanity had so generously carved for him. He simply needed to be sure the Light Carrier and any ability she had to deter him from his mission did not interrupt his progress, now or in the future. Sara Forrester should have been killed in New York. Because she hadn't, there were loose ends to attend to and fast.

"You believe she is weak," Tarsamon said, breaking the heavy silence. "Yet the Soltari would not have selected a weak individual as the protector of the light on Earth. I believe you gravely underestimate her."

"She is valuable indeed, strong in her character but inexperienced in this life." C-05 stepped back a full foot. "The Soltari hid her memory of other worlds and her experiences in them. She believes she learns as she travels without fully being able to recall her role as the head of the Alliance. I don't believe she is aware yet of her power. This is why there is an opportunity to get to her now."

"Pursue her then, before she becomes *enlightened*. And bring this woman to me. I want to see for myself if the spirit residing in her human form is as strong as I have known in the past, memory of it or not that she may have. I will know when I see her, when I can feel her energy. Her prior entrance into the darker side of Ardan sent waves rippling through one of the darkest energy realms that exist. You're either misinformed of her circumstances or underestimating her."

"My Lord, it would be nearly impossible to save her, as she will fight to the death. The reinforcements she has are numerous." C-05 paused, considering the aides Sara had at her disposal in Ardan, not to mention those in other realms, and how he could get her away from her team. "But…"

"Intercepting her path to the keys is of greater importance." Tarsamon turned again to face C-05.

"If I bring her to you, what guarantee is there that I will not be killed with the others on Earth?"

"Your life is meaningless to me with the exception of your ability to reach beyond the depths of the protected caverns of the Druids that I cannot. Your success at stopping the Light Carrier would be rewarded with the freedom from my forces in any of the realms you choose."

This had been the sweet reward that C-05 had hoped for in exchange for turning over the Soltari's prized possession to the Dark

Lord. But before he could choose what realm to live out an eternal life in, he had to locate the soul he had loved over time. She'd been separated from him by the Alliance at the failure of his last quest and sent to an unknown location. He'd considered tracking her, but in the numerous realms in time and space she could be in, it would take an eternity to find her. And no one who enjoyed the benefits of staying in Ardan under the protection of the Soltari would risk helping him. He was certain he could negotiate this piece, to help locate his partner, if he could bring Sara to the Dark Lord alive.

His anger stirred, heating his blood as he remembered when he'd lost his love. It hadn't been his fault that the number of forces they were sent to battle had been sorely underestimated. It was the Alliance's duty to have all the facts and provide them to the team members. No. They had divided an immortal love, punished him for *their* mistake. And they would pay.

Tarsamon paused to listen to the seed of fury taking root within C-05's conscience. Only when C-05's eyes lifted from the floor and the not-so-distant memory to meet his did he speak. "Go. Sara isn't stalling and you waste precious time. Remember, fail in your promised quest to intercept her path and it is your immortal life I'll own. I can get to her eventually, without you if necessary. The magical ones cannot hide her in the Druid world for very long."

C-05 turned and exited the gloomy cavern, his only companion the scent of dust and mildew pasted inside his nostrils, with his possible demise resting on the surface of his thoughts. And yet getting Sara away from her team was the only chance for him to reclaim what he'd lost. To him, the reward was more valuable than life alone in any realm. He hadn't wanted to pursue Sara. He had been caught off guard in the dark world, underestimating his abilities. His only bargaining chip to spare his life was to turn over any information about the quest and his ability to get close to the Light Carrier.

The only way she might let her guard down was if he could convince her he'd slipped, become too afraid. He thought she might believe him, perhaps show him mercy. Maybe she would trust him just enough to let him close to her.

He pulled his bottom lip between his teeth. *Just a little more convincing. That's all Sara needs. Just have to get her alone, away from her protection.*

A plan began to take root in the darker corners of his mind, an area he had not wanted to enter. He tried pushing the idea away but couldn't, fearing his own life was ticking by at a faster rate since leaving Tarsamon. C-05 scratched the back of his neck, feeling the cool sweat slide under his fingernails.

His skill to shift into another form would prove useful, but it would mean taking the life of one of the companions she trusted. No matter, he thought, drumming his fingers against the denim covering his thighs as he pulled the car into the last parking space in front of the hotel. This was war, undeclared, but definitely war. There were always unfortunate casualties in any battle.

For now, he'd wait patiently for the light of a new day to find the gateway somewhere by the river that would lead him to her. He didn't have an exact location but there were sure to be energy trails, signals that could be picked up if the passage she had sought had been unlocked recently. And he was certain it had. Since he'd arrived in Doune, the hairs on his arms would stand on end each time he thought of the gateway. He felt the strong sensation of electricity that glided within the air currents straight to him, fresh from the opening of something as powerful as a crack in time. He thought following her was akin to catching the scent of an animal and tracking it, except the scent he hunted was an energy trail and the animal was a much more valuable prize than any food or fur.

7

The sound of a man and woman talking drew me away from my peaceful state into a bewildering fog of sensation.

"She's awake," came the voice of a woman.

I searched to process where I might have ended up after the spiraling effect that had ripped me from Kevin's grip.

"Is she all right?" the man's voice asked.

"Oh, quite. Perhaps a little groggy, but just fine," answered the woman.

"Matt?" I asked, taking a shot in the dark. I peeled my eyelids back to get the first glimpse of my surroundings. At least my ears had not failed me. Matt was approaching as I tried to regain my senses. I sat up before my body was ready and the room began to spin.

"Not so fast, lass," said the woman. "Ye probably ought to sit for a moment before trying to set out again."

I turned to Matt, seeking answers quicker than I could phrase the questions. He touched my hands resting in my lap. Had it not been for the dizziness, the woman was right, I would have been up and out the door, looking for the other members of my team.

"Where are the others? Is Kevin all right?" I squeezed my eyes shut, trying to press a dull ache from behind my eyes before opening them again to focus on Matt's face. "Where are we?" I wrapped my hands around the edge of a cot, glancing at the crumpled blankets where my feet had been.

"Kevin and the others are with Mac trying to find information regarding the priests," he answered. "We arrived in an underground world called Randun, far beneath the group of rowan trees we saw, before you were pulled away. Remember?"

Beneath the trees? Had that been the tunnel I was spiraling through before blacking out?

"Yes, of course. I haven't lost my mind." I heard the rising temper in my tone. "Sorry."

In an instant, I felt very small considering the different realms of Ardan, Tarsamon's corner of it, and now, an underground realm called Randun. Were there others? Three medallions with three locations—Scotland, the Mayan peninsula, and Egypt. It left me to wonder how very little I'd considered of anything larger than my life in New York prior to this quest. Everything I thought I knew meshed together with newly discovered facts, was mingling together like a bad salad at a potluck. Ignorance might indeed be bliss. But if I wanted any chance of normalcy again, I couldn't just sit here waiting for it.

"We have to go," I said with some desperation. My eyes focused intently on Matt's. "There isn't much time before the shadows find a way in."

"Here, lass. Drink this. It will calm ye," the woman said, pressing a cup toward me.

"Thank you. But I don't need a drink or to be calmed. I need to find the members of my team," I said.

"You don't need to worry about the dark forces. They cannot enter here," she said.

"That is somewhat of a relief. If it's true," I replied. "Who are you?"

I sat staring at a very short woman, no more than about four and a half feet tall. Her long red-brown hair hung smoothly behind her shoulders and patient amber eyes stared back at me.

"Sara, this is Magdalene. She found us—"

"I was told to meet ye," she interrupted.

"She's given us a place to stay," Matt continued. "She knows about our quest, but that can all be explained later. Kevin asked that we wait."

"He doesn't lead this mission. Does he?"

Matt pressed his lips together, caught between a request from Kevin and my uncomfortable tension.

I inhaled a quiet breath that reached deep into my lungs. But it had little effect on my growing anxiety. There was indeed something to be concerned about. I couldn't pinpoint the exact reason, but somehow it felt like we were still in danger. It wasn't merely a sensation that time was slipping away from us, either, but something else. Matt didn't seem unsettled in any way. He couldn't feel the same sense of urgency as I.

My focus narrowed and my nerves cinched tighter than the corset I was still wearing. The last thing I wanted to do was argue with the members of the team about what path to take. The abilities I had been granted were provided as a means to guide me through the task to see the guardian of the key. With that task completed, I had to trust the heightened sense of feeling and intuition leading me to the next steps. Matt was a good friend of Kevin's and would gladly do what he'd been asked, believing it was best. And given that I had not been awake to protest the instruction, I couldn't really fault him.

I turned my gaze to Magdalene. "Thank you for your hospitality." I shifted my gaze back to Matt. "I'm sorry, really, but I can't wait. We are pressed for time and must continue on. Tell Kevin I will return by nightfall."

"Where are you going? This is unfamiliar territory and you can't be wandering about."

"I can't explain this feeling. But there is a strong pull for me to search out what is urging me outside. I can't sit here and wait." He let out a breath. "Look, I won't get involved in anything. I'll blend," I said, lifting the long skirt slightly with one hand. "And if I find anything worthwhile, I'll bring the information back. If I don't find anything, no harm done."

"I can't let you go. There is no one else to protect you."

"I'm an avid fighter. Besides, if Magdalene is correct, I won't need protection." I pushed myself to stand, swaying a little, and slid my arms through the sleeves of the long black coat, noting the additional weight of it. My sword had somehow already been fastened inside. Before exiting the doorway, I glanced over my shoulder to Matt. "By nightfall."

The air was cool against my cheeks but not as crisp as when we'd left Scotland almost a day ago. *A day. I've lost another day just in travel.* I stood in the street, eyeing the folks moving around me and trying to sense which direction felt most accurate. I turned to memorize the front of Magdalene's cottage, hoping I would be able to find it later.

A broken corner of thatched roof. Faded blue door. Got it.

The street was busy with people passing by, carrying baskets full of bread or vegetables, armfuls of folded cloth, and other trinkets that looked to be going to market, somewhere nearby. Daylight reflected in this place far beneath the surface that I had been pulled from, without any explanation as to how. The street bustled with several people, many no larger than Magdalene herself. My five-foot-ten-inch frame towered like a giant as I emerged from the candlelit flat. There were at least three other men out there somewhere who must be receiving the same gaping expressions from the town folk who passed them by, I thought. But I couldn't focus on Kevin, Juno, and Mac's location just now, and I sure didn't want to attract any further attention. I turned my gaze to the right, down a cobbled path that ran between two large buildings speckled with small windows, beckoning me in that direction.

I hadn't waited for an explanation of things to be wary of in Randun before the urge to leave Magdalene had rushed through me. It would have been wise to gain some insight into my new surroundings before setting off on foot. The muscles in my shoulders eased their firm hold with each step that carried me farther down the street, as my anxiety began to calm. Perhaps when Kevin returned, he wouldn't be too angry. I knew he would understand my need to go, though he couldn't possibly have anticipated I would, or I'm certain he would not have left the cottage without me. A twinge of guilt floated to me and left almost as quickly.

Several minutes through the town and the sky began to change from a bright white-yellow to a lighter shade of gray. There were no sounds, save that of a breeze that whispered past my ears. Cooler temperatures had set in and a dusty path replaced the bustling activity of the town I'd left behind. Trees that lined each side of the cobbled road had dropped off and now scattered across an open plain. A little farther ahead stood clusters of rock formations, not quite large enough to be mountains but close enough. The branches of the trees had been cleaned of any leaves, adding to the recent wintery feel of the day. I glanced up to see several clouds had settled in, much darker and denser than only minutes earlier. *How can it be that, so far beneath the surface of the Earth, there's weather?* It was as if I had not been pulled below ground at all but instead had taken a flight to another colder location, where a cluster of shorter people dressed in older attire resided.

The stillness in the air seemed even louder than the noise in the streets earlier and a light snow began to fall, silencing my footsteps beneath the thin blanket of white. I didn't know just how far I needed to go but decided that as long as there was light to see and I could brave the colder temperatures, I would continue on until what guided me forward had been satisfied. I heard footsteps following me and turned to see more of the same emptiness that extended the distance as far as I could see ahead. A few more steps and I heard them again.

"Don't hide. Show yourself!" I called, as my hand instinctively went to the hilt of the sword. No response. I waited as a cool breeze caught a few strands of my hair and a familiar sensation, as though someone had trailed fingertips over my shoulder and along the length of my arm, glided over me. I turned back again to find Cerys standing in the middle of the path. My mouth dropped open slightly and I heard a small gasp of surprise escape. It had been quite some time since I'd last spoken with the spirit that I'd learned had been my former love, my husband in a lifetime long ago, and an aide on the quest.

"Cerys," I whispered. "How did you find me here?" He walked closer and took my hand in his.

"My love." He paused, a gentle smile extending across his lips. "Let's walk together. I was able to reach you in your world. Why wouldn't I be able to reach you in this one?" He stepped in pace with me.

"Of course." I squeezed his hand. I was still trying to wrap my mind around the facets of the spiritual realm. "What brings you here?"

"A gift. And a word of caution." I turned my eyes from the path to glance at him. "You have done well to follow the guidance provided, as expected. But be very cautious of the evil that will try to deceive you."

"The dark shadows, the demons, we are protected from them in this place. That's what I've been told," I replied.

"This is true. However, be watchful of others." He stopped our walk and turned to face me.

My brow furrowed in concentration. "What others?"

"The demons and shadows are not your only enemy." Still holding my hand, he lifted and turned my palm upward, placing a dagger for me to hold. "A gift from the elves." He closed his fingers over mine, gripping the hilt. "The leader of the elves said you would understand the power of it when the time came." He released his hand.

"Eldor," I said under my breath, referring to the elf I'd met in Ardan, who had introduced me to my quest. He had also created my sword for this mission.

I pulled the blade from its sheath, eyeing the finely sharpened blade, the detail in the dimming light of early evening reflecting the same detail as the hilt of my sword. I returned the dagger to its sheath and placed it gently inside the fold of my coat. My eyes returned to Cerys's as he watched me.

"Please give him my thanks."

"Your message merely needs to be a thought to be received in Ardan. There is vision from that world into yours." He glanced down at our hands, still linked, and back to my eyes. "The time has come for me to leave."

"You've hardly arrived."

He smiled and placed a hand against my cheek. "He will not be angry. Do not worry," Cerys said. As he said the words, I saw Kevin's face in my mind's eye. "The evening grows later. You must go." He placed a lingering kiss on my forehead, turned, and took three steps before his image disappeared from view. I shifted my gaze to the sky, noting the convergence of thick, dark clouds.

If this is a storm, it's moving fast.

I turned to continue on the path, feeling drawn in that same direction that had pulled me this far. "Just a bit longer," I told myself, "and then I'll turn back." Something had led me out here for a reason. I felt it sure as the iciness of the snow upon my nose and cheeks. I was driven to follow that sense, believing it would lead to some piece of information about the key. The wind had begun to pick up, and with it, the snow began to fall heavier. *This can't be right. There's no way I'm going to find anyone or anything in this weather. Not tonight.* I lifted the collar of my coat, folded my arms against the falling snow, and turned back toward town. The wind increased, blowing snowflakes against my back. I ducked under a rock crevice I spotted on my way, to wait out the flurry. As I crept a little deeper into the darkened shelter, I could see the opening was actually a cave. If I had to sleep here tonight, it would suffice. But hunger and the desire for warmth in the growing cold were higher on my list of priorities requiring attention.

The dark cave came to life as the once solitary space filled with light. My eyes went to the source. A hurricane lamp lit up the entire inside of the shelter, revealing a much larger cavern than I had thought was here. I wasn't sure if I was startled more by the light and the fact that I was not alone or that the person staring back at me was Elise. *Not possible.* Elise wasn't due to arrive in Scotland with Aria until sometime today. She and Aria would have had no time to make it to the gateway, hike the distance to the rowan trees, and be on this path, much less in the same cave I took shelter in. Every sensation sharpened to the point of a pin as I became aware the questions I was forming had no reality-based answers. My mind was telling me this wasn't Elise. My eyes narrowed in agreement, searching for the edge of the mask. I stared, unable to speak, as my hand crept into my coat and rested on the hilt of my sword.

"Ah, you have become so much stronger," the voice said. Then suddenly, the image of Elise shifted away and, to my horror, was replaced by C-05.

"Shapeshifting again," I said under my breath. "Why Elise?"

He tossed the used match to the ground and turned his gaze on me, setting the lamp on the floor close to the wall of the cave.

"She was easy. I couldn't have taken her form while she was alive." *He didn't. He can't possibly have killed her.*

He smiled wryly. "Oh, that might work for other creatures, say night owls, hawks, and the like. Humans are different. The DNA, you know?"

I fought to put a block in place as he read the memory I last had of him changing into a hawk with what appeared to be a sprawling five-foot wingspan before diving off my balcony into the night.

"How did you get here ahead of me?"

"Your thoughts are an open book. When I arrived after you"—he paused, looking me over—"all the noise I usually hear had quieted after that little spin into Randun. And I knew I'd arrived. Only you are affected in such a negative manner by transport, Sara. Didn't you already know that? Ah, I suppose not. There is so much you don't remember, right? The negative impact has something to do with your particular makeup of energy joining with the electromagnetic fields of the passageway. It's why you feel it more than the rest of your team. Anyhow, you were out for quite some time, allowing me time to call you, shall we say?"

"The urge I had to come out here was you." I said the words with disgust ringing through them.

"If you aren't blocking your thoughts or under the protection of your team, it's much easier for me to reach you. Think of it as a reunion, from old times you don't remember. Besides, on Earth we never had much of a chance to get to know each other again."

Why was I listening to this? My heart sank at the thought Elise was gone.

"She didn't suffer," he said, hearing my thought. "In fact, you should thank me. She would have only held you back. Don't you think?"

I swallowed a sick feeling that had begun to well up in my throat and glared at the monster I knew had been lurking in this man since my discovery of his secret office, containing much more information than he had shared with our team. At the time, I had been led to the treasure of information—maps of all the locations of the keys sprawled across tables, Tarsamon's and my name linked in bold marker across a board—and now he had killed. Elise was beautiful, strong, and had been recovering from wounds she'd received trying to protect me from the evil that had been drawn to my home in New York. Evil that had been called to me by this man, who'd flown away from the madness. That just made the monster in front of me a coward.

"How long have you been allies with Tarsamon?"

"Hmm," he replied. His eyes cascaded down as if he was no longer in the cave with me but instead elsewhere, reliving another experience. "Does it matter at this point, Sara?" He glanced up. My senses told me a game was in play. I just didn't know what the strategy was yet.

"What do you want? The key?"

"You know, Sara, I like you. Really, I do," he said, pulling his sword and eyeing its detail. "If getting the key would resolve the dilemma I have found myself in, all the better. Sadly, though, it will not." I took a step back and drew my sword. "You see, you have made it further than expected and have become quite a hindrance to the Dark Lord's plan."

"Good. He should be concerned," I said, watching C-05 carefully.

He smiled. "I'm afraid you don't really know what you're up against. Fortunately for you, I do." He took a few steps to his left. I matched the slow pace with him step by step. My eyes were locked on him, trying to anticipate each move. "I can make it quite easy for you by killing you now."

I could feel him toying with me. But also that he underestimated my strength.

"You're weak because you fled to the other side and you know it," I said. "You have no power over me. And you have no power on Tarsamon's ground."

"Perhaps." He shrugged a shoulder. "But I did what I had to and I'd do it again," he said, lunging for the first strike.

Damn. A cave is no place for swords. A clash rang out, and then another, as our blades collided.

The moment C-05 had revealed himself, I knew there was no way out of this meeting without a battle, not after the way we had left things in New York and the fight for my life at his call. Steel clashed again, as we blocked and settled several times. I could feel the dagger's weight against my hip each time I moved, reminding me of the opportunity to obtain my second weapon. At that thought, C-05 blocked another strike and brought his blade into a guarded stance.

"Oh, he has taught you well," he said, referring to Kevin. "Would you like to take a breath, remove your coat perhaps?" he asked, reading my thought.

One of my biggest weaknesses was not blocking my thoughts. Kevin was a master at doing so and had intruded a number of times into my thoughts to remind me to keep a block in place. It was considered a defense tactic in a world of beings that could read each other's thoughts. Not having the need to use the technique on a consistent basis, I rarely remembered to engage the ability. Right now, I didn't trust C-05 enough to allow me the movement without him attacking me in mid-removal of said coat.

"Go ahead, I'll wait. I prefer the challenge," he said, stepping back and lowering his weapon.

I felt no immediate threat and cursed myself for believing him. No matter how often my ability to feel what others felt and the truth behind their words guided me, survival and logic battled against that intuition, and rightly so. I watched him carefully as he put his sword back into its sheath and splayed both palms as if to say, *See?* I lowered mine, never taking my eyes off him, and began to remove my coat, followed by the shedding of the heavy skirt while carefully slipping the dagger behind me into the waist of my pants. I'd gladly sacrifice warmth for the necessary freedom of movement.

"You won't have to worry about Kevin. He doesn't know where you are, can't feel what you're feeling now." C-05 paused, glancing down to scratch out some detail on the thigh of his pants. I could feel him toying with my emotions, trying to find a weak spot. The battle was still ongoing. The choice of weapons changed.

I glared at him. "I never worry for Kevin," I replied, keeping my tone even.

"I was wondering. Do you think he would feel more pain at finding your body or never finding you at all?" His eyes lifted from his pants to meet mine in a sickly glow. He was finding pleasure in this. Why? What was his angle?

His question sent a shiver through me.

"Then again, death is death, right? Oh, but your failure of the quest would lead to your immortal lives being separated by the all-powerful Soltari. I know that pain, Sara. I've felt it."

That's it. He seeks retribution. A couple of weeks prior to leaving for Scotland, I'd met with the Soltari and requested information be provided that had been hidden from me in order to lead my team well. They'd granted me the knowledge of my role in the Alliance and the power that Tarsamon held, but not of certain decisions I might have made as a member of the Alliance, or of my history with Kevin. But did C-05 know I had become aware of certain information or did he think it was still hidden from me?

"And yet you, Sara, still show allegiance to the Soltari, live by their rule, believing it true and honorable despite the threat of your and Kevin's existence together. You and your eternal love should share this understanding I have, to see the Soltari for what they are, nothing but cruel."

"You're a coward. Caving to the darker forces instead of appealing to the Soltari."

"As if that were possible! They had already relocated my partner before I was advised of the fact. Perhaps if you knew the pain, you would reconsider your past decision to agree with them."

A lie or truth? I couldn't remember making any such decision.

I felt that boiling point of anger in me hit the edge, rising to the surface of every pore and wanting desperately to send its force into one of the two blades I carried and expend the energy into the man in front of me. My eyes narrowed as the grip on my sword tightened.

"That's it," he said, satisfied he had irritated me back to his preferred game. "I quite expected killing you to be rather uneventful without your team, but now I can see you are proving to be a welcome challenge." In one swift move, he lifted his sword and took two steps to his left. Our eyes remained fixed on each other.

"Did anyone ever tell you that you talk too much?"

A shade settled over his eyes and his mouth twitched. "You understand that it is so much easier to allow the natural process of things to run their course, don't you? I mean the humans allowed the passage of darkness to be opened, failing to see beyond their pain, their anger." He shrugged. "Why not allow what was meant to be to occur? Why intervene in it, Sara?"

"You know as well as I the humans don't know what they've created. You were part of this side of the equation once, fighting against the greater imbalance of the dark energy that seeks our world. You switched so easily." Every nerve in my body was electrified like a live wire. "Maybe it's just that you were weak all along, destined to move toward Tarsamon." I saw a flash of irritation, or was it an edge of pain in his eyes that caused them to narrow into slivers? The look was so quick. If I hadn't been focused on every movement, I would have missed it. He raised his sword and initiated a slash, thrust. I blocked the maneuver.

We battled for what seemed like several long minutes. He could have struck me down as I began to weaken from fatigue. I didn't think he would actually try to kill me until he grew tired of the game. I hoped for an escape before that point arrived. My sword caught at the tip of his blade and lifted it up, creating a space to jab. I wasn't strong enough to lift the sword out of his grasp with mine, but I managed to jab him under his right shoulder. He winced. Rage swept across his face with the knowing that he'd underestimated my ability. The game was up. I drew my dagger, ducked, and jabbed it into his thigh before he could anticipate my next move or get the upper hand. With my hand still clutched tight around the handle, I yanked it out.

Blood began to soak through his pants, matching the small patch at his shoulder. He knocked the sword out of my grip and kicked it. The heavy steel rang out as it clambered a short distance across the rocky floor. He then set his sights on the dagger still tight in my hand. I bolted out of his grasp and fell, extending an arm out for my sword that had begun to glow a faint white light, like a beacon calling to me.

I felt a pull at my ankle, yanking me back toward him. I rolled to my back, my foot twisted slightly, still in his grasp. Using my free leg, I kicked hard at his chest, causing him to gasp. His gaze went to rage once more. He released my foot, opting for a better grip. That split second was all I needed for the few inches to reach my sword. He took two steps toward me and pressed a heavy boot on my left wrist, causing me to release the dagger. His sword was angled at my neck. With eyes boring into his, I swung my right arm forward, my sword now aimed between his legs. Would he slit my throat before I severed his femoral artery and any part in the path of my sword? He stood over me, aware of the precarious position while trying to read my thoughts.

Legs free, I rocketed a long-legged kick between his legs. He fell onto me and doubled over on his side. I grabbed the dagger and rolled to stand, but a steel grip at my throat stopped me. C-05 pushed my shoulders against the cold stone floor so that I was facing him and sat on my knees, pinning me under the weight of his body. The grip tightened around my throat. I released my sword with the intent to sink my index and middle fingers into his eyes. He caught my wrist and froze, glaring at me, seeming to enjoy the power in his hands and the opportunity to extinguish the life beneath him.

"You have proven more worthy at battle than I remembered. But we're done here."

The dagger. The fingertips of my free hand felt for where I'd dropped it to free the clamp around my throat. *There.* "Ah." I choked in a fraction of a breath and willed my strength to come to the forefront with the dagger now in hand.

C-05 bolted upright, eyes fixed in wide-eyed astonishment to the side of me. Black stars began to blink in the twilight of my consciousness as his grip remained in place.

Don't you dare pass out.

I struggled for more air and, from the corner of my eye, saw what threatened him. Karshan, the large gray wolf, one of my allies in Ardan, was stalking him in the darkest part of the cave. Two other animals that looked like cats followed directly behind him. An image flashed in my mind of six other wolves standing guard outside, their fur blanketed in soft white snow.

"She can't save your world if she's dead," C-05 called out in a controlled tone. The pressure against my neck was becoming more than I could stand. The key in jiu jitsu practice, I had learned, was to block an opponent first from getting their hands around your throat. Too late for that. I brought the hand with the dagger up toward his temple. C-05's grip tightened as I fought to reduce the distance between the tip of the dagger and his head. The darkness closed in a heavy curtain falling around me, and at the same moment, Karshan leaped for C-05.

I woke to the feel of something lifting me onto a soft, furry bed that moved beneath me. *So cold.* My body began to shiver against the icy breeze cutting to my bones.

"Take her to him," I heard a deep voice say. "They'll lead the way, for protection."

To whom? Who leads the way?

A rush of cold wind hit my face and blew across my back, causing the shivering to escalate into what felt like a violent shake. Something light and wet touched the exposed skin of my face and backs of my hands. I couldn't see anything in the pitch-black of night. I clung tighter at the warmth beneath me and closed my eyes against the blast of cold that stung at my eyes and ears. I couldn't feel my hands or the wind against my face anymore. As I drifted in and out of conscious confusion, my mind quieted to the sounds of padded feet hitting snow and the name Elise faintly being called in the back of my mind.

8

Kevin waited patiently for Sara to return by nightfall, detecting no threat and confident the shadows and demons could not enter this realm. As the evening grew darker, he had become concerned not because he felt anything ominous but because he didn't feel anything at all from Sara. Usually, he could sense her whereabouts, what feelings she was experiencing and, too often, hear her thoughts. He had reminded her to practice blocking him from reading her, but she wasn't used to the relentless determination it took to practice the task.

It was growing later and he had news to share with her.

Felt pulled to go. That's how Matt had described her calling to leave. Kevin rolled the words around with *by nightfall.* It was well past nightfall, working into late evening. A dinner of stew served with thick, crusty bread and ale provided sustenance but did little to settle his nerves. Kevin's growing concern and confusion regarding his inability to connect with Sara in any manner caused him to wish he hadn't eaten. He thanked Magdalene for the few bites he'd taken and sat quietly, staring into the fire, consumed in thought, while the others shared conversation. Juno had come over once offering to go find her. Kevin had some idea where to look. But with the snow falling heavier and no apparent threat at hand, he wasn't risking any members of the team wandering in a snowfall. Not yet. He expected Sara's return any minute.

Kevin knew the last thing Sara wanted was someone watching her every move. She'd already refused his offer to stay with him in New York until the danger had passed. She wanted, no, needed, her independence. He shifted and dragged his fingers across his chin. *Where the hell is she?*

But he remembered, as an immortal soul, Sara was sent to Earth not to create connections or bonds with others but to await a call to duty to get the three keys. It was the reason she avoided commitment, to follow her task. A bond with another, with him, would likely end in sorrow if she was distracted from her mission. And too much hung in the balance, he considered. Too many lives needed her to succeed.

"Damn it to hell," he muttered under his breath, referring to the condition he'd agreed to with the Alliance, to not remind Sara of their bond. Perhaps if she knew, she wouldn't take such risks. Then again, he reconsidered, his love was a bold and stubborn woman who'd do anything she felt necessary. Unlike himself, love came second with Sara.

They'd traveled lifetimes together to fulfill each mission at the Soltari's request. If he failed to protect her and caused the quest to end before the keys were found, he would be forced to hold true his oath to break the bond with her he'd kept for centuries. He hadn't wanted to take such an oath. He'd struggled with the decision for days before agreeing to the condition the Alliance had delivered. It was, in fact, the only way the Soltari would allow him to join Sara on the mission and for him to ensure her safety. *And how are you protecting her now? You don't even know where she is.* He growled under his breath and rubbed a knuckle on his lower lip. He couldn't wait much longer.

No one, especially the Soltari, could know how truly independent she was in this life and how difficult that made it for any partner teamed with her. No, he thought. He'd sustain any wrath for going against his oath to the Soltari, except to break his eternal bond with Sara. With her strong will, he thought, keeping her safe might prove more of a challenge than he'd anticipated.

As though a bolt of electricity had struck him head on, he sprang to his feet with a flood of emotion and thought, contact from the wolf he'd met in Ardan. He rushed toward the door. He didn't remember the name, having met the great beast only once and being completely taken aback at the knowledge that Sara was able to communicate with such animals. The first image was one that the wolf sent to him through his own vision—that of C-05 with his sword at Sara's throat.

"No!" Kevin roared, shoving the door open and running from Magdalene's cottage into the falling snow and empty street. In a single moment, he'd finally been able to feel Sara's fight. "Wait here," he called to Juno and Matt, who had followed him.

As Kevin raced down the cobbled path in Sara's direction, he felt the rush of emotion that spiked the wolf's blood to boiling and saw that C-05's ability to block him from tuning in to Sara's thoughts and feelings was ineffective in the wolf's presence. The fierce growl rang through Kevin's head, sending him flying in her direction at a faster pace. Every thought the wolf had flew into Kevin's thoughts as though floodgates had burst open. C-05 was forced to let go of Sara in order to try and escape. Kevin felt Sara's fight for consciousness. In his mind's eye, he saw the vision the wolf shared of C-05's body slumped over on its side. A pool of blood rested under his head like a crimson halo. But there was a vacancy in the image, a sense of disappointment that came with the vision. Had she killed him? Surely C-05 couldn't have survived what appeared to be such a brutal blow to his head. As a shapeshifter, he would have had to change his energy quickly to not be detected by the pack that had been waiting outside. He was fully aware of C-05's developed abilities, Sara's certainty that he'd joined the dark forces to aid Tarsamon, and he didn't underestimate the possibility that C-05 would try to read Sara's thoughts before coming to Scotland. But he had never considered that he would try to kill her. They were once on the same team, agreeing on so many issues.

The snow hit Kevin's face like tiny stings as the wind rushed past him. He shook off the cold under the adrenaline that moved him and heard Mac's voice calling behind as he nearly ran head on into the two enormous, black-spotted saber cats. The pack of wolves followed. She had once told him they were gifted to her as protection, with the ability to see into any realm. The cats slowed and ducked their heads in acknowledgement as Kevin reached them. He lifted Sara off one of the cats' shoulders. The other dropped her coat, sword, and dagger in front of Mac. Sara's hands were wrapped so tightly in the fur that Kevin had to peel them away, finger by finger, as though they were mummified. He gazed into her face to see there wasn't so much as a twitch from her. Her lips were blue, but Kevin felt a small sensation from her that she was present though unaware.

"Thank you," he said, nodding once. With Sara cradled in his arms, Kevin rushed past Mac, brought her into Magdalene's dwelling, and placed her beside the fire. He gently rubbed her arms and legs to accelerate the warming of her blood. Her pulse was slow but steady, and he breathed a sigh of relief as he sank back against the stone hearth. *Thank God she's alive.* He ran a hand through his damp hair and closed his eyes.

A movement startled him slightly as Magdalene placed two heavy wool blankets and a couple of pillows beside him. Kevin worked to tuck the blankets around Sara tightly and lifted her head to put the pillow beneath it, then leaned back, watching for any sign of movement. Magdalene returned moments later with a tray of hot tea, two cups, and what looked like pieces of torn bread.

"Perhaps this will help warm her," she said to him. "She hasn't eaten in quite some time."

Though he didn't doubt the little woman, Kevin knew Sara always prepared for outings by packing certain nonperishable staples.

"How do you know this?" he asked.

"I understand what the body needs. It speaks to me. And I can feel she needs food and drink," she answered. "This lass left in quite a rush." Magdalene smiled at him and glanced once at Sara before turning to leave.

Mac sat beside Kevin. "How does she fare?"

"So far her vitals are stable. She just needs to get warm." Kevin paused and drew in a deep breath. Mac nodded with understanding. "I've tried waking her. She won't respond."

"Go and sleep. Ye'll need the rest. I'll watch over her and wake ye if there is a change."

"I can't leave her." He paused. "She's strong. She'll recover," Kevin added, as though trying to convince himself. He hoped he was right. And damn her for leaving Matt, anyway, he thought. She didn't know she was risking their bond. All the more reason he needed to break the oath and share with her the memory of their past lives together. Not knowing could kill the risk-taker that she was. He withdrew the thought, loving her for the same strength that had sent her out in the first place and that brought her back to him. Alive.

Mac clamped a hand on Kevin's shoulder as he rose. The light in the room had faded to only what came from the recently stoked fire. A deep yellow-orange glow flickered across Sara's face as Kevin stared at her, willing her eyes to open. He knew the danger still existed that she had become so cold she could have been freezing, causing her to want to sleep. He knew he needed to pull her from that deep zone. He began rubbing her arms again, calling her name, quietly. He bent his head to her ear.

"Come back to me, Sara. I know you want to sleep but you need to wake up." He took her pulse again. Strong and steady. Good, he thought, as he placed his pillow next to hers to lie beside her.

The other men had made do in the same large room a few feet from each other, with the additional blankets Magdalene provided. Stillness filled the small room as he drifted to the realm of unconsciousness, unable to deny his own need for rest.

"Sara, wake up. I know you hear me. Wake up," a whispering voice directed.

I woke to a hand on my shoulder, gently shaking me. In the dim light, I made out the familiar shape of Kevin's face inches from mine. I blinked, my eyelids heavy, as though silver dollars rested on them.

"Here, sit up and drink this," he said, nudging me upward.

"No," I whispered. "Just a little longer," I said, protesting the movement as he propped me up from behind and held a cup to my lips. The warmth of the liquid felt good despite my lack of desire to move or drink. I took the liquid in tiny sips until one cup was finished and Kevin seemed satisfied, pouring yet another cup of tea.

"Where is he? Did I kill him?" I asked in a low voice, referring to C-05.

"We think so but aren't sure. His body is lying in that cave, after you stuck your dagger in his temple. But..." Kevin pushed a few strands of hair off my cheek.

"But what?"

"It seems the energy of his soul left an instant before you stabbed him. At least that's what the wolf believes."

Karshan.

"You kept calling out to Elise, saying you could hear her but couldn't find her."

"Have you heard anything from Aria? She's with her. She'll know if she's okay."

"No, not since we left for the gateway. Why?"

"I have to know they are safe. He said he killed Elise to take her form."

Kevin stared down at the ground, his brow furrowed in thought. "He took Elise's form? But why?"

"I don't know. Perhaps he was planning to reach me before I ended up in the cave and instead sought shelter from the snowfall."

"Drink more of the tea. I'll see what can be done to find out." Kevin pushed himself up and stepped toward Mac.

The two men spent several minutes talking in a whisper. When Kevin returned, he confirmed there was no way for either of them to reach Aria and Elise from the depths below the rowan trees. Kevin had tried to contact them through telepathy but had not received any response. Mac said that Aggie was able to get a message to him if there was something urgent and if she remembered the instructions he had provided. But because Mac had not heard anything from Aggie, he doubted if Aria and Elise had been in danger or were dead.

My concern shifted to Aggie. If C-05 had found her with Elise, would he have killed both of them? I pushed the thought from my mind, unwilling and unable to consider any ill will toward Aggie.

"I need to know about them."

It was possible C-05 had lied, and Elise was not dead. It might just be that he didn't need a person to be dead to shift into their form. I began to feel strongly that I needed to know the safety of the women before I could continue with the mission. It was distracting knowing C-05 might still be out there. And if so, what animal had he shifted into? Karshan and his pack would have hunted him down if they could have reached him.

"Try to rest for now," Kevin said, interrupting further thought. "We'll find a way to get an answer in the morning."

It seemed impossible that I would be able to sleep with Elise, Aria, and Aggie's safety on my mind. I pulled the blanket to my shoulder and turned to stare at the fire, as if each crackle of flame might ease my worry.

A tap on my hand snapped my eyes open in an instant. Magdalene was sitting beside me. She pressed an index finger to her lips, and her other hand waved me to follow as she stood and began working her way around the sleeping men. Kevin stirred as I rolled gently away from him and followed her to a room away from the main area. A bit of light peeked through a tiny little crack in a door left open. I ducked into it to find myself standing in a room full of candles. Each one had been lit so that the room glowed bright, as if it had been set ablaze by fire itself. In the far corner of the room was a stone hearth, heating a cauldron hanging in the center. On one side was a planked table with a cluster of greenery and a large bowl beside it. Steam was rising like tiny ghosts to the ceiling. I began to feel that the creation of something otherworldly was taking place while innocent folks slept in the other room.

"What is this?" I asked, my eyes searching every corner before resting on the pot.

"I can help you," she said, approaching the table. Without looking at me, she sprinkled an herb into the bowl of steaming liquid, followed by another that crackled as it hit the liquid. During our dinner with Mac and Aggie the night before, Aggie had begun to tell me of the stories the Celts had regarding the magic believed to be contained in herbs. It was thought that plants and herbs were a life force that were provided as gifts of the environment for such things as healing, visions, strength, and a number of other meanings. Aggie had not been able to finish sharing the details of the folklore after little Iain's curiosity had gotten the best of him and he'd stumbled downstairs to inquire about his mommy.

"Hand me the bayberry, just to your right there," Magdalene said, pointing in the direction of where my hand rested on the table.

"How can you help me?" I asked, handing her the only herb on the table near me. I leaned over and peered into the bowl.

"Ye really must try to relax a bit. I know ye don't believe in magic, lass, but did ye believe in dark shadows or talking animals before it was ye'd set out on this journey of yours?"

"You have a point," I replied. "How do you know about the wolf and the shadows?"

"How do you think I found ye? You're not the only one with connections to the spirit world. Your friends, the lasses that were to meet ye, shall we see how they are?" She pulled a sharp knife from a pocket in her long skirt and reached for my hand. I drew it back quickly. "No more than a drop of blood is all it will take. Won't hurt ye a bit," she said. I doubted that as I eyed the tip of the blade, flashing its razor sharpness under the flickering of candlelight. I wondered what other uses she had for the threatening object and hoped sacrifice was not part of the equation. I quickly measured my desire to know about Aria, Elise, and Aggie against the witchery about to be bestowed upon me. She held out her hand and gazed up at me.

A single drop of blood was a small price to pay for the knowledge, given it was reliable. If Kevin, Matt, and Juno trusted her enough to stay here, perhaps I could. I allowed her my hand cautiously, and she made a quick sweep across the tip of my fourth finger, where the silver ring bonded, and held my hand over the steam. I watched as it curled madly.

The steam lifted higher and the contents of the bowl started to boil in a most violent manner before settling into a calm state, as though it had never been disturbed. I glanced at Magdalene with her intense focus on the liquid, while I stuck the injured digit in my mouth, tasting the residual blood.

"There now. Come see," she said, turning toward me. "C'mon." Her expression mirrored that of a grandmother's with warmth and pride at her creation. I gazed into the pot to see a picture of the dinner Kevin and I had shared with Aggie and Mac. I blinked hard, closing my eyes tight and opening them again to see the image briefly before the pot boiled once more and calmed to reveal another frame of life—the gateway.

"Ask it what ye'd like to know," Magdalene said.

I pulled the finger from my mouth, still staring into the pot. "Elise, Aria, and Aggie," I said. "Where are they?" The pot rumbled and boiled, nearly spilling its contents over the rim. I stepped back as the steam whirled above our heads like that belching from a giant factory smokestack.

"Ask regarding one," Magdalene clarified.

"Elise. Where is she?" I asked, watching carefully as the boiling water settled into tranquility. A picture of a woman with red hair came into view, Aria, I thought, but before I could become confused by what seemed an improper image, I saw Elise. Aria was leaning over her as she lay in what looked like a hospital bed. I saw Elise's lips move, though I couldn't make out what was said, just before the scene faded from view.

"Aggie, is she safe?" I asked, looking at Magdalene. "I need to know, please." Magdalene fed another of the bayberry leaves and a ladle of liquid from the cauldron into the pot. I watched as it swirled a half circle and stopped. A faint picture of Aggie came into view. From what I could see, she didn't appear hurt, but the image was unclear.

"What does it need? More blood?" I asked. "Does it need something else to ask another question?"

"It shows ye what is important for ye to see," she answered as she glanced from me to the pot. "Quickly, see," she said. I leaned again over the pot and saw Aggie in her home, but nothing else reflected her state of being.

I turned to face Magdalene. "Thank you, really," I said. There was a sense of disappointment mingled with satisfaction in my tone. I was pleased to see Elise and Aria alive in the vision, but could not know Elise's condition or if Aggie was all right. She seemed to be. But the emptiness I had at not knowing about them was now quickly being replaced with discontent. I decided what Magdalene had so kindly provided would have to suffice. My conscience wasn't so ready to let it go, however. I turned to leave, but Magdalene caught hold of my wrist and wrapped a small cloth around my finger, knotting the two ends.

"We've known of your coming." She paused, still holding my hand in her fingertips. I shifted my gaze from the bandage to hers. "Those of us with the gifts of additional sight can help you while you are here, Sara. Ye must trust in those around you, while still being careful of others."

"I'm sure you're right," I said, nodding once and thinking of C-05. "The difficulty is in knowing one from the other."

"I can direct you," she said with eagerness. I glanced at the pot and back to her. I was a nonbeliever in magic and ritual. And compared to my allies, only a recent believer in the worlds I had visited. Though I couldn't explain what I had seen in the boiling water, I wasn't about to trust it until something else confirmed the vision that had been brewed up.

"My team and I are directed by powers beyond this world and I must follow that lead. Thank you." I lifted my bandaged finger in acknowledgment and turned to exit the doorway with her words in my head, along with Cerys's warning to be cautious of others.

I stepped quietly over the sleeping men and eased my way under the blanket, curling myself against Kevin, feeling his warmth and strength as comfort. The question about Elise's and Aggie's safety was fighting to keep me awake, to do something. I wasn't satisfied with the vision Magdalene had shown me, nonbeliever that I was. But there was little, if anything, I could do to resolve the matter in this world. I lay awake for several minutes, staring into the fire, listening to the breathing sounds of the men, while considering whether it was possible to go back to Scotland to bring Aria and Elise back with me to Randun through the same gateway. *What if I can't get back?* I couldn't take the chance and risk so many other lives if I wasn't able to return for the key. There had to be another way. My eyelids grew heavier. Kevin's arm tightened around my waist, inching me closer.

"Sh," he said at my ear, listening to my thoughts again. "Tomorrow."

Scents of cooking meat and baking bread filled the air as I stretched awake. Voices could be heard coming from a short distance away in the tiny kitchen. I had passed through it quickly on my way to Magdalene's witchery room the night before and wondered just how any more than two people could fit in the space no bigger than a large closet with a small hearth on the end. I walked toward the voices, combing the sleep tangles from my hair with my fingers. As I stood in the doorway, I saw Matt and Juno crammed next to each other at the tiny table, elbows touching, looking like a couple of sardines in a can. Magdalene was pulling out a fresh loaf of bread, while I eyed the plates at the table. Planted in the middle of the table were boiled potatoes, the remains of a loaf of bread with the end left in the pan, a bowl of what looked like blackberries, and some sort of meat that looked like Canadian bacon.

"Sara, you're looking much better this morning," Juno said. "Try some of this bread."

I smiled slightly, searching for a space to join them. "Thank you. I'm starved."

"Well, why not? Ye haven't set your teeth on anything since arriving, lass," Magdalene said as she put the new loaf on the table and pulled a stool from the side of the stone pit that functioned as both a stove and oven. "Here ye are," she said, directing me to a seat beside Juno. "There's room for all." If that were true, it would indeed be a feat of magic. I took the seat.

My gaze crossed from Juno to Matt. "I owe you an apology for yesterday, for putting you in a difficult situation at my leaving. I'm sorry," I said to him.

Juno turned to look at me, holding the piece of bread from going past his lips. I mouthed *what?* to him. He smiled and continued to shovel his food. Matt paused before glancing up from his plate.

"You owe me nothing," he said. "You did what you felt you must." Matt pushed his chair out, picked up his plate, and carried it to the small basin of a sink.

"Thank you. The food was delicious," he said to Magdalene, and promptly left the cottage.

"Is he all right?" I asked Juno.

Juno turned his head in the direction Matt had left and glanced back at me. "Oh, yeah. He's just a little bent. Thinks he should have followed you, stayed with you. He feels responsible."

"He's not," I said, reaching for the berries.

"Don't worry, shit rolls off his back faster than water off a beaver. But be sure, he'll never let you set off alone again." He scraped together the remaining food on his plate.

"There's no use stewing over something that's in the past. Where are Kevin and Mac?" I asked.

"They were outside discussing Mac's plans to go back to find Aggie."

Magdalene came around the table and leaned in to my ear, holding another plate of bacon in one hand and a wooden utensil in the other. "Sending him back is what's best. He'll be all right," she said as I scooted a dish to the side to make room for the plate.

I nodded with the realization that I couldn't stop Mac, nor did I want to. It was important to be sure his family was safe. I took a bite of the sweet bread that melted in my mouth. My stomach, unsatisfied with the tea, had grumbled its protest for more food, which I happily obliged, stabbing several small berries onto a fork followed by another hunk of bread. I wondered when Mac would return. From what I understood, we would need to not only have him present when we met with the Druids, but as the guardian of the first key, he would need to lead us to them. Until his return, we were more or less stranded.

No need to worry for him. There is time. Mac is well equipped to handle a trip back through the gateway. The thought entered my mind, but it was not my own. I turned to see Kevin in the doorway.

"You're looking well," he said, kissing me on the forehead. I smiled, pleased to see he was in good spirits in light of the fact we would be delayed a bit longer. With his ability to feel what I felt and in the time he had sent the thought from the doorway, he had assessed my condition beyond a glance. My neck felt bruised when I woke and, to my knowledge, was the only evidence of what had happened yesterday.

"I have an outing for us," Kevin said. "Do you feel up to it?"

"Of course. I'm fine," I replied. "When do you expect Mac to return?"

"No later than tomorrow, I should guess."

"Enjoy," Juno said, pushing his chair from the table. "But watch out for the shapeshifters I hear are lurking in caves." He narrowed a glance at me and turned up the corner of his mouth.

"You aren't coming?" I asked.

"Not this time. Matt and I saw some items for sale yesterday in the streets and are going to see what kind of weapons are available."

Kevin took Juno's place at the table while I finished breakfast. He didn't say where we were going, and I suspected that he was also being cautious around Magdalene. Being in the presence of people who had been expecting us meant neither of us could be sure if the people of this underground world had any supernatural abilities. Did he know of the witchery that had taken place last night? I could feel a new and disturbing sensation since Kevin had arrived this morning. Was he worried about Mac's ability to return? I stood from the table and met his gaze but nothing showed in his eyes. Still, a sense of imbalance circled in the air around him, as though the temperature had shifted a couple of degrees south and a coming storm was about to hit.

9

I still couldn't fathom that I was in another realm when it was so much like Earth. I glanced at the sky above, steel blue in color with a breeze that lightly touched my face at a temperature close to fifty degrees, I guessed. Had the location of the rowan trees really been a path to a parallel world? Unlike Ardan, I hadn't needed to sleep to travel to this realm. There was no other explanation for how I'd arrived except for some mysterious break in time, held in place by ancient, magical mystery.

As I stood feeling the sensations so much like home, I realized the urge that had pulled me out into the cold one day earlier had vanished. That sensation had left me as soon as I'd entered the cave and discovered C-05. I'd been warned by Matt and Kevin in the past not to underestimate C-05's abilities. Had he somehow been able to lead me to seek him out? How would he have known that Matt or any of my team wouldn't have followed me all the way to the cave? Maybe it was a chance he was willing to take. Whatever the reason, my awareness was sharpening. I wouldn't be caught off guard again.

With a bright sky to lead us, Kevin and I hiked down the same cobbled path out of town I'd taken yesterday, choosing a slightly different route that veered off through several trees and over a long, grassy hill. We had walked mostly in silence, the exception being his inquiry about the bandage still on my finger, to which he had merely raised a brow when I explained I had cut myself. We eased down the slope of the hill and began approaching what looked to be some sort of monument.

"The cathedral. It's beautiful. Don't you think?" he asked, breaking the silence.

"Yes. How old would you guess it is?"

"In this time, no more than a few years. According to Mac, he believes it is close to fifteen hundred years from our time."

"How can that be? I mean, how can he know it still stands? I've never heard of Randun in any textbook description of the old world." I stopped to stare at the details of weathered stone and mortar that rose high in the air with only a few windows in niches, noting also the sizeable graveyard just to the side of the structure. Kevin had taken a few steps ahead of me but, at the question, stopped and turned. I glanced away from the building to look at him. He smiled and reached out for my hand.

"Sara, Mac is a traveler to other realms as we are. You only remember Ardan because it's where you have visited recently and where you began this mission. But there are many other parallel existences."

"And have I been to this one before?" It didn't appear as though I had or something, anything, would have seemed familiar. Kevin only smiled and dropped his eyes from mine to the ground.

"I can't really say."

Can't or won't?

His eyes met mine again and evidence of something hidden behind a shadow of knowing crept into the pools of warm brown. He turned away, stepping closer to the cemetery ahead, leaving me to wonder why, when I'd asked weeks earlier for the Soltari to restore my memories, still others remained omitted. The entity had given back all of the information regarding the mission itself, my knowledge of the team members and that we had fought together on other quests, but important pieces like where I had been in previous lifetimes and my connection with Kevin were blank. The reason provided for this vacancy was so that I would not become distracted by any close relationship, allowing me to keep my focus centered on rescuing Earth.

As I came to the edge of the cemetery, a strong sensation abruptly shifted my attention away from further introspection.

"It's here," I said to myself, feeling the same sensation as yesterday.

"What's here?" Kevin glanced over his shoulder to me.

His ability to hear everything, thought or word, still surprised me.

"The sensation that called to me yesterday to seek it out." I felt my brow wrinkle and stopped walking, angling my head in the opposite direction. "I must have been distracted by the snowstorm to have gone in another direction."

"I wondered why you went out alone."

I glanced back to him. *Because I could.*

Kevin narrowed his eyes in response to my thought.

"I must have taken a wrong turn with the storm that had started."

"Or another element was interfering with your calling," Kevin suggested. I interpreted his meaning to be that of C-05 and his intent on intercepting my path.

Fifteen hundred years? I reflected on the span of time. "We are to meet the Druid priests in a cathedral? That doesn't seem quite right, somehow." To my knowledge, the Druids were not Catholic and would not have been found practicing in any cathedral.

Kevin turned up the corner of his mouth as we continued toward the end of the slope. I noticed a few of the headstones lying flat, scattered across the yard like toppled dominos.

"No, it's not likely we'll find them in the cathedral, but this is where we are to meet."

I stopped and turned to face him. "I don't understand. Why are we here if we need Mac?"

"I brought you here to show you something I think you'll be interested in seeing." I didn't doubt it, feeling the same sensation as I had yesterday taking root and urging me closer.

We walked several steps around the cemetery as I eyed the cathedral and its massive stones. Moss sprouted across the walls of the building, matching the same soft green over several headstones. We rounded the front of the structure and continued past it and the cemetery toward a cluster of oak trees. I glanced back at the cathedral, wondering if anyone was working inside. Something about the place gave me a sensation as though we were being watched. We stepped under the canopy of leaves and into the shade of the trees providing some concealment. I reached across to rub the chill of the cooler temperature away on my arms that had found its way beneath my coat.

"It's just a bit farther," Kevin said.

The shade abruptly ended as we stepped into a grassy field blanched with sunlight. An array of purple, white, and yellow flowers cascaded over a large cobblestone bed, the arms of which were reaching the tips of the blades of grass on a perfectly manicured lawn. A small path erupted beneath my feet, leading in the proper direction to admire, but not to touch the flowerbeds. Additional clusters of moss had also found a comfortable residence between the cobbled stones, softening each step. I followed Kevin as he led me through the garden and into a field void of any flowering plant and stopped dead in my tracks. Enormous standing stones stood clustered together, like tall figures glaring down upon us. The drive to touch them was more than I could bear. I took a few steps closer.

"Look at this," he said, reaching a hand out to an inscription.

I stepped beside him and saw that there was carved lettering I could not make out. "What does it say?"

"It's in Gaelic. It says, 'The Light Carrier will come on a day chosen by the spirits and three symbols will set in motion the path according to the Alliance.'"

"Well, at least we know we're in the right place," I said, glancing at the other stones for additional writing.

"Look, right here," he said, pointing to a few of the symbols around the carving. "It's a code. It's familiar but I don't remember." He paused, thinking. "Let me see your ring," he said, extending his hand toward mine.

"You know I can't take it off. It has been bonded to my finger since it was given to me."

"Then may I see your finger, please?"

I placed my bandaged finger with the silver ring on it in his hand, close to the stones. As he eyed my ring and then the stone, I felt a pull at my hand, urging me closer to the stone, a kind of magnetic draw. I drew my hand back in surprise.

"The markings on the stone are showing on your ring, Sara."

"While that is fascinating, I think we should step away from these stones. Didn't you feel it pulling at my hand when I got close?"

"Mac said the stone's power is not active unless he and all three symbols are present." One part of that equation was fulfilled. I'd kept the three medallions tucked deep down in my coat pocket. Was that why C-05 had wanted to kill me? If he took the symbols, he might not have the power to use them, but then I also could never fulfill the mission.

"It seems the power of these stones is stronger than either you or Mac might be aware and I don't care to press the issue further until Mac is here."

Kevin agreed that we didn't need any trouble, or to become separated from the others, if in fact there was some extraordinary connection associated with the stones. We turned and made our way back to the garden. I stopped, glancing behind me at the stones as an urge called me back in the same manner that had drawn me to the River Teith. The sunlight reflected over the tops of the monument, making them sparkle under the glow of sunlight. I felt myself falling into a relaxed, trancelike state as though I were daydreaming.

Kevin sensed the change and, without a word, took my elbow and led me away from the standing stones. While the pull to get close to the stones was similar to that of the river, this didn't feel like another gateway. Maybe it was meant as confirmation that we'd arrived, a sign we were on the right track.

We strolled through the fragrant garden on one of the brightest days I could recall seeing in sometime. The trancelike state faded and the heavy, sweet scent of thousands of blooms lifted on the breeze and filled my nostrils. I glanced over the colorful parade, admiring the beauty and wondering how it still held all the color as if it were spring following a snowstorm. How was that possible? I remembered planting the few herbs in the ten-by-ten area of my own garden and how hard it was to keep them thriving in the best environment. My heart lurched at the thought of home and how much I missed it. I missed my routine. What would it be like to have a cocktail with Kevin in the bar of that five-star hotel in California again, with its glorious sunset cascading through the wall of glass, or checking email or the day's appointments? And what about my patients who needed to talk through their problems for some hopeful insight?

"Sara." Kevin's smooth voice pulled me back to the beauty around us. His hand slid over my hair and rested on my back, urging me on.

"Why did you bring me here?"

"Yesterday, Mac said he needed to find the cathedral. Magdalene told us where we could find the closest one and we set out on a search for it and the Druids. But when I saw the stones, something told me they were more than just stones. I wanted to bring you to them, see what you felt, thought."

"I can't be sure if it's a passage. I don't think so and I don't really want to find out."

The sunlight beamed off the dew-covered grass, giving it a sparkle like a million tiny pieces of cut crystal. We arrived at the edge that separated the garden and the cluster of oak trees. I reached up toward the branch of one of them and selected a leaf to twist as a distraction from my thoughts.

"So," I said. "Are you going to tell me what it is you don't want me to know?" I asked, staring at the leaf as I pressed it between my forefinger and thumb.

"What do you mean?"

"You may block me from reading your thoughts, but you can't block me from feeling what you feel. What is it that is making you so"— I paused, trying to find the word to define the feeling—"anxious?" I glanced at him and saw a smile sneak across his closed lips, before returning to the leaf I began to curl.

"It's nothing for you to worry about and it's why I've blocked you from the thought."

"Oh," I said. "You know, it would be okay for you to put as much trust in me as you would hope to *get* from me."

He stopped then under the shade of the trees, caught my free hand in his, clasped it along with my other, causing me to drop the leaf. He stared into my eyes with that intensity I'd come to know. It was the only look from anyone that had the ability to move me to depths unventured, as though I were the sea that he was plunging straight to the bottom of.

"My decision to block you has nothing to do with my trust in you to handle what concerns me."

"Then let me in."

"No," he said softly, blinking once. "My job is to protect you in this mission and I will do so in every way."

Good. "By keeping things from me? What are you protecting me from?"

He raised an eyebrow. "You're misunderstanding."

"Then make it clear," I pressed.

"I simply don't want you to take on any concern I have. You don't need to carry that burden and you can't solve it, not the way you think you can. I'm not one of your patients, Sara." He loosened his grip on my hands and held them in his fingertips, stroking the tops of them with his thumbs.

I drew my eyes from his intense stare and dropped my gaze to the ground, sensing I was at an impasse. He was right. I couldn't solve everything, but I always liked to try. I wanted to help relieve what burdened him. The only choice was to get angry with him for not being completely open or to respect his desire to resolve the concern he had by himself. I nodded and flashed a quick smile and chose the latter option to put my trust in him.

We were well past the garden now, secluded in the quiet shade of the oaks, returning to Magdalene's home. I turned to continue through the cluster of trees to the grassy field that led to town but was stopped as Kevin placed a gentle hand on my shoulder, drawing me back to him. His lips were warm against my cool skin as he pressed them to my forehead, then to my temple. Lingering for a moment, he took in a breath against my cheek. His fingers reached slowly up the other side of my neck.

"Make love with me," he said in a barely audible whisper against my cheek. My voice caught in my throat and I let out a small gasp of breath. His touch was penetrating, disrupting my thoughts of what concerns he might have. I loved and loathed that he could sway me from one extreme to the other in an instant.

He was carrying a fear, I supposed, but of what? Had he seen something wicked in our future? My mind began to assume any number of things on this increasingly treacherous mission. Whatever it was that worried him, it seemed as though he needed to be close to me. Perhaps, too, he was merely distracting me from deep thought.

"Here?" I asked. He took my hand and led me deeper into the seclusion of the trees. Tall ferns rising up around us provided additional concealment from any passersby of the cathedral, not that a soul had been seen or heard since we'd arrived. "Kevin," I said, realizing I was wanting as much as he.

He stopped where smaller ferns grew among enormous trunks of tall trees, and spread his coat on the ground as a soft shield against the pricklier brush. I felt his hand at the small of my back, gently urging me against him. His other hand moved to the collar of my clothing and slipped beneath, then over my shoulder. I shrugged out of the coat, placing it beside his, and glanced down, running a hand across the dress cinched tight. *Damn thing.*

He laughed. "Easy enough to work around."

"You think?"

He eased me onto our coats, his hand still at my back. "Hold this," he said, lifting the skirt part of the dress.

I pulled it up until it was a pool of blue cloth crumpled at my waist, while his hands made quick work removing my boots and pants.

As he leaned over me, I pressed my lips just above the opening of his shirt, lifting it from the kilt. I drew my hands under as I extended my reach up his back, skimming along the well-defined, deep scar he had received in the dark world. I heard his breath quicken before he lifted my chin to meet his gaze. Flecks of gold shimmered over the warmest brown, consuming my own jade green under his fervor.

He captured my lips with his, working the kiss deeper and

spreading the fire into each slow touch. The heat began to rise in waves, causing the earlier chill to vacate. And once again, I was under his spell. No shaking it now with the chance anyone might see. To hell with a meaningless stranger, should one come exploring. He stripped his clothing off in what seemed one swift motion and long enough for a breath of icy air to frost the flames and lift our skin into gooseflesh before our bodies met again to share in the warmth. The contrast was only fueling my desire.

I understood his need to be together in this way, as if trying to merge two souls into one. His hand slipped between us and across my stomach, tracing an outline along my hip and thigh, before gently guiding my legs open. His stare held with mine even as he entered me, feeling the intensity of my emotion and desire mingling with his. So much was said without a word. I needed this. Not the mere physical act, though that had always been most pleasurable, but his closeness, his particular brand of intimacy. Our bond. The exchange was more than a heated coupling. It was a deeper interconnectedness, a knowing and understanding of what each needed to strengthen the eternal union of our souls. We moved in perfect unison, climbing to a peak we had sorely missed with the added company of the others on our mission. Tenderness swept through us as we claimed our connection under a canopy of shadows, while the leaves above whispered to us in the midst of our own soft moans. He brought me slowly to a climax that left my soul light as the breeze that carried through the branches, and then found his release, like a wave crashing into its welcoming shore. Moments passed with his fingers stroking across my forehead and mine at his back.

"I feel your mind is at ease," he said.

I lifted the corner of my mouth. "Was that your intent, aside from the passion you fed me?"

"Fed you? Hell, woman, you drew it straight out of me." He laughed.

"Don't think I've forgotten that you carry a burden of your own that I, too, hope to ease."

He rolled to his back, holding me to him. I rested my head on his chest with one leg lounging over his. He pulled my coat and makeshift blanket up to my shoulders. A thought flashed through his mind quick as lightning before he blocked it. I wasn't quite sure I had caught it, but it sounded like he was carefully containing a fear that I might slip from his protection again. I felt him touch the fingers of my right hand until he stopped at the bandaged one, gently lifting it.

"You said you cut yourself?"

"In a manner of speaking," I replied without lifting my head. His fingers glided up over my hand toward the bracelet he had given me back at the Cape. The protection it provided for him to find me gave him a sense of peace. I recalled the memory of its value when I'd visited the dark world and was almost captured or killed. I didn't know at the time if the shadows and demons were aware of the threat I'd become. The hairs on my arms rose at the memory of the burning sensation I'd felt at its activation.

"I can't imagine what you were doing between the time you fell asleep to the morning that you managed to cut yourself."

With the other injuries I'd sustained in my fight with C-05, I didn't think he would notice a slight wound on my hand. Then again, I was the fool for thinking any detail would escape his scrutiny.

"You don't have to imagine," I said. I recalled the event of being awakened by Magdalene and the steaming pot requiring my donation for the chance to see about Elise, Aria, and Aggie and let him draw his own conclusions.

"Sara, I would suggest you not join in any other witchery with our host or anyone else we may run into while we're in Randun. I don't really know what these people are capable of just yet. Better to wait until we know more, don't you think, love?" He stroked a hand over the length of my hair.

"I suppose so. She seems rather harmless," I said. "Why would she carry any ill will?"

"Perhaps she doesn't. But there may be others that would not look too kindly on the sort of practice you engaged in last night. History has me cautious. Witchery was viewed with awe by many, and not with any sort of affection, if you catch my drift." I lifted my head to look at him.

"We are in a different world," I said. "But perhaps hanging isn't out of—"

"Shh," he said, putting a finger to my lips, interrupting my final thought on the matter as he shifted from beneath me and reached for his clothes in quiet haste. "Block any thoughts from being read," he whispered. His eyes had locked onto something moving beyond the trees.

I grabbed my pants and quickly slipped them on under the dress that had remained in place. Kevin reached for his sword. I pulled the dagger from my coat and waited with him, listening. Someone was walking along the same trail we had minutes before.

"It's near. I can feel the trail of her energy. She's been here," a voice said.

I peered through an opening in the trees and almost gasped out loud before Kevin reached to cover my mouth.

Four men had found their way along the very same path we traveled, one of which looked like C-05. A closer glance proved the man resembled him, and too much so. The hair was different—not the snow-white buzz cut but a sandy blond. The eyes were a bit more angled on the outside corners and the thin lips were the same. There was enough resemblance to make my skin crawl. A smaller person, no taller than Magdalene, was leading him and two other men through the garden. Their guide was probably a town resident who knew the area.

Do you think they're looking for the standing stones and the inscription? I asked in thought to Kevin.

Likely. But until I can be sure who the others are, we need to remain unseen.

Can he sense our energy?

Not sure. New body. It takes time to adjust to all the levels of heightened sensory he once had. He knows you were here. That's enough for me.

There was something in the way the men carried themselves, in the energy they put off, that felt as though they had blood on their minds. *Hunters. They're hunting.*

My focus shifted away from the guide to the one resembling C-05 and the other two men with him. Both were of decent height, about five foot seven or so, and unlike the average four-and-a-half-foot-tall person in Randun. I began to doubt if they were from the same village as Magdalene at all. Instead, it was more likely they were from Kevin's and my world.

One of the men had a scruffy-looking beard, somewhat baggy clothing, and medium-length sandy-brown hair that sagged over his eyes. He looked as though he had been in his clothes for days, probably smelled like it, too, by the unkempt appearance. His lip curled on one side as if he'd been woken against his will. His posture was such that his shoulders rolled forward slightly. I didn't take this man for much of a threat, until I saw the flash of metal under his shabby tan coat.

The other man was a little neater in appearance but not by much. A dull green wrinkled shirt was tucked into his khaki pants. Without a kilt, would the town folk assume they didn't belong? Would they see them as intruders or visitors? The man's lean, muscular physique showed beyond the unkempt appearance of his clothes. He walked with purpose behind the shabbier partner. His hair was longer and pulled back into a black leather binding, similar to the one Mac wore.

Kevin and I watched as the men went through the garden to the standing stones. Kevin touched my arm and moved his index finger to his lips and then to his forehead. We fled the refuge of the oaks and went around the grassy hill under the protection of trees that edged the field, not speaking until we safely arrived at Magdalene's cottage.

"I'm convinced C-05 is still alive and in Randun," Kevin said.

"There's only one way to be sure," Juno said. "We go and see for ourselves."

"You think there's a chance he shifted into another form before his body died?" I asked. *Why not?* The man I'd seen at the cathedral was a close rendition of C-05. "He could be anywhere and we wouldn't know him if he was standing in front of us. How else could there be something so familiar about a man I've never seen before?"

"I suspected he took another form," Kevin answered. "But I didn't know he could shift into a human form this soon after he left the cave." His attention came back to me. "C-05's energy would remain the same. It would feel the same. And your senses would tell you that much, Sara. And if he found the standing stones, you can bet he's asking the residents about any other visitors and where they might be staying." Kevin angled his head toward the other men.

Juno played with the point of an unusual-looking knife on the palm of his hand. His eyes may have been elsewhere but I knew the look of concentration well enough to know we had nothing but his attention.

"We'll need to move soon," Matt said.

"Tonight," Juno added, not looking up. "But first, you and I will make a visit to that cave."

"When is Mac expected back?" I asked.

"This evening, he thought. He knows we will need to meet at the cathedral." Kevin leaned forward, resting his forearms on his knees.

"Once we know he has come through the gateway, we can communicate our location to him telepathically," I said.

"I don't think we are safe in doing that now," Matt said. "With C-05 alive, he has the ability, if he chooses—"

"He chooses," Juno interrupted.

My mind raced through the possibilities of how C-05 could be alive and what image he would have taken to escape. *I did stab him, right? And with Karshan there, well, there simply wasn't time for him to select another body to inhabit. We need to get under the protection of the Druid priests, but that could be longer than expected at the rate we're going.* Magdalene entered my mind.

"We can't Sara," Kevin answered. "I don't want to involve her any more than she is. It could be too dangerous for her."

"She's the only person who knows where we could go. She said last night that she can help, that others have been told of our arrival," I said. Juno and Matt looked up at me with concerned expressions.

Juno stashed the knife in its leather sheath. "We'll have to set out on our own tonight," he said. I could hear the rhythmic pattern in his head, like machine-gun fire, as he began assimilating possible options and locations around the cathedral. Matt and Juno had the experience, the know-how to escape a hunter.

"Sara, it would be safe for you to assume that anyone you come in contact with is quite capable with a blade," Juno said. "Do not under-estimate anyone. Keep your blades on you at all times and your shield of light at the ready. And Kevin is right, we can't involve Magdalene any further."

I nodded in reluctant agreement. "Yes." My gaze shifted to the ground as my thoughts tried to argue over what I knew was right.

"In the meantime, we'll need a place to hide until Mac returns," Matt said.

A slight movement from the corner of my eye drew my attention to the dark kitchen area. I hadn't sensed Magdalene's presence and was surprised that neither had the others. Without moving my head, I glanced at Juno, then back to her. Magdalene stared in my direc-tion from just inside the doorway of the kitchen, out of view of the men and quiet as a mouse. This time I sensed her fear as she listened closely to the conversation. Perhaps she had been there all along, hearing every word.

"I realize you believe we are protecting Magdalene by not involv-ing her further, but she's too involved as it is. We'll need to protect her," I said.

"She was aware of our arrival," Juno said, giving my suggestion thought. "It's possible anyone who wants to find us already knows we are here. I won't have her safety on my mind, knowing those who seek us will come to her, especially with the harm I suspect has been brought to Elise."

There was silence in the room as each contemplated the addi-tional baggage of another person to look out for. We had plenty on our shoulders as it was and even more now with the men we saw at the cathedral. None of us knew what specific abilities they might carry.

"I can help. I know where ye can hide," Magdalene said, stepping into full view. "We'll have to leave tonight under the cover of dark. There are many who are quickly becoming suspicious of who ye are," she said, glancing at us. "There is talk. I've heard it at the market just today."

Four sets of eyes rested on her with the knowing that there was no other option but to have her join us.

The rest of the late afternoon afforded us time to gather the necessary food, cloaks, and weapons. After a dinner of vegetable stew, bread, and cheese, Magdalene handed me a flask of cherry brandy. "It's for warmth, lass," she said, patting my arm. I tucked it into a fold sewn into the black wool cloak she let me borrow as an extra layer of warmth with a hood attached.

"You have been so kind," I said to her. "Forgive me for asking, but why do you help us?"

"I suppose the lack of trust would be expected." She paused with a gaze as if trying to find another answer in my expression. She sighed. "I help because I believe in your purpose."

"Who informed you of our arrival?" I searched for any indication she would be trying to hide a name, a micro-expression that would give her away. But I detected no attempt to conceal any information. A heavy knock sent my attention to the front door. Silence fell over the little flat. Matt reached for the door handle and waited as Kevin and Juno drew their swords.

10

I stood next to Magdalene in the room off the kitchen, dagger in hand. In one quick dash, I could recover my sword standing against the wall in the main room. Nothing about the knock felt ominous, but the air prickled with the electricity of heightened awareness. Being on guard was a precaution the members of our team had to take, knowing the danger that hunted us on the quest for the key.

I had been feeling an increasing responsibility for the safety of our small group but had to relinquish that responsibility to Kevin, Matt, and Juno as their assigned task. I shot a quick glance at Juno. A familiar voice entered the cottage and I quickly sheathed the dagger, stepping from the darkened room into the entry of the tiny cottage.

"Mac. Thank God you're back!" I said, hugging him. I searched his face for any signs of grief and found none. In the shadows just behind him, shades of fiery red hair belonging to Aria flowed from under her hood in a swirl of color. She stepped to the side and appeared beneath the single lantern that hung at the doorway.

"Inside. Hurry," Magdalene said, ushering them past the entrance and closing the door with haste. She slid a wooden beam down, nailed to the side of the door, for use as a lock.

I hugged Aria tightly. "What a relief you both made it through the gateway and are okay. What news do you have about Elise?" I asked.

"She's alive at New York Presbyterian and in good hands," Aria replied. I felt a slight release of burden lift from my shoulders. At least Elise would be safe.

"What happened?" Juno asked. "Will she be all right?"

"Yes. The battle before you flew out of New York left her weak. C-05 paid a visit the next evening saying he had important information for you that was life-or-death and demanded to know where you'd gone. We weren't about to tell him anything. Not when our guides in Ardan would have already shared with us any suspicions that would put your life at risk. So we knew he was lying." Her eyes shifted to Kevin. "He moved so fast. We fought for only a few minutes." She turned to me. "Sara, he's become stronger."

"What happened to her? What did he do?" Juno pressed.

"He slammed me against the wall and went after her, knocking her to the ground and cutting the side of her throat. He bent over her, like he was sucking out her breath, and flew out of the place before I could tackle the bastard. He missed her jugular by millimeters, according to the doctor."

"I'll kill him next chance," Juno said.

"Yeah, get in line." Aria paused, understanding his concern, and touched his shoulder. "She's doing well."

"Come in and have some food," Magdalene said. "It's getting late and we will have to leave soon." She hurried into the kitchen.

I turned to Mac, who had just begun conversing with the other men. His eyes softened and a faint smile crossed his lips as he read the concern on my face.

"Aggie is well. So is Iain," he said, touching a hand to my shoulder. I breathed a sigh of relief and nodded.

While I could tell his concern for his family was eased, there was a shadow of worry that still hung in his eyes. Before I could ask, he turned to Matt, answering a question that must have been posed before I approached. I left the men to their conversation and made my way to the kitchen, where Aria had retreated. She was hovering over a bowl of stew, tearing a piece of bread. I glanced at Magdalene, pouring tea, as she reached for another cup.

The air in the kitchen was almost as heavy with tension as the room with the men. Magdalene handed me the cup, never looking up. I breathed in the scent of ginger in the steam rising up.

"You're sensing danger?" I asked, blowing across the cup.

She pressed her lips together and glanced to Magdalene. "Magdalene was just explaining that she believes the one with the blond hair may know exactly where to find us. It seems he was asking around about a tall, lean woman with long dark hair and green eyes." Aria paused. "Every moment here puts us at a greater risk for an encounter with the man suspected to be C-05," she added, downing the last spoonful of stew. She pushed away from the table. "He isn't the type to attempt to fight all of us alone."

"That blond-haired man," I said, remembering the man at the cathedral, "has brought with him additional reinforcements. Kevin and I saw them earlier today." Aria looked at me, puzzled. "We don't know their strengths, couldn't read them." I shared the mental image of C-05's body on the floor of the cave. "If that's in fact C-05 asking, then it won't take him long to pick up on our energy. He's too close. We have to leave now."

I stood and reached for the wool cloak lying across the back of the chair.

At the same time, the men approached the entrance to the kitchen, as though confirming my sentiment. We bundled up in the cloaks provided by our host and layered them with coats we had brought with us, rolled a few blankets, and tidied neat bundles of food. We were to hike a mile out of town, where we would meet up with a contact Magdalene said she had with horses.

Aria and I followed Magdalene into the room where I had been invited to view the witchery brewed up in the boiling pot. The men entered steps behind us. Empty now of cauldron and flame, the room looked like nothing more than a library. Books stood neatly lined along shelved walls. Magdalene went to the farthest corner of the room, stepped behind a single bookcase holding several stacked bowls and clear containers of different-colored liquids and herbs, and waved us to follow. She peeled back a moss-green cloth that cloaked a wooden door and, with ease, unlocked it and heaved a shoulder into it once, then again, shoving it open into a dark alley separating her building from another similar grouping. As the door cracked open enough to squeeze through, a heavy pounding at the front of the cottage rang out. I turned to see Juno arching an index finger toward the door. He mouthed the word *go,* as all four men slowly drew their swords and fell into the shadows behind us.

"Lady Mara. Open the door. We have a warrant for your arrest for the practice of black magic."

I heard the words followed by more pounding as we quickly stepped outside and around a corner. I reached for the dagger and held it tightly inside my cloak.

Lady Mara? I recognize that name, but from where? The adrenaline pulsing through my veins pushed me faster down the street to avoid the men who had come for Magdalene. How many beats on the door before they used force, only to find no one home? *Hurry.*

Then I remembered. Lady Mara was the name of the owner of the antiquities shop in England that I had visited just a couple weeks ago on a trip to England for a charity benefit. Behind the storefront, the shop was a place where every sort of weapon could be found. Some were created to be DNA specific to an immortal warrior. Lady Mara had given me the smaller of two rings I wore and explained it would block the energy found in the symbols from being read by any dark entity. At the time, Lady Mara had a face as wrinkled as any sundried prune, but with each line was bestowed the wisdom of ages. Maybe even fifteen hundred years of it. I glanced at the brown and black stone, then at the back of Lady Mara's, Magdalene's, head. The height was the same. *No, she couldn't be the same woman. It simply wasn't possible.* From behind me, and louder this time, pounding could be heard as the two men charged into the dwelling.

The night air had grown crisp and the wind had just begun to pick up lightly. I glanced into the black of the evening sky. *No stars. Thank god we have a guide.* We made our way through the alleyways, being sure to avoid the cobbled streets lit at each corner by a hanging lantern.

We moved into the cover of the grassy fields and into a dense thicket of trees, all the while keeping quiet, with the exception of Mac and Magdalene, who held a conversation in low tones. I fell deep into thought wondering how quickly Tarsamon was placing his demon forces within our world since our departure. Or was he distracted from consuming the humans and focused instead on stopping us from getting to the key of enlightenment? Clearly, his forces were blocked from entering Randun or we'd have surely met up with them by now. But what was happening in our time? How many more people had the shadows consumed? That world, my world, seemed so far away now.

Magdalene's lantern was the only light to guide us through the dark cover of trees that cascaded over the hillside. The sound of our footsteps was muffled over the dead leaves dampened by the recent snowfall. The smell of moss and bark filled the air, and I welcomed the clean scent, taking in a deep, cold breath. Aria's red hair glimmered faintly in the glow of the soft firelight as she stepped just behind Magdalene. I took a few longer strides, catching up to her.

"How were things when you left?" I asked.

"Hmm? Do you mean Scotland or the States?"

"Both," I said, contemplating the time frame from New York to our arrival in Randun.

She paused a moment to step through the ferns that had become thicker and taller in the last couple of minutes.

"The shadows had tracked your energy and were trying to set a course for Randun. Aggie and I think so, anyway, before some unknown force blocked them at the river."

"They couldn't have tracked my energy, or that of the medallions that opened the passage to Randun," I said, rubbing a thumb across the ring Lady Mara had given me. But how had C-05 managed to track me? I had been warned upon receiving the ring there was a limit to the ability it had to conceal that energy. What that limit was I didn't know. "They must have been ordered to track you and Elise."

"However it happened, Tarsamon has set his forces on locating you, or us, rather. But he hasn't stopped his consumption of the life force energy on Earth, either, just shifted his effort. Here, let me show you."

Aria stopped to focus on the image she wanted me to see. In my mind's eye, a swarm of shadows hovering high above the town of Callander, dipping down near Doune Castle, could be seen. They blended with the darker cloud forms.

"They're close," I said as we continued on our trek. "They'll be waiting when we return. I'm certain."

"Perhaps. But we can't worry about it. We've got to get you to that key. If you believe you are guided, you must know a path exists beyond any challenge that awaits us when we return."

"I do."

The certainty of my response was surprising even to my ears. My belief was strong that the mission would continue despite any amount of danger. It had to, or the death of a planet would be on my shoulders for eternity. One fact was certain—as a member of the Alliance, I had already planned for the challenges of the mission long ago, anticipating life-threatening consequences. There was no turning back. No fear that could stop this adventure that had been set in motion long before we had arrived in Scotland.

We broke through the forest-covered hill into open space. No light but the glow of a single lantern swaying.

"We are to meet just over there," Magdalene said, lifting the lantern to her left. I drew the hood of my cloak forward with a crisp breeze that picked up and glanced ahead. As we came closer to the meeting point, I could make out the faint outline of a fence and a small farm-like cottage just behind it. A glow came from a window, perhaps illuminated by no more than a single candle or two.

Magdalene led us along the fence to a covered area and beyond a large opening to a stable, where the scent of hay and fresh forage filled the enormous space.

"Stay here," she said. "I'll return quick as a lightning bug." She left the lantern to light the area and closed the heavy barn door while she went to find her contact.

From what little I could see, there were eight stalls. Aria and I set down our blanket rolls where we stood and waited while the men unloaded their gear, choosing sleeping arrangements near several bales of hay close to the entrance. The sound of footsteps and the heavy wooden door sliding open had all eyes refocused at the front of the barn.

A somewhat portly man about five feet tall entered. His hair was sandy blond and nearly touched his shoulders in a disordered array of flyaway pieces around a perfect and plump oval face. I wondered if he had been woken from sleep. Bushy eyebrows in a shade darker than his hair rested above deep-set eyes that quickly assessed the lot of us, lingering on Aria and the flame-red hair before shifting his gaze in my direction. Magdalene stepped from behind him and whispered something to him before turning her attention to us.

"This is my brother, Lorne," she said.

"Thank you for providing us shelter," I said to him. He nodded with an expression that was clouded with suspicion, his eyes darting at each of us.

"You're safe here, but I can't say for how long. I can provide ye only four horses." He gestured to the stables and to those we could take with us.

"That's most generous," I said. "We will stay only the night and wish to bring you and your family no trouble." I could feel his tension, the risk he felt he was taking at letting us use his stable.

"How do ye know of my family?" he asked, irritation apparent in his tone. He turned to Magdalene without waiting for an answer. "I told ye not to speak of anything to 'em. If word gets out, ye know well enough of the trouble it could bring. The whole town will set to destroying my livelihood."

"She didn't say anything. I assure you," I said. "She only mentioned a contact. There is no reason to be angry with her."

"I'll decide with whom my anger will be, mind ye," he replied.

"I told ye of their abilities," Magdalene said quietly to him.

It wasn't that I knew everything about him. In fact, I knew very little except what I could feel from him. At the forefront of his mind was the concern for the safety of his family, his wife and two young sons. His offer to help Magdalene was due to her incessant pleading and the obligation he felt toward her as his sister.

"Yes, well. That may be so, but the less talk of it, the better for all of us. Good night," he said, turning abruptly to leave.

"Pay no mind to him," she said, glancing at our small group. "He knows of the danger that surrounds your task and prefers to be left out of it."

"We understand," Matt said. "Go and stay with him. Perhaps it will ease his mind a bit to talk with you."

"Are ye quite sure?"

"We will be fine here. And thank you for your help," Mac replied.

I smiled and nodded to Magdalene.

Once the door to the stable was closed, I took in a deep breath and peeled off my coat, leaving the wool cloak for warmth. Aria unrolled her blanket and settled into a dark corner between a large pile of hay and the side of the barn while I located a spot to call my own. Kevin was in conversation with Mac, strategizing the best plan for tomorrow, I guessed. He hadn't said much of anything during our hike, and I felt the same concern I had earlier rising within him. It was as if a distance was beginning to grow between us as time moved us closer to the key.

"We should keep watch," Juno said to Matt. "I'll take the first shift."

Matt nodded and began to make himself as comfortable as possible in a pile of hay, near Aria.

I didn't want to reach out for Kevin if he wanted space, no matter the reason. *I'm being foolish*, I told myself. *It's just this silly insecurity again.* Without knowing what worried him, there was just no way to win the argument going on in my head whether I was right about what I was feeling from him or foolishly reliving old insecurities of abandonment. I gave in to the quiet whispers between him and Mac that pulled me into the fog of sleep.

In a matter of moments, I'd drifted into Ardan, a world I'd come to know well. Instead of the usual dark path I often found myself walking just before a guide would find me, I arrived in a very brightly lit and empty space. Faint images of tree branches encircled the space, like a gray frame against white. The challenges that had faced me upon prior visits—the battles using swords and energy against the dark shadows—were gone. My recent visits were meetings and communication to aid in the mission. Now I found myself alone, waiting for whoever had called me to this world.

A tingling sensation raced from my neck down the length of my spine. I swung around just in time to see something had shifted in the distance. I narrowed my focus and watched as a faint outline of tan emerged. My hand instinctively moved to the hilt of my sword and then fell away, as the focus became clear and the warm feeling I received only in the presence of Cerys flowed through me. I closed my eyes and breathed in the air as though it touched every cell in my body and joined with it, then opened my eyes to see him standing inches from me.

"Sara, it's good to see you are well recovered," he said, touching a hand to my cheek. My thought flashed to the moment he gave me the dagger just before I entered the cave to find C-05.

"I have missed you," I said, searching his eyes and holding the feel of his touch as long as I could.

"I am never as far as you might believe," he reminded me. "He loves you deeply."

An image of Kevin entered my mind. I glanced down and back to Cerys. "Do you know what worries him?"

"Of course. And so do you. Your thoughts about him are correct."

I scanned through the crevices of my memory. The only occasion given to such inquiry was in the forest, when Kevin and I had been alone. My eyes stopped searching the air around Cerys, as if to find a fact hidden somewhere behind him, before meeting his stare.

"Do you hear every thought?" I asked.

"No, my love. As I've said, I'm closer than you believe."

How did you…? But the words melted off my tongue before I could finish the thought. Had Cerys seen Kevin and me in the forest together? I stared deeper, seeing something familiar in his gaze. Before I could define it, I felt his touch once more, sending another wave of warm distraction through me.

"I've come to deliver a message," he said, pausing to be sure my attention was fully on him rather than what worried Kevin. "When you wake, be prepared. You will be challenged to prove your strength, utilize your abilities. Do not let fear overcome you." The light of the room we stood in began to fade, as a black fog settled over us.

"No, no, no. Not yet!" I called out as he started to disappear, reaching out one hand toward the now empty space. I spun around to see that Cerys was indeed gone. "Just a little more time," I whispered, pulling my hand back. I closed my eyes as complete darkness and a deep sadness washed over me. I sunk my head into my hands and felt a large hand slide around my waist. I jolted at the touch in the blackness that consumed the room. It grabbed tighter and pulled me against the solid feel of a man whispering in my ear, just before I rocketed an elbow into his ribs. I felt a momentary release at my waist, as hands quickly grabbed me by the shoulders, this time pulling me around. A hand covered my mouth.

"Sara, who in God's name do you think it is?" Kevin's voice flowed as an urgent whisper into my ear and with it the brush of his lips. Sending me a thought would not have succeeded in reducing the perceived threat, given that I had momentarily been caught between dimensions of sleep and wakefulness. My conscience hadn't fully returned from Ardan when I had felt his touch at my waist. I relaxed at the realization I was still tucked in a stable on the other side of the hay bales where Aria had settled earlier. I nodded as Kevin removed his hand from my mouth.

"Sorry," I whispered, blinking as if I could see him. My eyelashes were wet, though I couldn't recall crying in my sleep. Kevin kissed my forehead, took my head in both hands, and gently drew me close against his chest. I breathed in his scent—warmth and musk—that comforted me. I closed my eyes. God, how I wished I could give all of myself to him. We'd lingered in each other's touch more than once, but to sacrifice my emotions to his trust? Impossible. Cerys's words floated through my mind like a banner across the sky, *Do not let fear overcome you*, until I drifted once more.

11

A scream rang out above the barking of orders from the demons below. High above the commotion, Tarsamon watched from the balcony off the tower he called home as the smoky haze shifted across the blood-orange backdrop of sky. Dark shadows poured from the blackened clouds that hovered, as though the sky itself was bowing before him. The light rarely shifted on the other side of Ardan, a place that had been closed off by the Alliance. He was allowed to live in an area roughly the size of Rhode Island, but that space hadn't been enough for the plan that had taken root the moment the doors of freedom had been shut to him. The building of his forces required so much more, an expansion into Earth, another source that could feed the element of energy and a passionate desire to ravage light. His evil army of shadows and demons wouldn't have to wait much longer for their hunger to be satiated with the malignant energy so readily available in the careless humans.

The choice for Earth had been made long ago and the time to take it was now. There wasn't another place that housed as much raw energy as that world. The discourse that had developed over centuries had created a great deal of anger and fear that ruled most of humanity, allowing evil a passage into Earth. The humans had chosen the path. He was simply fulfilling the final destiny. Tarsamon turned from the fury and screams below and began to pace, contemplating the challenge that stood in his way.

While he could thank the humans for making an easier path for him to enter, Sara Forrester was progressing on her quest at a faster pace than he'd expected and providing quite the skid to his plan in obtaining the energy on Earth. *She's human*, he thought. *Easily removed.* So why was she still alive? Her team had the power of the Soltari backing them. Now that C-05, a former member of the Alliance, had severed ties with the powerful forces and joined with him and his forces, a new opportunity presented. Tarsamon's effort to enter the Druid-protected realm had proven it to be nothing more than a locked door. C-05 delivered to him messages, information from inside Randun that he otherwise would not have been able to retrieve. But C-05 was only as good as the intelligence he had prior to turning against the Alliance. His value would eventually run out. No matter, he thought. Right now, C-05 was able to breach the protected barriers in Randun that kept his forces from getting to Sara.

A loud screech from below caught Tarsamon's attention. He angled his cloaked head toward the sound. Beatings of the hairless dog-like creatures that made up a good portion the demonic population were often necessary to ensure compliance and order during training. After all, angry souls that had not worked out their evil in life still needed a place to reside after they left other realms like Earth. But order was still expected and under the strictest rule. Free will could only cause chaos in the already angry souls under his control. That energy needed to be channeled and put to productive use.

Tarsamon brushed the commotion aside to return his attention to the problem at hand, Sara Forrester. His pacing continued as a way to organize his thoughts or alter the plan. A soul couldn't really die in the dark realm, being that it was already dead. The evil world was a growing society that would inevitably require the acquisition of new territory, new energy for sustenance. The fact that entering Earth had been so easy and the transition was occurring was evidence that darkness among the humans was indeed thriving. And why had that been the case? The Alliance had not been doing their job well. He would have expected some sort of a battle upon entering Earth. Instead, his forces had swept in with a hush and gradually overtaken one human life at a time, fitting in well with the mood of anger that had already spread like a disease among the population. Could there be discourse within the Alliance, a weakness that might be penetrable? He tapped a bony finger on the sleeve of his folded arms, considering another possible opportunity to strengthen his position.

A minor inconvenience—the Light Carrier being called to action—had set his sights in a direction away from Earth. He relaxed at the thought of the Soltari needing to pull such a resource, a human, of all things, to aid them. It meant he was gaining traction.

Prior to Sara's arrival, his focus had been the growth occurring in massive numbers. When she'd made the mistake of entering the dark world, her effect had been minor. Striking the blows to the demons and shadows reduced their sustainability, extinguishing them. But her presence had sent rippling effects into the energy field of Ardan, giving him another strategy to learn from her and what mattered to her.

Tarsamon stopped pacing to eye the business below. Angry souls, looking for reparation, he thought. They would get it soon enough. For now, continue building the forces, consume the life that was left, and of course, stop the Light Carrier. Not necessarily in that order. There was nothing to worry about, unless she obtained the first key. Tarsamon shifted his thoughts to C-05 again.

C-05 had failed in his first attempt to execute Sara in Randun. Even as a human, she was stronger than he'd thought and was being guarded by those in Ardan. He'd expected as much, but why hadn't C-05? Sara was the Soltari's strongest weapon against evil. Did the entity really think a human with an immortal soul could stop him? Tarsamon turned at the sound of steps behind him as C-05 passed through the doorway, as though he'd summoned his presence by the mere thought of him.

"It's evening in your world," Tarsamon said. His booming voice sent a chill crawling down C-05's spine as if demon fingers had pricked him with sharp claws. "You look different. What brings you here? It's not a place you prefer, but one that has not shut you out, either," he said, enjoying the sense of fear he could feel from his guest.

"Yes. There was some difficulty that forced a change in my appearance. I've come to inform you that I'm in place to meet the Light Carrier and her team. I've found the cathedral and the standing stones that confirm her arrival. The energy at the stones has been opened and, as you know, can only be opened once it has connected with the Light Carrier."

"Good. Do you still underestimate the power you are dealing with?"

"No. I have brought with me"—he paused, considering the two men who were aiding him—"resources that can enter once the Light Carrier is granted access beyond the gates of the cathedral." *Resources?* He reconsidered. *More like obedient dogs. Just...like...me.*

"You trust someone to help you?"

"They were once soldiers of the Alliance. They've rejected their rule, the continuous battle, but haven't been shut out. Yet."

"Like you."

The reality of the comment linking C-05 to the two men struck him like a slap. He'd been respected by the Order once, but there'd be no chance of recovering any dignity or respect after helping Tarsamon. The effect of which he'd not fully considered, and there wasn't time now.

"You understand once she's obtained the key, you will not be able to take it, and her strength increases?"

"Yes." He didn't need to tell him that he hadn't been able to track her from the cathedral. But there was one way he could get the key. It was an unlikely chance, but still one that existed.

"I will expect that you will not have to plan for such misfortune," Tarsamon replied, reading C-05's thought.

There was silence between them as both scanned the world that was to become C-05's new home, until he'd finished his quest. It was a grotesque realization that leaped up at him from the pit of terror below, as the faceless demons collided in small fights with the hairless dog-like creatures, snarling and drooling like rabid beasts. Blackened shadows fell around them and spread across the ground. The scene below was worse than any hell he had imagined in the churches he'd attended as a boy, sermons given to instill the same fear into him that he could feel crawling up the walls around him now. Life was irony in a bitter moment. And if the walls could speak, he was sure he'd hear them say, *Told you so.* All he wanted to do was close out the ear-piercing screams, growls, and other undeterminable sounds that crashed into each other and lifted into the air. Though he tried to imagine a life here, C-05 didn't believe he could ever get used to the idea of living in a world like this, no matter how short a time it might be, and his world, Earth, was already dying.

Tarsamon turned to face him. "You're not having second thoughts?" he said, breaking the silence.

"Of course not. What is meant to be must be. The humans have selected this course of action, whether they are aware or not. It must proceed as intended."

"Indeed, it must," Tarsamon said. "Let me show you how it proceeds in your world," he added.

Tarsamon extended his hands up and over the balcony, pulling them apart as if to stretch an imaginary rope between them. The long sleeves of his black cloak hung in points, dangling from blackened wrists. C-05 watched as a hologram-like scene took shape in midair. He recognized it as one of many metropolitan cities, New York, perhaps. People were busy making their way through the streets to what kept them occupied, but it wasn't the chaotic environment that held C-05's attention. He peered closer. It was the struggle he saw in the people that wouldn't let him turn away. So many of them carried themselves slowly and heavily, weighted by a black-shadowed demon that clung to them. Dark circles clung under their eyes, looking as though they hadn't slept in days, maybe weeks. *They look like the walking dead.*

"They grow weaker. It's part of the process of consuming the energy of the spirit," Tarsamon said. "It's a weak and primitive culture that gives in to fear and anger. Best to consume while they are young."

C-05 felt his stomach move toward his throat and swallowed hard, suppressing the bile that inched up. As much as he feared for his own life, he knew his part in contributing to the suffering was wrong. He shook his head, reminding himself the occurrence was inevitable. He couldn't have stopped it if he wanted to. Only one person could do that, the one person he was instructed to kill.

Tarsamon closed the floating image and turned to C-05, his shadowy, dark face reading every feeling and thought that passed through him.

C-05 knew well enough he could not block anything from him, yet blanketed his face with a stoic expression anyway, despite his obvious transparency.

"They grow restless," Tarsamon said, casting his gaze once more over the balcony toward the evil below. "My interests lie primarily with the Light Carrier now, as she is the one threat to controlling the light in your world. She is a setback to the time frame to complete the consumption of life, but one that you will remedy."

"I understand," C-05 replied.

"I know that you do."

C-05 woke in his hotel room in a soaking cold sweat, shivering. He spun the clock around on the small table beside the bed to see the time was three a.m., the usual hour his spirit returned from travel to parallel worlds. He strode into the bathroom needing a splash of water and to relieve himself. As he glanced in the mirror, he saw his color had gone to a pasty white. Did Tarsamon see the same fear that stared back at him now in the mirror? He never liked the path he'd chosen, but there had been no choice. He had to bargain with Tarsamon with all the information he held or risk losing both life and soul. He'd never expected he would be the one who had to stop her.

"You *are* a coward. And now you better follow through," he said to his reflection. "You should have let them have you when they caught you." He bent over the sink. When he came up, it wasn't just his new reflection in the mirror he saw, but the Dark Lord that settled over his shoulder, bringing back the fresh taste of fear from his dream state and a question of how he would fulfill his promise. A promise that was to save his life and forever torment his soul.

He didn't feel lucky to have escaped the gray wolf. He'd had no choice with a body lying crumpled and lifeless on the floor of the cave. Sara had done that. She might not remember him now and the decisions they'd made together across lifetimes, but she was capable of killing him. It was by sheer luck that as the great wolf lunged for him, the large black crow, usually a sign of death, had flown too close to the entrance, likely seeking shelter from the storm. A second longer and his soul would have been captured by the wolf. He'd flown toward the main gateway that led out of Randun. Since his soul had entered once, like a key fitting a lock, it was an easy pass through. Just beyond the entrance, he'd brushed against the first man he saw idling in a small boat on the river and picked up the trace energy he needed to mirror his appearance. The man had brushed him away, furious at the proximity of the black bird for distracting him from casting the fishing line from the quiet inlet he had found. It had been sheer luck that the man had similar features to his own.

Prior to joining with Tarsamon, C-05 had stationed a few allies Sara would need in Scotland, the Yucatan, and Egypt, among other locations. He'd done a lot of research to narrow down the specific location of the keys. And he had done it all for her, to aid her on the quest. With the tide having changed, having extra resources about might come in handy after all. A few white lies to tired soldiers and they would do anything he asked. Each of the two men in Scotland were strong physically, but also excellent at battling energy as soldiers serving the Alliance. C-05 swiped another handful of water across his face and reached for a towel. He wouldn't get back to sleep with the pressure from the Dark Lord being applied, as if he were a bug caught in the tight grip of a child's fist. For the first time, a new thought sprung to life—was it at all possible to get out from under Tarsamon's hold with his own life?

12

A whinny from one of the horses woke me to the flickering glow of the lantern Magdalene had left the previous evening. Its light reflected shadowed movement as Mac began pulling a mare from the stable.

"We'll need to leave before sunup," he said to Kevin over the protesting horse.

"They're wanting their breakfast before you work them," Kevin replied, reaching into a wooden barrel for oats.

I put both hands to my eyes and rubbed what little sleep I had received away. Two of the horses had already been pulled out of their stables and were beginning to toss their heads at the bustle from the two mares. Mac and Kevin were standing beside them. It had been a rough night, with the hard floor and sadness that had not really left me since Cerys's departure. *Toughen up. There's no room for feeling distraught right now.*

"Sara," said a voice behind me. I turned to see Magdalene setting a clay pot on the ground. "I brought fruit and hot cereal. Ye'll want to be sure to eat," she said, handing me a bowl.

"Thank you. Are you in a great deal of trouble with your brother?" I asked. I was hungry and gladly accepted the bowl and spoon.

"Nay. Not much troubles him for long. He understands what ye must do and how I feel I must try to help. Don't ye worry none over it."

"That's good to hear."

"Aye. I'll say. The Scotsman's anger is fierce but short-lived."

"Have the others eaten?" I asked, glancing around. I only saw Juno brushing hay from his clothing and assumed Matt and Aria must be outside.

"They have. Eat up. You'll need your strength," she said.

I nodded and smiled slightly, touching a hand to her shoulder as she bent to spoon the steaming cereal into the bowl.

"I'm grateful for your help."

"It's not much. But whatever I can do for ye, I will."

"What other magic do you practice aside from seeing images of folks in your boiling pot?" I asked, blowing across the spoon.

Magdalene heaved the pot aside and sat beside me, leaning against a hay bale. "Ah, that. Well, ye see, there are many plants, flowers, and such that have great healing powers. I've been interested in the magic since I was a wee girl and me mum showed me the powers contained in knowing," she explained.

"Oh, so it goes back a ways in your family, the practice of the magic, that is?"

"Yes, as far back as me grand-mum. She was a priestess, ye know."

"Do you keep your knowledge a secret from others?" I desperately wanted to know if magic was accepted or shunned in this world.

"A priestess is respected for her healing powers." She paused. "As long as it is believed ye are one." She raised a crooked index finger in front of her face. "I don't shout about it, ye know. But I like to carry on what me mum taught me."

"Of course. I think it's good that you do."

A loud neigh from one of the mares startled me from the residual fatigue I had awoken with, interrupting further conversation. I heard Mac exclaim that the horses were getting more restless. I knew we would be leaving shortly and hurried to finish the breakfast.

"Here, take this," she said, handing me a red berry. I rolled the circular object in my hand just before she curled my fingers around it and shook her head. "It's from the rowan tree. It offers ye protection, lass, under the white witch."

"Thank you," I said, uncertain whether I believed in the magic I held in my hand. Still, I could use all the help I could get and tucked the berry inside the pocket of my cloak.

"There's a well just outside if ye'd like to freshen up," Magdalene said, handing me a cloth with a tiny embroidered flower in the corner. She pointed beyond the door as she turned to leave.

I stood and headed outside to find the well, hoping the cool water would wash away the last remnants of sleep and sadness that hung over me like a personal shroud of darkness. I caught a glimpse of Matt and Aria in close discussion just outside the corner edge of the barn and pretended not to notice, sensing that if I drew their attention, I might be disturbing a private moment.

The air nipped at my cheek and I pulled my cloak around me. Steam rose from the well, creating a white mist against the still-dark sky. I pulled up the bucket, took a drink, and splashed the frigid water over my face, effectively shocking me out of any stupor of sleep. The water had little relief from the unusual sadness clinging like molasses to my soul. *Is this a residue from the dream of Cerys or something more?*

I didn't need any distraction on this mission. Damn if I hadn't slipped and fallen for Kevin. I had no intention of falling in love, ever. Who needed the complication, the pain that came with loving someone only to have him leave? Thinking back, I'd been under Kevin's spell since I'd opened my eyes to those soft brown pools staring over me in the hospital as my attending physician. He had said once before that we'd come so far, we had a history together over lifetimes that I didn't remember. And for good reason, I thought, swiping the cloth over my face. This task that faced us couldn't take the burden of love getting in the way. I'd just have to refocus, set my sights on the mission, and keep love from clouding the task. A stabbing sense of separation, of loss, ran through me at the thought.

I swept one more icy splash of water across my face before turning from the well and heading back into the barn. Inside, I dug for the small hairbrush that was tucked in the satchel of things I'd brought and began working out the tangles in my hair, cursing them as the brush stopped with each tug. The knots hadn't been there when I went to sleep, and it was as though some mysterious evening bird had made a few matted nests among the locks. I spotted Juno rolling up his gear. Kevin and Mac had disappeared from the barn, readying the horses, I guessed. I sat down to attend to resilient tangles, losing patience as each moment passed. Within moments, I felt a hand cover my own that held the brush.

"Can I help you with that or are you trying to pull it out one patch at a time?" Kevin asked.

"Sure. Thanks," I said, letting go of the brush. He picked out a couple of pieces of straw and tossed them to the ground before carefully working out the last two knots in silence. He ran the brush through the full length of hair and smoothed it once with his hand. I turned to face him as he sat beside me.

"We'll be leaving soon. Are you ready?" he asked. Before I could answer, a shout from outside came rolling in.

"Your horse, she's leaven' ye," Mac called, holding the reins of two horses in hand. Matt and Aria were saddled on another horse.

Kevin voiced an expletive before racing out. I threw on my coat and followed him to the door, watching as he took off after the horse. Juno was already in hot pursuit, riding to catch the mare in mid-flight, eventually managing to slow it. Kevin grasped the reins and leaped into the saddle, then headed back toward the barn, where I stood near Mac. The horse, evidently disturbed at being caught from fleeing, began to rise up in defiance. Kevin tightened the reins to gain control, walked her around a bit, mumbling words as he leaned forward, engaging in a private conversation with the graceful yet unruly beast. A few minutes later, he returned and reached an arm down to me. I grasped it and hauled a leg over into the saddle in front of him. With everyone settled on his respective horse, we began our trek through the dark toward the cathedral. Kevin and I rode in silence for a few minutes.

"Where did you learn to ride?" I asked, breaking the growing awkwardness in the silence between us.

"Ah, my father took me to a ranch when I was a kid."

"And you liked it enough to become a good rider, I see."

"No. I hated it," he said, laughing under his breath. "The ranch was owned by a miserly woman who didn't care at all for kids. She was doing my father a favor by letting me stay awhile, when he would set out on his rounds and tend to the horses." He shifted in the saddle. "Veterinary medicine," he added. "The only way she felt comfortable having me there was putting me on a horse to keep me from exploring her property and finding trouble."

"You? Finding trouble? Hard to imagine." I wondered what he must have been like as a boy, before and after his mother had been taken from him at such a young age. Had he retreated into himself or released his painful emotions in anger and defiance? He grasped my waist a bit tighter and leaned his head close to my ear.

"I was wickedly feisty," he said in a whisper.

I bet.

"How much?" he said out loud.

"Stop reading my thoughts," I said.

"Darling, if you don't want me to hear you, impart a block. It's a simple exercise."

"So is not listening."

He laughed at my ear. "I see you're still testy. What is it that's disturbing you?"

"I might ask you the same thing. And perhaps we could solve both of our issues."

His mood had changed since we'd been in the forest together, walking through aisles of flowers in the garden near the cathedral. I had suspected the fight with C-05 had caused him to fear losing me. But he had to expect such danger on the mission. And what was it that he was keeping hidden from my view? If I was testy, perhaps it was because I wasn't sure what it was that worried him.

"You might ask and I wouldn't elbow you in the ribs," he said. I raised an eyebrow at that. "It wouldn't be important for you to know anyhow," he added.

"Really? And why not?" I asked. *Why wouldn't it be important to know what worries you?* "When I said I was sorry, I meant it," I added in reply to his rib comment.

"I'm not angry about that. It's more important that you release whatever you are holding so you can remain fully focused when we arrive at the cathedral." He shifted in the saddle and I felt him press closer to me. "I feel your sadness Sara, but why?"

"I don't know. Since last night, I've felt something hanging over me."

This time I put a block up so that I could keep my thoughts private. It was easy to believe I could just let the nagging feeling go, push aside the sadness. But that wouldn't be truthful. I couldn't let a sensation like this one go. When I felt an emotion that had no reasonable explanation, it generally meant it wasn't my emotion but someone else's that I had tuned into. In the past, evidence of such feelings had come to light soon enough through some action or comment by the other person. I wondered about this one and if, perhaps, because Kevin might be carrying a fear about losing me, I was picking up this feeling from him. Maybe he wasn't blocking me as well as he thought. His arm wrapped slightly tighter, pulling me even closer against him, and I felt the warmth of him penetrate through the outer layers to my skin. The sensation sent tingles gliding down the left side of my shoulder and back as the fine hairs rose in response. It was that very connection I wanted to understand, and how he was able to cause me to feel at such a deeper level than I'd ever felt before. I angled my head slightly back into his neck. *To give all to someone, what would that be like?*

I love you. I heard his thought. We had never spoken the words to each other. He had feared I wasn't ready for the commitment that often followed. But I had not been ready for what I would feel when he said or, rather, thought it. The thought was felt exactly as if he had spoken the words. In spite of the affection I carried for him, fear raced forward, chasing away any other feeling and crippling the tenderness that had just swept over me seconds earlier in the safety of my private thought, as though it had been stolen from me. If I could, I would plunge a steely knife into the fear that kept me from knowing true love, removing the boundaries of protection created in a forgotten and painful childhood. But I also had a job to do. One that didn't have room for such complication of emotion. Unable to block being read in a rush of feeling, I knew he felt both emotions of tenderness and fear from me. I extended a hand behind me and gently stroked his cheek.

I can't say what you need to hear. Not yet, my love. I hoped my thought wouldn't cut too deeply. I was sad at the inability to deliver what I so wanted to say and angry at the sheer emptiness of the words that took their place. A tear dropped silently onto the back of my hand covering his over the reins and I realized the sadness I carried. My inability to give back to him was like a spell cast over me that I couldn't remove. Not yet, anyway.

You will, he thought, as he kissed the back of my head and continued the rest of the way in silence.

The sun was beginning to rise over the grassy hills in the distance as hues of pink mingled with shades of orange to chase the remaining deep blue-black of night away. Our breaths fell out as ghostly clouds that faded into nothingness in the icy air.

At least it isn't snowing.

As we came up over the largest of the hills, I could see we were close to our destination. The gravestones stood like dwarfed soldiers waiting to be called to duty, as they rested in the shade of the enormous walls of the cathedral. My eyes searched every hidden corner, every shadowed wall for movement or a sign of the man who resembled C-05 and his counterparts as we approached the grove of oaks at the base of the hill. I touched the rowan berry in my pocket, as if the mere thought of it would provide an additional layer of protection, should it be needed.

Kevin guided the horse between the trees, following Mac, while the others traced a path behind us, until Mac held up a hand indicating we would be going the rest of the way on foot. He and the other men dismounted and tied the horses' reins around smaller tree trunks, leaving them to feed on what remaining grass was scattered about the forest floor. I felt the previous sadness bury itself deep in the darkest corner of my soul as I slid off the horse and followed closely behind Mac and Kevin. Emotional healing would need to be tended to at another time. In a quick moment that surprised even me, I'd exchanged pain for duty. There was simply too much focus required for finding the key to be bothered with the collection of pain building in the recesses of my mind.

Heading toward the front doors of the massive cathedral, I stole a quick glance at Kevin resting his hand on the hilt of his sword, ready for any surprise attack. Juno marched beside him with the same ruthless look of determination, while Aria and Matt walked closely beside me. Out of curiosity, I held a palm out to see if I could generate the white-blue sparks that had created my shield in another place and time when I had battled in the darker realm of Ardan. In an instant, a flame lit at my fingertips. I closed my fingers into a fist, saving my defensive energy for when it might be called upon.

My gaze shifted to the entrance ahead. The copper strands of Aria's hair caught the beams of the rising sun and glowed like a flame against the shade of the building beside us as we approached the massive arched doors to the cathedral.

Mac knocked a couple of times before lifting the circular metal handles and shoving a shoulder into the heavy doors to open them. We weren't expecting anyone to welcome us. Knocking just seemed like the thing to do in case anyone was present. But as expected, the great hall appeared dark and void of visitors. Instead, it was a draft that blew through to greet us as we stepped inside. An icy chill clung to the current and raced down my spine, as though the cathedral housed its own prickly-fingered spirits with the aim to skim across our energy and assess the details of our business. Kevin stepped beside me, Juno flanking the other side, while Aria and Matt proceeded down the main aisle toward the altar, eyeing every corner for a stranger or C-05.

"This way," Mac said, angling his head to the left to face an arched hallway. As we approached, nothing could be seen beyond the blackness that closed off any curious wanderers. On both sides of the hall entrance stood a knighted soldier, empty of course, with no face beneath the bucketed helmets they wore. If we were in Scotland, visiting one of the castles, it would look as if they were placed for effect, and I thought it odd that the soldiers appeared very much so in a time when knights were most likely always active soldiers. I tapped a finger against one of the steely arms to be sure.

Hollow. Good.

"That could be threatening if it were real," Juno said. I glanced at him and smiled, as he eyed the sheer size, not much larger than his own.

"I believe they are meant to be," I said. "Do you feel that?" I asked, turning to Kevin. He nodded in reply. There was an element of energy in the room that did not belong to any of our team members. I waved a hand over the face of one of the rigid figures plated in armor. The figures shifted abruptly into a guarded stance, blocking the entrance with their swords and causing me to step backward. Mac, Juno, and Kevin drew their blades. Aria and Matt's footsteps were approaching quickly behind us.

"No," I said, holding a hand in front of Mac and Kevin.

"Your ring, Sara," Mac said, not taking his eyes off the knights. "Has it changed?" I glanced at my hand. The ring contained an inscription signifying me as the Light Carrier that was visible to those aiding in the mission. To anyone else, the ring appeared as a simple silver band with squared off edges.

"Yes," I answered. "The inscription is illuminated in white."

"Who seeks passage?" asked a hardened voice from the armor.

"The Light Carrier," replied Mac, "in the name of the Soltari."

"Provide the sign," demanded the voice. I took one step forward and slowly extended my open hand. The ring, locked in place on the fourth finger since it had been given to me, still glowed with the lettering of another language. I held my palm flat, fingers up, in front of the figures. In military fashion, both knights lowered their swords to allow passage and returned to their at-ease positions, becoming the decorative figures standing watch once more.

The previously darkened hall lit with the blaze of torches along the length of the corridor, as if a magical force was welcoming us. We stepped past the guards and I glanced behind to see that the cathedral, from which we had come, was now completely dark, urging us forward. Kevin grasped my elbow, gently angling me between him and Mac.

"I'll not be handled, thank you," I said to him. His hand dropped away. Juno, Matt, and Aria fell in close beside us.

As we moved through the dimly lit corridor, swords drawn, my eyes scanned for any movement. Our footsteps echoed off the walls. It wasn't more than a couple hundred feet or so before the corridor opened to a labyrinth of mysterious halls and chambers.

"Shall we randomly pick one, or is there a method to these mysterious rooms?" I asked, directing my attention to Mac.

"Stay close," Matt replied before Mac could answer. "I see several things occurring, some at once." He stopped, interrupted by the sound of grinding stone. We turned at once to see the walls closing in around us, forcing us into one large, empty chamber and pressing the light completely out. I felt Kevin move directly behind me.

"We'll need to spread out," he said.

"Once I can see where I would move," replied Juno. At that moment, a white glow slowly began to absorb the blackened chamber and I turned my gaze to the source. All through the walls of the cavern were what looked to be several pairs of glowing white eyes glaring down upon us.

"Matt, Juno, what do you see happening with this?" I asked. "I can't feel any sensation from them," I said.

"They don't directly pose any danger," said Mac. "They are the watchers, keepers of the caverns and eyes of the Druids."

We had fled the shadows into Randun, hiding in Magdalene's home and treading through the night and early morning. The smell of the humidity and horses stuck to my clothing and permeated my senses. My patience to get to this point was emptied like a lake sucked dry in a desert. The sadness that resonated through me was gone, replaced with a determination to get to the Druids. Our world was running out of time and I wasn't going to stand around to be stared at.

I stepped toward the numerous glowing eyes. "We seek the Druid priests. Allow us to pass."

As if in answer, the stone floor shifted beneath our feet. My arms flung out, trying to maintain balance, as another movement of greater strength followed behind the first, landing me on my back. The floor began to vibrate. I grasped for anything to hold on to but was left empty-handed with the others as the dusty stones beneath us cracked open and tilted downward. We tumbled forward and began sliding uncontrollably in different directions. A pit of darkness below the cavern was all I could see as I began grasping for a crevice to hold. The last sound ringing in my ears was metal sliding against stone.

Our weapons.

13

"Shit," I said under my breath, landing in another room of darkness. I coughed out a chest full of dust that had come crashing down with us.

"Ye can say that again." It was Mac's voice that filled the blind stillness that surrounded us. The floor felt solid, but then so had the one I slid from. I pressed flat palms on the ground around me, groping for a sign of anything, including my sword. My fingers fumbled for an object other than dirt. *Do I still have the dagger?*

I took in a deep breath, rising to a standing position carefully. A faint light began glowing in the corner of the room, reflecting the same rough stone-covered walls Mac and I had just left.

I glanced behind me to see his image in the hint of light that illuminated the space. *Where are the others?* My eyes shifted to every corner, seeking an exit or opening before scanning the ground. Spotting my sword a short distance away, I retrieved it in a couple of steps.

"Are you all right?" I asked, extending a hand to help Mac up. He nodded in reply. "What do you make of this?"

He shrugged his shoulders. "Well, the Druids would not make it easy to get to them, aye? I can't sense anything in here. But I do know I'll need to meet the keepers of the key with ye. The watchers should be leading us there." He stood and brushed a hand over his pants, causing a small cloud of dust to lift into the air. The fall had left a fine powder of gray across his hair as well.

"I'm not worried," I said, and wondered for a moment if that were indeed true, not seeing any of the rest of the team. "As prepared as you are with knowledge of this mission, it couldn't prepare you for what we would actually come in contact with." I found his sword and handed it to him.

"Now," he said, looking left then right, "I don't suppose there's a door leading out of this room?"

"I'll check over here." I turned in the direction of the dim white-blue light that hung in midair, like a mysterious ball of magic. Mac proceeded to the opposite side of the room, calling out first to Kevin, then Matt. I pressed my ear to the thick, rough wall, hoping to hear any sound that might lead us to the others. Instead, a loud *whoooaaa* sound settled around us. The wind whistled through the cave, as though an ancient and enormous sarcophagus had been opened, releasing age-old spirits among us.

"Something's coming," called Mac above the noise. He lifted his sword a bit higher. I gripped mine tighter and stood beside him. My ears began ringing as the sound grew louder and more intense. I fought against the desire to hold my sword ready or sheathe it to protect my ears. I settled for wincing at the ear-piercing noise, as if that might help reduce its effects.

A trickle of water began to drop and quickly increased in volume from the ceiling in five individual locations against the wall opposite of where Mac and I stood. I couldn't pick up any sensation from the energy source. But then again, my ability to sense anything had been unreliable since arriving at the cathedral.

We watched in stunned silence as the fall of water defied gravity in the expected puddle on the floor. Each stream, instead, began building upward, molding into a clear, solid form in the size and shape of a person. When the flow of water ceased, the results were tall, glass-like figures of men in long, transparent cloaks. I shot a quick look to Mac without moving my head and returned my gaze to the elaborate water features that had begun moving closer.

"Do you sense a threat?" I whispered.

"No. But I trust my abilities here as much as you."

All five figures closed in around us and stopped. I shifted my stance to get a better view of each. I, too, sensed no threat yet kept my sword tightly gripped at my side. It had been crafted by the elves using the finest steel and blessed by the powerful Soltari, but I wondered if the element of water had been considered as a possible evil I would battle in the blade's creation.

"Light Carrier," said one of the transparent vessels in a smooth, deep voice. "Fulfill the task and the key will be granted."

"Where is my team?"

"Unharmed and waiting to be called upon to protect you again," said one of the other figures.

"You will have no need for the protection of the Great Warrior while you are here," said another of the figures. "The task that lies ahead is one for you and the guardian of the key."

If I had no need for Kevin's skills, that meant I was not in any danger of dying. And yet the weight upon my shoulders urging me not to trust those words felt as heavy as ever.

Two of the figures leaned closer to us. One glasslike hand was placed on Mac's shoulder. And from the figure that faced me, a hand extended toward my face and touched beneath my chin. The sensation felt as though I'd been nipped by a cool puff of air.

"Your first task of strength will involve trust," one of the figures said.

Of course. Trust was my weakest trait, and lack of it had caused plenty of pain in my life by creating distance from those I cared for. Lack of trust was now to be a test of strength. *Will I be strong enough? Have I learned enough over time to succeed now?*

Without warning, each clear form dropped and water crashed to the floor, dispersing across the stone and sinking into its cracks and pores. I redirected my attention back to where the dim light hung and beyond, to the wall that began shifting its heavy mass, as stone upon stone ground loudly open.

"After you, Light Carrier," Mac said, directing his sword in front of him for me to lead the way.

I sheathed my sword and cast a smirk at him as I stepped ahead. I felt my way along the dark passage, flattened palms pressed to the walls as my senses sharpened to pick up on any prickling sensations that might be in the air. The corridor curved slightly left before the wall gave way to open air.

As we entered another chamber, there was plenty of light cascading down from some unknown source, illuminating the center of the room to reflect black and white solid cement figures of angels lined in three rows of seven. Some held hands closed together in front of their faces with heads slightly bent forward as if in prayer. Others, rather dark and menacing, held in both hands what looked like scythes, tilted in an angular fashion, possibly guarding against something yet to come—one could only hope. Still others revealed both hands covering their mouths. All of them had wings that were pulled in close, resting against their sides.

"You'll see him again," said Mac, breaking the silence of our careful study of the room. "The Soltari wouldna' keep Kevin away if they thought it was important enough to bring ye together in this life."

Does he know of the agreement Kevin made to be allowed to join me?

"Is this a vision you see with a second sight or a belief?" I asked.

"I dinna have the second sight Juno and Matt have. It's something I know."

There was a sound in the Scottish lilt of his voice that held confidence. I smiled at the comfort found in his words and wondered if he had said them to remove any distraction before the challenge. In the short time I'd come to know Mac, he appeared to be a person only concerned with the immediate situation. What he was not, however, was someone to say anything he didn't mean. I shifted my gaze over the room after assessing the angelic figures in front of us.

To our left, an array of weapons waited. Among the antique-looking spears and axes were floating spheres of fire and blades of multiple lengths and widths. I crossed in front of one dark angel to get a better look at the collection, leaving Mac staring into the eyes of one of the stone figures.

"Select your weapon," came a booming voice that echoed off the walls of the large room. For an instant, I didn't want to select a weapon.

You have a job to do, so do it.

"Then, select the proper succession," the voice added. Mac moved to stand beside me.

"Ye must choose a weapon, Sara. Only I can choose the proper succession. We battle trusting I have selected correctly," Mac said, turning the corner of his mouth up as if to add, *lucky me.*

Battle?

"You?" I asked, surprised to learn I was being asked to trust someone who seemed easy to trust.

"Ye didn't think ye'd be the one to have all the fun on this adventure, did ye?"

"I thought as the guardian you would have been provided all the answers needed to gain access to the key."

"Ye'd be the access to the key. I'm only to bring ye to the task. Go ahead. I'll battle whatever comes at us."

"Wait," I said, carefully selecting a spear. I proceeded to one of the angels that rested dead center of the others. I held my hand up in front of the angel, hoping it would move like the guards had, but there was nothing.

"Sara, it isn't in your hands. Trust, remember?"

I nodded and stepped back to the tools.

Not this one.

I extended an open palm toward the fireball as it glided toward me and hovered above my hand. "Your turn," I said, holding out the floating ball of fire. His eyes shifted between the sphere and back to the angels, contemplating which might be the correct match. I was finding it more difficult to release control over the choice to be made. I took a deep breath in, closed my eyes, and released the tension in one breath.

As my lids lifted, I saw Mac in front of one of the black angels with hands covering its mouth. "Here," he said, as I took a few steps closer. He lifted the ball from my grasp and placed it inches from the face of the angel. The figure shifted, slowly moving the hands away from the mouth. I watched as it came alive, standing on the stone block it had been resting upon. Its wings lifted and extended up and out. A loud scream pierced the silence. Mac and I stepped back as the angel moved toward the center of the open space. The angel's hands reached across as if to brace itself, continuing the scream, but instead brandished a black spear.

Wrong. Everything about what was happening felt entirely wrong. But I didn't know what to do to intervene. Then I remembered, I wasn't supposed to. I had to trust.

At least we were only dealing with one figure at a time. The high-pitched scream closed out all other consideration or thought. I gripped a spear in time to deflect a jab from the stone figure. I might have to trust, but I wasn't going to let the enraged angel stick me while Mac figured a way out. I glanced quickly behind the winged creature wielding its weapon in the air to see that all of the closed-mouthed angels had been awakened and were now moving about freely, with purpose and equivalent shrieks of distraction. I lost sight of Mac as seven of the twenty-one moved toward the center of the room, and concluded I'd been premature in my original assumption involving a battle of one.

The room was growing much smaller with the moving figures. I took a step back and bumped into Mac as he launched one of the fireballs straight ahead. It slammed into the wall in front of us and exploded into a massive flame.

Jesus! I lifted an arm to shield my eyes. There was no heat, but the blast was plenty bright enough.

The seven angels stopped shrieking and formed one line facing us. Mac lowered his hands. A whispering hum fell over the room. The sudden quiet was deafening following the screams. I made a mental note to get my ears checked once I returned to current civilization, while being sure to thank the powers that be that I was gifted with telepathy.

"What next?" I asked.

"I don't know. That seemed to be the best first choice."

"Until they opened their mouths," I added. "Why did you throw it away?"

"I wasn't sure where to place the thing, and I couldn't very well think about it with the screaming."

"They haven't returned to their positions and still hold their weapons." I waited, uncertain why until I realized this task might not be a battle we were intended to fight.

"Mac, they didn't really try to fight. Think about it. If this was a battle intended for us, they all would have attacked." I glanced at the still figures and back to Mac. "Perhaps it's a riddle?"

He stood silent for a moment, considering. "In that case, perhaps the weapon is not one that is so obvious," he said, gesturing to the collection of fighting instruments. "Look at them." His gaze was focused on the angels. "One group is praying, others rest hands over their mouths, and the last wields a scythe."

I could see his mind ticking away as he went down the checklist of possible solutions. "You think they represent unseen factors?" I asked, looking at him.

"What if the scythe represents a destructive force?" He paused and pointed at an angel covering its mouth. "Words are wasted, so ye don't use or rather need them."

Telepathy.

"And instead, ye used something greater than any tool found in the physical realm?" He pointed at the angelic figure praying.

"Faith," we both said at the same time.

"By our standards, it's a crude rendition but representative of what most would do faced with difficulties to overcome, right?" I asked.

"I suppose," he replied. "Your weapon of choice then?"

"Is faith."

"I don't see a weapon like that here."

"You're trained in the Druid beliefs, aren't you? You're a high priest, yes?"

"Aye. But religion is not what is being called for here."

"Religion is not faith. Faith is what you put your belief in. If I were from a world not as advanced as Ardan, faith would be all I would know to use." I turned toward the angels. "Your challenge then becomes quite easy as far as succession is concerned," I said.

He had already figured out the sequence—eliminate the destructive force, no need for wasted words, and lean on faith.

I picked up another fireball, a representation of light, and handed it to him. He moved with confidence toward the stone figures that held the scythe, placing a small part of the light from the ball of fire at the feet of each of the seven, and stood back. I let go of a breath I hadn't realized I'd been holding when none of the figures moved. Seeing that all was calm, he proceeded toward the next set of seven that had previously uncovered their mouths and shrieked. Mac crouched down and placed the fire at their feet. Having similar results, he approached the praying angels and followed with the same delivery, then stepped back to join me.

The light of the flame was absorbed into each of the stone figures, as they came to life, lifting their wings in the same manner as the first seven, the tips of their wings touching in the now cramped space. Their solid forms grew more transparent until all that was left were the faces that floated around us as mist, reminding me of the Soltari.

"*Leig as. Leig as.*" Whispers bounced off the walls as the transparent faces slipped into the cavern walls.

"What are they saying?" I asked.

"Set free. Their spirits have been released."

"You did well," I whispered, turning my head slightly toward him and keeping an eye on the disappearing faces.

"Aye. I thank ye for your trust in me. But we aren't finished yet."

Further comment was cut off by the sound of stone grinding together, creating a point of exit. As Mac and I rounded the darkened corner, the gleaming eyes of the watchers stared out at us. *Eyes of the Druids,* I reminded myself. I glanced at them as my shoulder brushed the wall from which they peered and I rounded another turn, following what seemed to be a spiral sloping downward. I could hear Mac's footsteps behind me as the passage grew narrower and darker.

I wondered what other information he had about the keepers of the key and turned just in time to see Mac's hand fall away from my shoulder as the wall shifted inward, separating us.

"Follow where the watchers lead." Mac's voice trailed off as the distance between us grew.

14

"**M**ac! Can you hear me?" I placed two flattened palms against the porous ridges of wall at my back and an ear between them to try to listen for a response. Nothing.

I had never felt as alone as when I had first stepped through the seemingly empty forest of Ardan, until now. The comfort I had come to find with Kevin, Juno, and the rest of the team, the knowing that I was not alone on this path to obtain the key, was a great source of strength I had not realized I'd had until this very moment. A terrible sense of fear crawled up my spine at the thought I could not simply step out of my circumstances, get a cab, catch a flight, and return to New York. I had no choice but to put all of my trust in the higher power of the Soltari, hopefully guiding the outcome in this realm and any other that held the last two keys. God, what I wouldn't give for a cup of hot tea, the mushy comfort of my pillow-back sofa, and to be able to let all worry slip from my mind.

"Where are the others?" I said to myself. "Or anyone?" I extended an arm as my palm and fingers crept along the curve of the wall. I continued to follow the direction it led, grateful I wasn't claustrophobic. It wasn't the closed-in sensation I found most disturbing but the deafening silence. The smell, too, had changed from a deep, woodsy and almost stale air of an aged church to the fresher scents of rain and moss. If my eyes failed me, I would swear I was outside. There must be filtration of some sort, air holes that fed down into this cave.

After several more steps, I realized the spiral was taking me farther down the chasm with Mac's words, *your trust*, ringing like church bells in my ears. While my ability to trust had been fractured from a young age, I knew I didn't have all the information needed to solve the tasks ahead of me. There was no choice but to trust the Powers That Be that I would not only find the other members of this quest but also come out of these deep, dark caverns alive. Was I under the protection of the Druids yet? I'd seen the watchers, the eyes of the Druids. But were they the protectors or mere informants?

A brief surge of strength returned as I continued stepping my way through the darkness farther down toward what felt like the center of the Earth. A quick flash of nausea rippled through my stomach, followed by a brief encounter of dizziness. I stopped momentarily and sucked in a deep breath, wondering just how far down I really was to feel physical symptoms.

I closed my eyes, took in another breath, and opened them again with the hope the sensation would disappear. A sudden shift where my hand touched the pebbled surface had me withdrawing, as the wall face began to move. *I'm going to need oxygen and soon. I'm beginning to see things that aren't really here.* The sound of a moan rang out as a lumpier texture began to take shape, as though the rock had suddenly started to develop a raging tumor.

Need light. My phone.

I reached for it deep in the bottom of the inside pocket of my coat and pressed randomly for the right app that would turn it on.

Where is it? Come on.

I pressed my back to the opposite wall and felt a breath on my face. I dropped to the floor, gripping my phone, and angled the light against the wall.

"What in the holy hell?"

A face, complete with wall-textured eyes, nose, mouth, and accompanying body, was emerging from the solid structure as if it were self-constructing out of clay. I crawled in the only available space and pitched myself against the farthest end of the hall-like area, searching for an opening. All the while the sound of a single groan turned into more.

Block the energy. I slid the phone back into my coat, brought my hands together and let the creation of a bluish-white flame play at my fingertips. The fire lit instantly, waiting for me to manipulate it for my purposes. I pulled my hands apart and down as the shield took shape around me. Three figures, instead of one, were standing in front of me. The same three I recognized as the men Kevin and I had spotted at the cathedral.

"How could you possibly have gotten this far?" I asked.

"It wasn't without a challenge," the man who resembled the former C-05 replied. "It takes much more effort to become part of the inanimate objects of nature when you can shift. Wouldn't you agree?" He angled his head in the direction of the other two men. They smiled through closed lips in response and stared through me like dogs waiting for the attack signal from their master.

"And Karshan? How did you get past the wolf?"

"That wasn't easy, either. Time happened to be on my side."

Sheer luck that's due to run out. So, he is C-05.

"Your dark energy would have been detected by the watchers when you entered the cave."

"You might think. But you aren't close enough yet to those who protect you. I've done my research at length, Sara, to know who you are to meet with, while you're just prodding along with your team and your guardian."

He tracked my energy trail. There's no way he knows more than Mac.

"My companions here"—he lifted a hand in their direction—"are concerned that you need assistance."

"I don't need anything from you or your dogs."

Where is the way out? There had to be an opening, along an edge. *Perhaps up above, somewhere?* The path didn't end here. It couldn't. Though I couldn't see behind C-05, the entrance to this cave might still be open.

My thoughts were interrupted by a slam that had hit my shield with the full intention of shattering it. The intensity rocked me on my heels. I started to back up until there was nowhere else to go. My palms lay flat against the stone, searching the crevices for a break or a seam. But that, too, was interrupted as a black cloud hit my energy field again, this time encircling and eating away at it.

Come on, Sara. Strengthen the shield. The light brightened for a few moments before dulling.

"Goddamn you," I shouted. "You don't have to do this. You don't have to work against us."

"If you knew the truth about what you fight for, who you fight for, you might think otherwise. The Soltari has a dark side, Sara, or Tarsamon would never have found an exit from your beautiful world."

What does he mean? What exit? Don't listen to him. He wants to create doubt, negativity, to make you weaker. It's the Dark Lord's way.

My breath was getting heavier and I didn't know how long I could continue with the light of my shield fading. I couldn't risk losing the energy I had left in my protective field in order to create a more powerful ball of fire to hurl at C-05 and his men. I pushed his words from my mind and felt another slam.

"You like to fight," I said. The defensive shield had faded and the illumination around us had returned to that resembling dim moonlight.

"Mine," was all C-05 said, taking one step toward me before catching my heel in the center of his chest, knocking him backward. The other two men stepped forward. I turned and angled a hard kick into the side of one of the men's knees, causing him to go down in gripping pain.

"No. She's mine," C-05 growled. The last man stepped back. I would have drawn my sword if there had been room to fight. The first guy was still down, groaning and holding his knee. If I'd judged the angle right, it was probably broken. If the increasing moan was any indication, I'd put a bet that it was.

I pulled the dagger from the sheath, my eyes fixed on both men.

She's got no place to go. C-05's thought had slipped into my thoughts.

"Right," said the man, obviously skilled in telepathy. He stepped toward me along with C-05 and grabbed my arms at the elbows. C-05 pried the dagger from my clenched fist and roared.

"Aarrgh." He dropped the blade and grasped at his hand that had a red welt matching the handle of the dagger.

The elves must have put the same blessing of protection on the smaller blade as they had on my sword, one that wouldn't allow anyone to handle weapons created for me.

Don't touch my shit.

Without waiting, I bent forward using the weight of the man at my elbows and brought my leg up so that the heel of my boot landed in his groin, causing him to release me.

Before I could get up, C-05 pushed me the rest of the way to the ground and sat on my back. "You can be so ugly, darling Sara."

I angled my foot into the floor for leverage and, with all my strength, heaved my torso backward, pushing him into the wall of the cave. He grasped my hair, yanking me back against him. A small groan escaped from my throat. Before I could attempt to maneuver out of his grasp, the sound of stone upon stone ground out. The wall had moved but where? The floor began to rock. Had C-05 experienced that upon his entrance to the cathedral? The eyes of the cave I'd seen earlier reappeared. Anticipation of the same event that had separated Mac and me from the rest of the team settled over my senses. I elbowed my opponent in the ribs. With my hair still firmly in his grasp, I let the pain of it rip into my scalp as I angled my head to the side and, with a closed fist, hit him square on the bridge of his nose, causing a release. I grabbed the dagger and slipped it into my coat as I ran for the opposite wall, my fingers clinging to any grooves they could find and with all the strength I had.

As I held tight, I turned my head to see the floor open up. The three men scrambled to climb away but nothing could save them from being swallowed into the depths below, as the floor began to slope and an audience of blue-white eyes watched. I heard the screams of the men travel downward, as the ground closed again into one solid piece. I dropped from my perched position and saw a small light illuminating an opening at the end of the wall and stepped into it.

I braced a hand against the wall to steady myself, feeling the dizziness return. *If C-05 can penetrate the walls of this place, what else can he breach? What are the limits of his ability?*

I grabbed my head with both hands as a stabbing pain ripped through my head, causing me to collapse to my knees on the floor. Pain shot from one side to the other, as though a hot poker was being inserted through my skull. My eyes began to well up with tears at the intensity beating through my head. I glanced upward to see the watchful eyes glaring at me from the walls and a dim light coming toward me. Another sharp stab of pain blew through me and I held on tight to my skull as if it were going to separate from my body.

"They said you are finished and I could come to you." A childlike voice resonated beyond the pain. "You're going to be all right now. I promise."

Through eyes narrowed in pain, I saw the face of a young boy staring down at me. He patted my head lightly with a tiny hand. As he did, the pain began subsiding. *He can't be more than five or six years old.* From beneath the hair that fell over my eyes, I could see him squat next to me.

He tilted his head to peer more closely at my face. "It's time. They told me to bring you to them."

I took in a deep breath, glad to be free of pain. Resting my hands on my knees, I lifted my head to look into his eyes, a bright green, lit with the purity of innocence. His hair was the color of dark coffee with red hues that clung to his head in small, soft curls. A feeling that I'd met him before rattled through my still-recovering brain. *Did I counsel him at the crisis center? And I find him here? Impossible. What in God's name is this child doing in such a dreadful and potentially dangerous underground world?*

"Who told you to bring me?" I asked.

He smiled softly, lips pressed together. "You'll see. C'mon, they're waiting."

"What's your name?"

"I don't know. It hasn't been chosen yet."

My gaze shifted downward as I tried to make sense of his reply.

He extended his small hand for me to take and I did, rising up from the floor. A sensation of overwhelming tenderness flowed through me at his touch.

"Do I know you? Are we already friends?" I asked.

"Not yet."

I raised my eyebrows and glanced toward him. But he never looked up.

At a loss for words, I brushed the dirt from the seat of my pants and followed him as he turned to continue on the path I had been on moments earlier. A soft yellow glow of light streamed up the corridor. We took two steps down into a small, empty room with a single wooden door on the opposite wall. I paused to scan the area, checking for any other walls that might be changing.

"It's okay," he said, tugging me in the direction of the arched wooden door. I smiled down at him. The boy's tiny hand closed around a large circular metal ring and he pulled the door open. A blast of air and bright light hit me hard. All I could see were streaks of green and yellow-white light. My eyes blurred against the harsh and sudden change in environment.

What is this place?

As my eyes began to adjust, I could see the streaks of green were actually several soft ferns. Children dressed in white cloaks sat cross-legged in rows of three on either side of a stone path, intermixed with lines of rich green grass. The air was sweet with the scent of recent rain. I glanced beyond the rows of children to a clear wall of transparent water behind them, separating us from the rest of the world outside. To my right was a mirror image of what I had just viewed to my left. As the boy continued to lead me slowly up the path, my jaw fell slightly open at the sight beyond the wall of water. I stopped and released his hand.

Stepping carefully past the rows of children, I approached the glasslike wall. *It can't be.* Kevin, Juno, Aria, and Matt were standing on the other side a short distance away, swords drawn in defense of something. Mac wasn't with them. A few yards ahead in front of Juno was C-05 and his two companions who had been yanked from the cathedral halls and apparently deposited outside.

"Kevin!" I called out. "Juno!" Each call was silenced, swallowed into the fall of water that kept me from them. I turned, glancing down at the faces that stared with stoic expressions under white hoods and remained motionless as the realization that I could do nothing for my team filled my heart with some desperation. The feeling, however, was short-lived as I remembered my duty to obtain the key.

The little boy who'd led me to this garden of sorts waited on the path. In the short time I had been distracted, he had acquired a lit candle from God knew where and was holding it between both hands. His hood was pulled over his head, hiding the lush curls beneath it. And standing beside him was Mac.

Thank God. I made my way toward them. The boy extended a hand and wiggled a curled index finger for me to bend down to his level. As I did, he held the candle out for me and turned his attention toward the end of the path.

"Go ahead," he said. "They're waiting. I'll see you again soon." I felt my eyes widen in surprise. A soft smile hid beneath the lowered eyes of the hood.

What can he possibly mean? I have no time to care for a child on this quest. He must be mistaken.

"Sara, the priests await ahead," Mac said, diverting further intro-spection. He lifted his chin toward the end of the path.

"Yes. Right." *The key, Sara. The key. Stay focused.*

The flame of the candle flickered wildly, lying flat at times as I stepped with Mac toward the figures waiting ahead.

She's here. Close. I can feel her. The thought pierced my concentra-tion. The ability to read thoughts was indeed intact. A movement from the corner of my left eye caught my attention. Just beyond the wall of water, C-05 and the two men who accompanied him were stalking through the terrain. Tall shrubs flanked their backside out of view of the rest of the team. One of the men stared up and down the wall, and I wondered if the viewpoint from outside was of brick and mortar.

It must be. He only senses me. He can't see me. He suspects there's a way in. As though in answer to my thought, the man reached a hand out and felt along an invisible edge, as though with a flip of a switch he might open the wall that separated us.

"Sara, we must continue." Mac's voice pulled my attention back toward the aisle where the figures waited. "The team will handle them."

I nodded, slowing my pace as I approached four men and a woman standing in a line in white hooded cloaks. I searched the faces of each. The woman, who stood at the end of the line, stepped forward with cupped hands, extending them toward me. She nodded once and I handed her the candle. She stepped back as the man in the center greeted Mac.

"Guardian of the key, welcome."

Mac bowed his head and spoke in Gaelic. And though I did not speak the language, the translation in thought was clear, as though I had always spoken it.

"*From the depths of time and through the transcendence of lives, I deliver to you the one chosen as the carrier of light by the all-powerful Soltari. The bestowing of the first key of enlightenment shall be held by this soul to be carried through the quest of the third and final key, whereupon all three keys will be received by the world to claim Earth from the powerful evil seeking to consume it and restore the balance between darkness and light.*"

The man in the center extended an open hand toward me, palm facing up. I glanced into his face to see a smooth complexion with wrinkles slightly contouring the corners of his lake-blue eyes and placed my hand in his. Closed lips remained unmoved behind the soft white beard that hung nearly six inches or so below his chin. The ring on my fourth finger continued to illuminate the lettering engraved in it as my palm pressed flat against his.

"Sara, you have come the distance, and even with so much doubt that you would actually arrive," he said. "If you remembered who you have always been and could shed this earthly form, all doubt would leave you."

I knew there were pieces of my memory hidden, such as the many lives I'd shared with Kevin, but what did he mean by *who I have always been*? How much was being kept from me?

"Tell me. Show me what you know, please," I said.

A gentle smile pulled across his lips. "It is not within our power to release information before it's time. The Soltari determines the appropriate time. You are granted the key of light and the knowledge contained within it. Protect it. The combined power of all three keys depends upon the energy of each one." His palm left mine and I let my hand rest at my side while he closed his hands together and brought them to his lips, as if in prayer. I waited with growing curiosity, watching each movement with extreme interest. The priests on either side of him produced a crystal ball the size of a baseball and, without glancing away from me, passed each to him.

I felt as if I were about to witness a magic show, but without any ohs or applause to follow. This was the well-practiced magic of the high priests, and none of the attendants would be surprised at what emerged. I, on the other hand, had no knowledge of the rituals or folklore of these individuals.

The man took both crystal spheres and tossed them straight into the air above him. They defied gravity, hovering above our heads, then crashed together and lit into two blazing spheres of light, like two miniature versions of the sun. I returned my gaze to the priest's eyes staring into mine. He extended one hand and reached upward to claim a single burning orb. He held it inches from my face. I froze, entranced by his movement. But I felt no heat, nor the singeing of my retinas in response to the fierce illumination erupting from it. The light dimmed, until complete clarity and movement could be seen within the orb.

"The light senses your energy and is awakening to reveal its truth to you. You shall carry the mark and energy of the seven suns that have dawned in this realm prior to your quest. This energy is one that can only be held by you. It remains with you until you choose to pass the energy to another source."

Before I could wonder what truth might be contained or what other source he meant, a picture began to develop, a small world growing in a glass ball. Tree by tree, a forest appeared and then the paths so familiar to Ardan. Sparks of light beyond the shadows lit within the crystal. I lifted my eyes to the priest. He continued to stare through pools of blue with a knowing I couldn't identify. And as I peered closer into the picture forming, I saw Cerys speaking with me. His face began filling the globe, closing out all other images of Ardan, and slowly transformed into Kevin's. I nearly stumbled backward at the sight and sensation that consumed me. The two men were the same soul. *How?* I felt Mac's hand press against my back, steadying me. There were slight differences. The longer hair Cerys kept and his bright cobalt-blue eyes were now replaced with Kevin's shorter cut and eyes the color of umber. *Of course.* I hadn't tied the resemblance together before. Maybe I wasn't meant to. But seeing it now reminded me of the familiarity I had found often in Kevin's touch that was so much like that of Cerys's. Kevin spoke only one word in the globe, "Arwyn," a name that, upon hearing, I knew to be my own.

"That's not possible," I whispered under my breath. But even as I uttered the words, I knew it was not only possible, it was a fact that the spiritual identities, Arwyn and Cerys, were our true selves, and not the limited identities we had assumed on Earth, as Sara and Kevin. A flood of emotion started to consume me. A memory had returned, providing the truth of who Kevin and I really were. I fought hard to suppress the sensations demanding to come forward. There wasn't time or energy to deal with my connection with Cerys or Kevin. I needed to remain focused on the task, the mission. I didn't need to be confused or challenged with a sense of longing or a bond. Was that what I was feeling? A bond? I was aware I had been married to Cerys in one of my past lives, maybe others, but this feeling wasn't that kind of bond. It was much deeper...eternal.

"No," I whispered. My head was light as air, floating between a state of disbelief and knowing. "It's too dangerous."

"My dear, your eyes have been opened to the truth of what is. What has been revealed to you is what the Soltari has chosen for you to see, as a means of strengthening you for the mission. It is simply impossible for a lie to exist."

"How?" I asked, racing to understand how Kevin could be here and Cerys could be in Ardan as a guide, yet both were the same person. "If that's true, where does the spiritual form of me reside?"

15

The priest reached for the other suspended orb and held it at chest level, placing a palm on my forehead. His fingers curved over the top of my head.

"Close your eyes, Arwyn, Light Carrier of the Soltari," he said. "This will not cause you any pain."

I did as he requested. A small center of warmth that filled my solar plexus extended down the length of my legs and back up, radiating heat through my chest and neck. The hairs on my head felt as though they were standing on end. I had resisted the urge to open my eyes but couldn't hold out any longer. *What the hell?* A sickening sensation fell over me as my gaze settled on a large beam of orangey-yellow light transmitting from the orb he held directly to the center of my being.

I slammed my eyes shut. None of the guides in Ardan had provided information on how the key would be delivered, and I never thought to ask. The furthest thing from my mind would be to assume I would be carrying it within. My stomach turned again at the thought, as I fought back the desire to interrupt the ceremony by retching. I slammed my eyes shut, searching my memory for the fresh rain scent I had smelled minutes earlier. Though there was in fact no pain, the stench of burning skin beat down every memory and filled my senses. *Fresh rain. Fresh rain.* The scent of singed flesh diffused any attempt at mental trickery.

"Succeed in your task and protect the light within," came the same voice from the white-bearded priest. The room began to spin and I opened my eyes. I wouldn't be able to hang on. I swallowed hard and prayed for a breath of fresh air. Darkness closed in. *What the hell is going on?* And then silence.

Reaching a hand in front of me resulted in feeling empty space. I was certain I was no longer standing upright. I pressed a flat palm to the ground and closed it into a fist. It wasn't the feel of the stones that made up the path that my hand enclosed, but soft spears of grass. I peeled my eyelids open slowly to see I was indeed outside. The walls of the cathedral stared back at me.

"Not yet!" I heard a loud whisper. "We have time. Just hold off. There are too many right now," said a voice. My senses tuned in to an energy I had become all too familiar with. C-05 was near. I struggled to regain full consciousness and find a place to hide. I reached for my sword but found the sheath empty. I thought I still had the dagger, but quickly realized I'd last felt it in the inside pocket of my coat that was also missing. Was I strong enough to use jiu jitsu? I rolled to my side and lifted my head to assess the area.

"Just over there, beside the rowan. Do you see?" Matt's voice floated into my ear just as Kevin's face came into view.

"Hurry. We've got to hide," I said to Kevin as he bent over me. "C-05. The men. They're here," I said, trying to warn him.

"They were," he replied, crouching beside me. "But when they didn't find you, they gave up fighting and blew past us, moving deeper into the forest. Can you stand?"

"Yeah, I think so." Kevin extended his shoulder under my arm to help me up, but I placed a hand gently on his chest and locked my gaze with his, allowing him to read my thoughts.

"I can't believe they revealed that. You know then?" he said, refer- ring to the knowledge the priests had given me of him and Cerys as one and the same person. "And you know that your name is Arwyn?" I could sense his hesitation and excitement, wondering if I remem- bered more of Cerys and Arwyn, our spiritual selves.

"Yes." His eyes dropped to the ground in contemplative thought. "How long have you been aware that you and Cerys are one?"

"Since you first arrived in the ER the night of your accident. The memories rushed to me the moment I began CPR." He paused. "You know I was not able to tell you what I knew?"

I nodded. I suspected, too, that had I been confronted immediately with the reality of my true ties to another realm, I would not have hesitated to check myself into a mental hospital for evaluation.

"I'm not angry that you didn't tell me," I said. A memory returned to me about the day at the beach in the Cape where I had spoken to Cerys just before Kevin had come outside. Kevin was able to pick up on the emotions I felt when Cerys had been present and had asked, "You love him?" At the time, I'd responded yes. I felt some comfort that Kevin was aware I loved him, even if I couldn't yet speak the words.

Mac appeared from behind Kevin. "Sara, are ye all right?"

I nodded. "You?"

"Yes, fine. We'd better go. Ye are no' safer now that ye have the key."

Kevin helped me up, though it was not so much for the physical effort that was needed. I was plenty strong enough. His assistance was to feed a compelling desire to touch, no matter how minor the connection, that resonated between us.

I could see Aria, Juno, and Matt keeping watch close by on the outer boundary of the cathedral. Juno turned in our direction. I shivered as the cut of an icy breeze found its way beneath the canopy of trees surrounding us and through the layered clothing. I crossed my hands over my shoulders, rubbing them for warmth. *Where are my coat and sword?* I scanned the ground for a sign.

"Looking for these?" said Juno as he reached me with both of the missing objects. He handed me my sword wrapped in my coat. "They looked like they had been tossed over there," he said, pointing in the opposite direction of where I had awoken, mere steps from the entrance of the cathedral. *How did I end up outside?* I thanked Juno and slipped the coat on with haste and followed the men the short distance to where Aria and Matt were waiting.

I glanced to Mac. "Where can we go?"

He grunted once. "A safe house. Maybe. If I can find one before nightfall."

We couldn't return to New York, not until the remaining two keys were collected. Tarsamon, C-05, and the dark forces could too easily find their way to us there, with no protection from the priests. In Randun, at least the dark shadows were prevented from entering. That fact had to be driving Tarsamon mad, unable to enter this world or connect with me except by way of C-05.

C-05 and whoever he had hired were yet another set of challenges to be reckoned with. Would he make another attempt to get to me? Now that I held the key, he'd have to kill me to eliminate the power of it. There was no way he was taking it from me. We hiked the distance back to where we'd left the horses tied earlier, in the thickest part of the forest.

"We canna go back to Magdalene," Mac said, breaking the silence as we approached the horses. "We'll need to rely on the aid of those in Ardan for additional protection." He mounted his horse. "For now, we need to seek shelter at one of the inns along the road and be watchful. We'll leave in the mornin' to find the next gateway, or sooner if staying the night becomes too dangerous. Be ready to move at a moment's notice."

"Won't we need to return through the gateway leading back to Scotland to get back to our time?" I asked. "I suppose that would be where we would part ways."

"My dear, I am to travel with ye to all three of the locations, as will the guardians of the second and third keys," he said, pausing to reach inside his coat. He pulled out an object and slipped the cloth down a bit, revealing the handle of the dagger, and handed it to me, having retrieved it at some point while I was assembling myself with coat and sword, I assumed. "The job of the guardian is to guard the keys until they have been *released*, not just until they are collected by you."

I pondered this for a moment, never having considered reaching the end of our quest. I hoped the knowledge of how the keys were to be released would somehow be bestowed upon me. Kevin and I climbed onto the back of the horse and began what might be a long trek to the nearest inn across a vast hillside. I leaned back gently into the warmth of Kevin's chest, burning like the heat of a furnace in spite of the cold.

We were nearly out of the shade of the forest, heading in the opposite direction of the hills we had crossed on our arrival to the cathedral, when the sound of beating hoofs came up from behind. I turned my head, looking past Kevin to see Magdalene riding with some speed in our direction. She brought her horse up between Mac's and the one Kevin and I were riding.

"Since ye've made it out of the cathedral, I take it ye were successful?" she asked, pulling on the reins. The butterscotch-colored mare shifted its head side to side, showing its displeasure at the abruptness of her direction to halt.

I smiled. "Did you suspect we wouldn't be?"

"Ah, no. But glad to see ye anyway."

"Were you waiting for us?" Juno asked.

"Ye might say that. I'm lookin' out for the horses, to bring them back when you're done with them. Can't take them beyond Randun, now can ye?" She shifted in the saddle. "Ye'll be needn' to find a place to camp and soon," she said, glancing up at the sky. "It can get a wee bit challengin' in the dark."

It was almost dusk when I had awoken outside the cathedral. There was no more than a fading orange glow on the horizon now, quickly being swallowed by evening.

"Aye, so it can," Mac said. "We're headed for one of the inns."

"That's good. Don't expect they'll all be welcomin', ye know. Most of the townsfolk know of the stories of the Light Carrier and that her presence may bring danger their way," Magdalene explained, brushing the hair back from her eyes. "By the looks of this troop, anyone could guess who ye are." I thought of her brother's expression upon seeing us. At the same moment, I heard the decision that passed through Juno's and Matt's minds to camp and also that Mac wouldn't allow it. We'd keep moving through the night so as not to be sitting prey for C-05 or anyone he brought with him. "I know of one that is not afraid to house ye and provide a bite to eat, but we must hurry. It's not the closest."

Do you trust her? Kevin asked me in thought.

As much as you do.

Mac glanced at Kevin for a quick approval. From the corner of my eye, I saw him nod once.

"Lead the way then," Mac said.

Magdalene clicked her heels against the horse's underside and called out "Ha," as she set off toward the inn with our team following close behind.

Kevin leaned into me and wrapped his arm tighter around my center. The feel of his weight and warmth of his body against mine were more than a welcome comfort. They sent desire pulsing through me like the blood through my veins.

Later, love, when I can have you to myself. He answered my want for him in thought, reminding me he could feel what I felt. Heat rose up my neck and ears and I was glad he couldn't see it. Was nothing private unless I blocked my thoughts from him?

Within what seemed a span of twenty to thirty minutes and plenty of darkness, we arrived at a small inn off the dusty path and behind several tall birch trees, almost as though the place was purposefully hidden from view. I slid off the horse with about as much grace as someone falling off, grateful for the dark and my long legs that prevented me from actually landing in a face-plant. I'd managed heels and dresses numerous times, from business to glitzy events, but for some reason, the dress that had come with my arrival to this other world was nothing more than trouble I'd soon be rid of.

The inn was a simple two-story home with aged, oil-rubbed wood paneling that extended from floor to ceiling. Stairs against one wall led to a partially open second floor. A fire crackled with low-burning flames from a hearth, while hurricane-style lamps burned on tables, adding to the glow of the firelight that cast shadows on every wall. The air was comfortable and warm, but a chill still floated somewhere through those temperate currents and with it the sense that something wasn't quite right. All seemed well enough. Before I could give it another thought, a small, plump woman in long skirts and apron entered the room, fastening a cap to her head. Upon seeing Magdalene, she dropped her hands and ran up, arms extended, and greeted her with a kiss on each cheek.

"She hasn't heard the rumors," Aria whispered. "But does think us unkempt," and casually pointed to her head to indicate no cap before tucking her hair behind one ear. Matt stepped closer to Aria. Something had developed between them in the last couple of days with his manner appearing much like Kevin's toward me, protective.

"Maggie, my friend. How've ye been? Let me look at ye, love," the little woman said.

"Aillie, these are my friends Aria, Mac, Juno, Matt, Kevin, and Sara. They've traveled a great distance. Might ye let them stay a bit? Just a night?" asked Magdalene. The woman's dark, round eyes looked each of us over quickly, pausing at the swords visible from inside our open coats. While our clothing had changed upon entering the portal, it wasn't the most flattering attire of the women of the town or outlying area. Upon closer look, the long skirt didn't fit into either farm-girl category or well-to-do town folk but would blend into a crowd without drawing much attention. Besides, I wasn't planning on staying long enough to lift more than a few eyebrows.

"Aye. Friends of yours are welcome. Come in. Come in and have a seat," Aillie said, gesturing for us to sit at either of two large round wooden tables. "Ye must be starved. I'll bring out some stew and ale." She shuffled into the kitchen with Magdalene following close behind.

"Do you think she's filling her in or keeping—" Juno began but had been interrupted by the crash of a pan hitting the floor. I stood up to see if I could help, glancing at Juno.

"I'm sure that's just what's happening." I smiled and turned toward the direction Aillie and Magdalene had disappeared, but Kevin caught my hand.

"Leave it to them, love," he said. "It's best if it resolves however it is meant to, without our intervention." I glanced at him before turning back to sit beside him again.

Are you sure I can't smooth it over a bit? I asked him in thought.

Not likely. You're the stranger. Remember? Best to let it play out as it should and allow Aillie's trust in Magdalene to work between them.

It went against my natural instinct not to attempt to restore cohesiveness, but he was right. I sat down beside him.

We ate heartily and drank ale until my head was light. The warmth of the room and lull of the spirits made my eyelids heavy. Aillie's husband's particular brand of ale was a bit stronger than what Magdalene stocked at her place, and he kept pouring until I smiled and leaned onto Kevin's shoulder to steal a moment of calm beneath closed eyelids.

I woke to the soft touch of fingers running down the length of my arm in the pitch-dark of the room. As I stirred, the mattress crunched under my weight and the fingers stopped their descent. I could hear the familiar voices of the others downstairs, still talking, and a hearty laugh from Mac.

Did I pass out? I've never done that. But I didn't recall making my way upstairs to find the bed. Maybe Kevin had carried me.

"I've wondered about you," a voice whispered. I wasn't fully awake and still had residual effects of the ale lingering, keeping me sedated enough from asking what he could possibly mean. *Am I dreaming?* I turned onto my side and bumped into a strong male frame and forced my eyes open. A dim light revealed a small opening in the window of the old room and I shivered in response to the frigid temperature that seemed to suddenly take up residence all around me.

"Why in God's name do you have the window open?" I groaned, curling into the warm body beside me.

"That's right. Come to me. I can do more than keep you warm."

Now fully awake, I resisted the urge to bolt from the voice and the bed. My mind shot into full gear.

Think, think, block your thoughts. What little light shone into the room and across the person beside me reflected a similar physical resemblance that might have been convincing, but the energy I felt was indeed not Kevin's.

16

"She's so much stronger than I had imagined," C-05 said.

"May well be, but it will be all of our lives if we don't stop her, and soon," one of the two men said.

"Like hell we're stopping her now, with her protection the power of that key," the other man added. "We'd be lucky to come out of that alive, I tell ye."

"Shut up," C-05 said. Irritation had sunk far beneath the surface of his skin and was a burning sensation he couldn't cool. "We need to be smart about getting to her. Now, let me think." He paced the grassy area hidden beneath the oaks, gazing out at the coming night. "You." He pointed to the first man who had spoken. "You brushed against Kevin when we were dumped out of the cathedral. Did you capture any residual energy that could be used?"

"Kevin, the one with the longer dark hair, yes?" the man asked.

"Yes," C-05 gritted between clenched teeth. His mood had grown darker each moment he continued, and faltered, on the path to get closer to her. He didn't dare go back to Tarsamon without Sara, knowing it would be the end of his life if he showed up without his prize. He could feel the Dark Lord growing impatient. Thankfully, the Druid priests had created a safe haven the dark forces couldn't enter, working as much in his favor as hers. A nagging sensation kept pinging at him that Tarsamon wanted to know his status. It was a signal he needed to return soon.

"Now that she has the key, what power does that give her?" one of the men asked, interrupting his thoughts of Tarsamon.

"I don't know for sure." C-05 shoved a hand through his hair. "I hadn't gone far enough in my research to determine the power of each key because I never anticipated having to know, much less fight against it."

The fact was C-05 had never expected to be on a path to hunt down and bring the Light Carrier to Lord Tarsamon. If all had gone as planned, he'd be directing her toward the next location of the keys, providing additional resources to help her on Earth, and keeping her away from the very darkness that wanted her captured. After all, they had been allies once. That was before he'd slipped and gotten caught in the darker territory of Ardan by Tarsamon's legion of demons. Sara had been the only bargaining chip he had in order to be set free from Tarsamon. Would he really ever be free? The shell of an existence that awaited him when he brought Sara to the Dark Lord would be as though he were living in pure hell. Because once one's energy had turned away from all light, there was nothing left but anger, hatred for all things, and a wicked, ravenous desire to consume more light-giving energy, like a blood-thirsty vampire on the hunt.

Even now, far from the grasp of dark shadows and sunless sky, he could feel the light he carried, what he loved about life, leaving him and growing darker than he'd ever known. Was it possible for it to return? Or would he become one of the lost souls trapped in Tarsamon's realm for eternity? He thought of the surly beasts that chased him before he'd run out of breath trying to find the exit back to his world and wake from the nightmare. Of course, he had never found the way in, and here he was trying to track the one person who could save his life from the wrath of evil if he failed to deliver. Then, he considered, there was his beloved. What would become of his Isobel? Trapped, he'd never have an opportunity to find her. And if by rare chance he did, in the state of darkness he was in, she wouldn't want him. Light cast away shadows. It shone on darkness, chasing it away into grim corners to hide like the crippled, cowardly soul he was quickly becoming.

C-05's spirit wasn't dead yet, though. He hadn't given all of himself to the Dark Lord, not yet, because he still knew the sensation of loss. He still carried the ability to care for at least one other—his love. She was the reason visions of sadness and anger pulsated through him. The Soltari had held ransom his eternal connection with Isobel just as they were holding Sara's and Kevin's. C-05's hands began to shake. He balled them into fists as he felt desperation race up his arms into his shoulders.

"You." He lifted a chin in the direction of the taller of the two men. "Sara and her team won't be able to go back to Randun."

"We saw to that well enough," said the man, referring to his earlier direction of the town constable to Lady Magdalene's door, claiming witchcraft was being practiced.

"Shut up and listen, carefully. That means she needs shelter. Where can someone hide nearby?"

"Why, that'd be the old Ockburn Inn a ways up the road."

"We ride there first. Take the energy you collected from Kevin earlier in your fight and put it to good use. And understand, you'll need to be clever in your approach with the protection she has around her." C-05 realized this might be asking a bit much of the man. "Don't confront her. There's only one way for her to give up the key. We have to get to her before she and the team pass through the portal back to Doune."

"If ye dinna want me to confront her, how is it ye think I'll get the key?"

C-05 could see the man's thoughts ticking away across his face before he heard his thought. *Look like Kevin. Don't confront her. One way.*

"You want me to lie with her?" The man looked from C-05 to his partner, shocked.

"Whatever it takes to stop her."

"But she's no' going to believe it's me, or, uh, Kevin, ye know."

"She will if you use the energy wisely. Make...it...convincing."

"And if she isn't convinced?"

"Ye'd better get your balls out o' her bed," the other man said with a laugh.

"Then be ready to kill her." C-05 pulled himself into the saddle. "I'll give you a signal when it appears okay to enter. We'll wait for you outside."

17

I pretended to be asleep and stirred slowly, turning away from the figure beside me. As my eyes sharpened to the shadows of the room, the stream of moonlight reflected my coat lying on the chair next to the bed. I stretched my arm slowly in the direction of it, reaching fingers as discreetly as possible to the pocket, hoping the right one, the one with the dagger, was closest to me.

"Where are you going?" The voice was a little stronger now, not quite the whisper I'd heard upon waking.

"Mm, just so tired," I lied. As soon as I had realized it was a stranger in my bed, I was as awake as if someone had dowsed me with ice water. Without knowing who or what I faced, I chose to go along with the stranger's game long enough to retrieve a weapon. I could feel the weight of the dagger in the nearest pocket. Just one solid reach and...

"Not before I've had you," came the voice and he moved to press his weight on top of me.

Goddamn it!

I reached another inch to retrieve the blade, grasping it between the tips of my forefinger and middle finger. I brought my hand back to my side, sliding the icy steel under my naked body just as I became immobile from his weight. I sucked in a breath as my skin adjusted to the sensation of cold. In one swift movement, my wrists were pinned to the mattress. The bracelet I wore began to heat in the spot it rested on my arm and its light began glowing as the only beacon in the room, sending a silent signal to Kevin of the danger, if he wasn't groggy from ale. *Remain calm. Think your way out of this. And if he tries anything, he's dead.*

"This is lovely," he said, stroking a thumb across my wrist and over the bracelet while holding my hands clasped in one of his. "Just a little too bright on an already moonlit evening." He reached another hand up, fiddling with the clasp.

"How can I please you like this?" I purred, suggesting a release. I would need to maneuver myself quickly to gain the upper hand.

"I'm sure you won't disappoint," he said.

Murderous thoughts multiplied at his words. I felt the blood pulse through my veins much faster while I kept them hidden from view of another potential telepath. One couldn't be sure. And from what I could see in the moonlight, the man appeared to be able to shift his form. But the energy sitting over me now wasn't C-05's. It was unfamiliar to me.

Stay cool, Sara. Think your way out.

"Then touch me once more to be sure, like you did when you woke me, will you?" I said.

He released the proper wrist for me to reach for the dagger. If he hadn't, my knee would have encouraged him. I pressed my hand to the mattress, lifted my torso closer to him, and in one swift move, grabbed the dagger from beneath my back. I whirled it around, wielding it into the closest part of his body, as he grasped for control of my arm. A warm spray of wetness coated the side of my face. A groan came from him as he slumped over my chest. I struggled under his weight, trying to shift from underneath him. Bringing my knees up, I pushed his weight off me. He rolled and hit the floor with a resounding thud. Another groan and gasp, then silence from the mound on the floor. Could he be pretending to be dead? I couldn't know for certain with the lack of light. I waited, listening for any other sounds.

Footsteps raced up the stairs. The door flew open and Kevin stood in the doorway next to Matt, who was holding a lamp.

"Jesus," one of them said.

I grabbed at the quilt, wrapping it around me as I stared over the bed in horror to see I had landed my mark well into the left side of the victim, surely puncturing the lungs and likely the heart, since he was no longer moving. Blood had left a trail from the edge of the quilt, across the planked floor, and was soaking into a rug beneath the man. But the horror was in what was happening on the floor. The body initially looked like Kevin, but as it died, it shifted into a different image of a man. The sharp, rusty smell of blood pierced my nostrils as my other senses returned. I swallowed hard.

My vision was slightly disturbed by spots on the bridge of my nose. I swiped a hand over it and stared at the naked body of the man lying crumpled on the floor. From the vantage point of the bed, he appeared so vulnerable. Only a moment before, it was I who had been in the compromised position.

I thought about the respect for life I held, never believing I could harm anyone, never mind murder them, and remembered C-05. That fight hadn't been the same as this one. The battle with C-05 had been for my life. And who could be sure whether this one would have ended up the same, had I missed my mark?

Matt bent down to check the man's pulse and confirm he was indeed dead.

"Answer me, Sara. Are you all right? Is any of this your blood?"

What?

Kevin's voice drew me out of the daze I'd been in and I shook my head. I had killed someone and that went against every moral fiber of my being. But given the circumstances, it was going to be him or me who ended up dead. I wasn't going to be violated. And well, there was no other way for this situation to have ended. It was going to be him who lost. It had to be. Too much was at stake. From now on, anyone who stood in my way or tried to harm me would have to die.

"I'm okay," I mumbled, nodding. All the while, my thoughts were reverberating, *not okay*. I glanced around the bed, then to the floor. My dagger rested in the center of the sheet, coated with drying blood. Kevin reached across, wiped it on a piece of unfamiliar clothing strewn at the edge of the bed, and turned to Matt. His words were a distant sound as my mind wandered back to the body.

The man on the floor didn't appear to have a weapon in the room. The only evidence he'd brought anything with him was what must be his shabby shirt at the end of the bed. *Maybe he left his sword outside? Fool. Is someone waiting for him? C-05?* Kevin stepped to the open window, stared, and closed the wooden shutter. *Would the guy have tried to kill me?* It didn't matter. He wanted to harm me, pretend he was Kevin for some reason I couldn't think of. There were individuals that didn't want to see me complete the quest. And for that reason, I was being hunted by shadows and demons and even C-05. *He has something to do with this. He has to.*

As I continued to stare at the lifeless naked body, I wondered if that was the face of one of the men I'd seen with C-05. I couldn't be sure. There was no sensation. No fear. No remorse for removing the soul from the man. The lack of emotion was a tool of strength I carried to succeed in the quest, to do what had to be done and resist any weakness that would sway me from my task. I knew now the reason my life had started out so rough—to toughen me, to build a wall of strength. And now I felt nothing, not even relief at killing a predator. As my eyes moved over the body, I realized I would not find solace until the mission was complete.

My heart was returning to a normal pace at the realization it was safe. I watched as the transformation finalized into one of the men I'd indeed seen with C-05 at the cathedral. From the doorway, Matt signaled to Mac and Juno downstairs, hoping to leave Aria with Magdalene and Aillie and reduce the chance of bringing any further attention to the dead man in the room.

"How did he take your image?" I asked Kevin, pulling my eyes from the corpse to look at him.

"I don't know. During the fight, this one and I brushed against each other when C-05 and the other man rushed off. There must have been an exchange of energy that he used to shift into my form."

"We'll take care of him," Matt said to Kevin. "I'll find some rags so you can clean up." He ducked past Mac, who stood in the doorway with Juno behind him.

"It's nothing," I heard Matt say over the balcony. "Just a little upset stomach from nerves and too much drink." He threw in a hearty laugh. "The lady's not used to good ale."

Good. That might explain someone carrying a rug out of the room.

After tossing the clothing on top of the body, Juno and Mac rolled the man in the large rag rug, colored in dark hues of green, red, and rust, that rested beside the bed before heaving one end on each of their shoulders. Kevin shut the door behind them as they carefully stepped down the shadowed stairway. Small creaks in the floorboards echoed their descent.

Kevin turned from the door and raised an eyebrow and cocked his head at me, still grasping the quilt.

"What?" I asked.

"Are you hurt?"

"No, I don't think so. I can take care of myself."

"So it seems. We've got to clean you up. It looks as though you stepped out of a horror movie."

*Well…*I thought. I began scooting off the bed just before a quick knock came at the door followed by the opening of it a mere crack. Magdalene peeked a head in and, seeing it safe, entered with a medium-sized bundle of torn cloth. Her jaw dropped. She snapped it shut and rushed over, dumping the rags on the bed beside me.

"I'll fetch ye some hot water for a bath," she said, patting my knee and turning immediately to leave. With the latch of the door, I glanced down at my bare shoulder to see it covered in blood.

Kevin brought the basin over with a pitcher of water that had been left in the room and sat beside me. He began wiping my face, carefully avoiding my eyes. I sat in silence, watching his eyes as they shifted over my forehead and neck. I sensed he needed to know what had happened. He turned the cloth and brushed my cheek near my mouth and his eyes met mine. Not wanting to speak of the details, I allowed him to view the memory as I went over it in my mind. When I was finished recalling it, he placed a hand on either side of my head and tipped it forward, kissing the top of my head.

"You are very lucky he played your game," he said.

"Or I played his."

"Yes. Either way, had he killed you"—he paused—"or anything else, there's no telling what might have happened."

"You actually believe there was a chance of that?" I said, implying there was no way I would have allowed the man to take me in any way. I shook my head. "I know you. Your energy. Anyway, I don't want to think of it. It's done. What I'm worried about is, if that now deceased person knew where to find us, C-05 and his living partner must be stalking outside. They can't be far."

"I'm not leaving you. And the others will be even more watchful. Juno and Matt are searching the grounds."

"As they dispose of the trash?"

"Yes. It's a good thing we're leaving tomorrow," he said. There was a knock at the door and I was feeling the urgency to put my clothes on if there was going to continue to be interruption. I pulled at the quilt and wrapped it tighter around my body as Kevin cracked open the door.

"May I come in?" Mac asked in a lowered voice. Kevin glanced at me for approval before opening the door wider.

"I'm all right," I said before Mac could ask. "You should get some sleep."

"Good. And I mean to." He paused, stole a look at Kevin, and then turned his attention back to me. There was a troubled feeling resonating in the air around him, a deeply concerning one. He wasn't sure whether to sit or stand and settled on the former, selecting the chair next to the bed.

"Magdalene has a bath ready for ye, so I won't keep ye," he said as his eyes glided over the side of my face that Kevin had been working on. I reached forward and put a hand on his forearm.

"Whatever it is, you can tell us," I said.

"It isn't so much what I need to tell ye. It's what I need to know." Mac paused and pulled a thread from the inside knee of his pants and glanced up, narrowing his eyes on mine. "There's no easy way for me to ask. Did the shapeshifter, did he, uh, touch ye deeply, take ye, rather?"

"No. You can be sure of that," Kevin answered for me. But Mac's eyes remained fixed on mine.

"No," I said. "He didn't even manage a kiss before I realized he wasn't Kevin."

"Thank God for it." Mac released a breath he had been holding since asking the question and glanced up to Kevin and back to me. "Then the key is still safe."

"What do you mean?" Kevin asked.

"A shapeshifter's goal is specifically to fool their prey, for that ye know." Mac leaned forward, resting his forearms on his thighs. "Because ye have the key, if he lies with ye, well, it's believed he can absorb the essence of the power of the key."

"Why wouldn't he just try to kill her? Wouldn't that have been easier than trying to rape her?" Kevin asked. His eyes darted to mine and back to Mac.

"Aye, ye might think so. But since she holds the key, if she is killed, the power of the key doesn't die with her. It is released, making the key active in the world. A single key is no' very powerful alone, but active just the same. And they wouldna' want that, Tarsamon and the dark forces, that is."

Mac shifted his glance from Kevin to me. The immediate silence was growing awkward as I considered not only the new safety granted me in holding the key, but also that my death was perhaps the only way to release the power of the keys.

"Well then, I'll leave ye to what is the remainder of the evening and bid ye some rest."

"Wait," I said. Mac halted his approach to the door. "When you said if he lies with me, he can obtain the power of the key, are you saying the key could be taken forcefully?"

Kevin had been standing at the window, having turned his attention outside since Mac's last comment. His head snapped around at the question.

"No." He paused. "The belief is ye must give the energy willingly. When ye give your body, ye give the energy contained within it. It's why he chose to shift into Kevin's image."

I glanced to Kevin. Our eyes met in understanding. He closed his eyes and turned his head away.

"Sara," Mac said, placing a hand on my upper arm. "The pure of heart will never take the light from ye, never hold the keys. The energy cannot transfer to them. The responsibility of such a burden is to remain with the one chosen to hold their power. None of us want to carry it. Only the dark forces will try to fool ye into giving that power away." I just stared past him, my eyes drifting downward at a small pool of blood remaining on the floor.

"The power combined in the keys would kill them," I said. "They have to know they couldn't contain the energy within their beings."

"In time, the light, or rather, the specific energy the key is created with would destroy anyone else who tried to hold it. They are willing to give their soul to separate the keys from ye, because it means they are forever removed from the power of the Soltari. Having that much strength puts them in command. But"—he paused—"they can only hold it, even for a short time, if ye give it to them willingly."

"Well, that will never happen, under any circumstances," I said.

"You'll have to be sure it doesn't, no matter what happens. This quest has just begun and the path we take to get the next two keys will become more dangerous."

"I've been made aware of that fact. But I suppose it doesn't hurt to be reminded." Then again, I didn't need a reminder this soon after stabbing one man's recent attempt.

"Well then, I'll be leavin' ye both to your evenin'. Good night."

I glanced up at Mac and forced a smile as he closed the door, leaving Kevin and me in silence.

A moment passed before I stood to open the door toward the bath. Kevin fell in close behind with an oil lamp in hand, avoiding the short train of quilt that scooted across the floor behind me.

"Where are you going?" I asked.

"I told you I'm not leaving you alone."

"I think I'm safe to take a bath," I said in the doorway of the room with the tub. "You should go get some sleep, too."

"I'll get some sleep with you when we're done here." He raised his chin in the direction of the tub. I stared at him for a moment. Not a single moment to myself? For the remainder of the quest? It could have been worse, I reconsidered. It could have been an arrangement with someone I didn't like or love. "Your water is getting cold," he said.

I sighed and gave in, turning toward the room with the glow of a candle coming from it. Kevin closed the door. Letting the quilt slip from my grasp, I stepped into the tepid water.

"You know, I don't believe you have ever had to release the stubborn part of your personality for anyone, until now," he said quietly, placing the oil lamp on the wooden table in the room. Its glow flickered warmly, casting shadows against the walls.

"I want to be angry with you for being too protective, but I can't," I said. "I understand."

He reached for a small glass bottle of something liquid and pulled open the stopper to smell. Approving, he brought it over to the tub and kneeled behind me.

"Lucky for me," he said into my ear. The corner of my mouth turned up as I narrowed a glance at him. The mild annoyance I'd begun to feel slipped from my mind and drifted away into the warm water.

After picking up an oval-shaped wooden bowl, he dipped it in the water and placed his other hand gently under my chin, tilting it back toward him, and proceeded to wash my hair. His touch sent tingles down my arms, reminding me of Cerys. *One and the same person.* The image of Kevin's face imposed over Cerys's flashed in my mind. It occurred to me that I hadn't loved Cerys and then Kevin. I had loved one soul over thousands of years. And here we were together, again, in this world. The thought of the connection caused my closed eyes to fill with tears, that a love so strong could be sustained for not only more than a lifetime, but several. *Can anything separate us? Yes. Kevin made an agreement with the Soltari. But what were the terms specifically? Can they be undone?*

If the theory of parallel universes held that there was another virtually identical copy of each person and that our planet existed with only slight differences in another realm or universe, then where was the copy of me? The question plagued me again. Kevin and Cerys did not occupy the same space or world, but they were the same person or entity. A gentle flow of water over my face distracted any further thought on the matter.

"Hey," I said, smiling as I brushed a hand over my face. I opened my eyes to see him looking at me. One of the residual tears fell from the outside corner and across my temple.

"You are always thinking. Sometimes too much," he said, grinning at me. He set the cup down and began stripping his clothes and tossing them away from the tub.

"The water might be a bit cool for your liking," I said, leaning forward.

He stepped in, sitting behind me, and gently guided me back against his chest. "I don't think it will bother either of us in a moment."

His solid form behind me was a comfort. He poured the remaining liquid into his hands. The scent of fragrant oil containing rosemary and lavender filled the air. He reached around me in what might have been a hug and rubbed his hands together before stroking them up my arms, across my chest and letting them follow a slow path between my breasts, erasing any trace of the ill prospect that had tried to seduce me earlier. His lips brushed against my ear, and a small gasp escaped my lips.

They'll hear us.

"Shhh," he said, hearing my thought.

His fingers drew a few wet tendrils of hair away from my cheek as he slipped an earlobe between his lips. He paused and put his lips to my ear again.

"You're mine," he whispered. "Always will be. Everyone within earshot of this bath already knows it."

He pressed his lips behind my ear before trailing soft kisses along the side of my neck. I lifted my hands from his thighs and reached back, tilting my head to meet those lips. One hand held me firmly against him while the other slid lower across my stomach. The water sloshed over the sides of the tub as he shifted his leg, allowing mine to open and give him better access to what would soon be my hushed undoing.

18

I woke early to the sound of voices below the staircase. The faint hint of early-morning light crept in from the seams in the shutter of the window. The room was freezing despite the low fire still burning in the tiny hearth in the corner. I realized Kevin must have gotten up in the night to throw a couple more logs on the fire. I had felt him stir at some point and woke briefly to his fingers gently tracing over a mark on my right side, just under my rib cage. The flicker of firelight danced in the room.

"They marked you when they gave you the key," he had said, referring to the Druid priests. The memory returned of the light entering my body and with it the less-than-pleasant stench of burning skin. My reply to Kevin was a muffled "Oh? Okay," as I curled into his warmth. I flipped the covers back and viewed the red marking. Burned into my skin like a branding iron to a hide was the oval shape of an eye with a flame in the center. I had been given the light of understanding to pass on to my world once all of the keys were obtained. When all was said and done, would I bear the mark of each key I would carry?

"Good morning, love," Kevin said. He was standing fully dressed with his back to me, leaning over a table, staring into a paper of some sort and did not turn when he spoke. I began to shiver without any warmth left in the bed or in the air.

"It's a cold one. That's for sure." I raced out of bed and proceeded to dress quickly as gooseflesh erupted over my body. My clothes had been placed on the stone that framed the hearth and I welcomed the small bit of warmth found in them. He turned to face me, pressing a smile through closed lips as I rushed to dress. His eyes smoldered as they roamed from my lips and down to my breasts and thighs.

"If only there was time," he said, turning his attention back to the paper. I slipped on my shirt, pants, and boots, foregoing the dress. I might get a few dropped jaws of horror on my way out of the inn but I didn't care. The last damn thing I needed was some obtrusive material getting in the way of a possible fight or slowing me down in any way.

"Good morning to you," I said belatedly, brushing a hand over his back. "What is it that holds your interest so intently?" I asked, peering over his shoulder to see a crude drawing of a map. He sighed. A sound I rarely if ever heard him make. It meant he had been in deep thought and was emerging from the depths of another place far from here.

"He's out there, waiting for you, plotting. I can feel him," he said, referring to C-05. "The only small consolation is that he won't kill you. Not now." He glanced up.

"Would they really try to take the key, as Mac said?"

"I don't know." He stepped back from the table. "If you were given something so valuable, I have to believe the Soltari would have imparted some form of protection to prevent such a thing from occurring, knowing the darkness will hunt you." I stood behind him, wanting to give him space to continue his concentration, but slid a hand up the length of his arm before resting my cheek against the back of his shoulder, while my palms pressed to his chest, gently hugging him against me. Perhaps I might want to visit the Soltari in Ardan and inquire about further protection from the dark forces and any possibility in obtaining the key.

"What's this?" He turned into my embrace. "The woman who never seeks comfort in another person is desiring it now?"

I paused in consideration. "Tell me about Cerys and Arwyn."

His other hand closed over mine. "I can't." The words were barely audible. "It's part of the vow I've taken to not share memories with you."

"Or what?"

"I've told you before. I can't share memories with you because the Soltari believes it will interrupt the path for the keys. Too much emotion."

"Is that what you believe?"

"No. But it doesn't matter what I believe. If I helped you to remember, they wouldn't allow me to be here to aid in this quest." I opened my mouth to speak and snapped it shut. "And I won't risk anything not to protect you."

I dropped my gaze from his to our hands. He pinched my chin between his fingers, angling it up so that I was looking into his eyes. "If anything were to happen to you, you know I would come for you," he said.

"If anything happens, I'll get back to you and our team." He whispered a kiss over my lips. "Tell me what has been eating at you," I said, pulling back to look at him. That bothersome sensation I felt from him had returned.

He turned his head to avoid my stare. I placed a palm on his cheek and brought his face back to mine, urging him with my eyes to share what drove at him so deeply not to confront me.

"I can't let anything happen to you," he said.

"It won't. We are fighters. All of us."

"You don't understand what is at stake."

"I think I do. I have the weight of the world to carry, and should I not be successful, that world ends. That's a lot at stake."

He shook his head. "Forget the world for a moment. Us. If anything happens to you..." and he stepped sideways out of the embrace.

"What? What happens to us if I fail? And don't tell me you are bound from saying because of the Soltari. Because if you do, I won't believe you anyway."

He angled his head toward me and froze me with a stare. "If anything happens to you that causes you not to succeed, we will be separated by the Soltari. Never to be joined again."

So, it was true what C-05 had said in the cave. What was itching under Kevin's skin, that he couldn't scratch, was the worry that we would be separated forever.

I studied him, the intensity flowing through him. "That's bullshit. I sacrifice my life to take on a world of demons and evil, and if I fail, not only do I lose the world and all the lives in it but I lose eternal love with you? A punishment for failure?"

"The Soltari can't afford to lose the energy contained on Earth. It's a growing part of the multi-universal energy, a very positive force. Consider it a punishment for allowing yourself to become distracted. And I'm considered a contributor because I wanted, no, I needed to protect you."

"I will not lose you, no matter the outcome of this quest. Be sure about one thing—I will do everything in my power to succeed on this mission for the lives that depend on it, but I will never lose the bond I have shared or will continue to share with you. So get that thought right out of your head. Our separation won't happen."

"You can't go against the Soltari, Sara."

"I won't have to if all goes as planned. Besides, I never would have agreed to a condition like that to make this journey for the keys. They sent me here, then changed the rules of the agreement for you to join me." I reached a hand to his cheek and pressed my forehead to his. "Do not worry over it any longer. Fight with me to fulfill this quest. No matter the outcome, you will never lose me. You have my word."

"My love. You may be stronger than you know but you are not powerful enough to stop the Alliance from enacting an order on behalf of the Soltari."

We shall see. And then again, maybe we won't have to.

He put his hand to the back of my neck and pulled me to him, pressing his lips to mine. Need and desire blended in a single kiss. And in the silence, a solemn promise was made to stay by my side no matter what battle would come our way.

Kevin eased back. "We need to leave."

I reached for my coat and found the dagger had been cleaned and replaced in its leather sheath in the inside of my coat pocket.

I tucked it in the crook of my pants at my low back, feeling it safer on me than in my coat, being that it had been separated from me once. With the sword strapped in place, I stretched my arms through the sleeves of the long coat.

"Ready," I said.

"No dress?"

I shook my head as he opened the door. The smell of cooking porridge, bacon, and coffee wafted up the steps, along with several voices.

There was no talk of the deceased guest during breakfast and I was glad for it. I didn't know if Aillie was ever aware that there was another temporary tenant on site, or that he had left under the cover of night wrapped tightly in a most colorful and missing rug. What I did know was that I wanted to put the event behind me and never again think of it or what might have happened if my aim had been off.

"This is the place Aria and I returned to. A point of passage exists in this area," said Mac.

We'd arrived at the location he and Aria had come through two nights prior.

I nodded. "We'll have to hike until we find it," I said. "I don't feel a pull like I did when we were here last." I turned to Magdalene. "Thank you. We couldn't have made the trip without your assistance."

"Can I go with ye? I can help."

"Even if I wanted to, I can't take you through the gateway."

She glanced down and nodded. "Then take these." Reaching into a small satchel, Magdalene pulled out a fistful of red berries. The one she'd given me earlier was still stuck in the bottom front pocket of my pants. I curled my fingers around them. "They will grant ye the protection of the white witch, no matter how far ye must travel. I might warn ye, though, they are none too pleasant a taste, but then that's not why ye'd eat them."

I thanked her with the hope I would not need them, before

turning and heading toward the others, who had already started walking through the thick grass in search of the portal. Kevin remained only an arm's length away.

"How will I know if ye succeeded?" she called out.

"That pot of yours should tell you," I shouted back and waved.

We wandered through the tall ferns until we came within several feet of a cluster of rowans.

The portal might be in there.

"Wait a minute," I said, turning to Mac. "We can't go back through the same gateway. You and Aria said the shadows were already in Doune. They will be waiting at the River Teith."

"It's the only way out, Sara," Juno said.

"She's right," Mac said, turning to address the others. "We won't be able to go back to the gateway at the river."

"Not without one hellacious fight," said Matt.

Two things entered my mind—C-05 would know that Doune would be the only path of entry back to our world, and if we couldn't use the gateway at the river in Doune, how would we get Elise? How else would we get to the next location on the Yucatan Peninsula? As much as I didn't want to admit it, we might have to go back to the River Teith.

"We don't have control over where the gateway leads, right?"

A few blank stares were returned.

"Give me a minute," I said, taking steps away from the group. I glanced to Kevin. "I need direction from the guides in Ardan."

When I'd first set foot on this mission, I'd been told by one or two individuals in Ardan that there were many guides to aid me. "I'll be safe alone for a few minutes." He stopped following and let me continue on, keeping me well within his sights. I sat down and leaned into a large, solid oak, absorbing what little time alone I'd been granted. I'd never tried to reach my guides outside of Ardan and only once that I recalled had Cerys contacted me during the day, rather than in the usual dream state. I reached into my coat pocket that still held the three symbols and closed my eyes in concentration. Maybe I'd be able to get a message, a feeling, anything. *Who am I kidding?* Pressed for time and feeling a bit foolish, I opened my eyes to see Eldor, the leader of the elves, approaching from a short distance away.

That worked?

His smooth, long brown hair caught the gentle breeze that whispered through the air and lifted on one side, like a single wave of hello. The vision of him against the bright sunlight seemed so much like a dream that I wondered if I had dozed.

"Eldor. It's good to see you again," I said, standing. His eyes were a tranquil cerulean blue and penetrating, just as I remembered.

"Sara, it's been some time since we've spoken. I see you've done well in obtaining the first key." He smiled. "Walk with me." He held a hand out and glanced past me. I shifted to see Kevin in the distance. He nodded once and turned away. A brief exchange between them signaled I was safe enough for Kevin to leave.

"May I have the symbols?" Eldor asked.

I glanced at my palm still clutching the medallions. "I've got to get us through the gateway. But the shadows…"

"My dear, you still do not trust enough." He paused and turned to me with an open palm. I placed the symbols in his hand as we continued to walk, heading out of the tall blades of grass and into the shade of the forest. "The three symbols you hold in your hand were to open the primary gateway and obtain the first key. The power of the first key unlocks the gateway to the second, and the second to the third and final key in Egypt. Each key knows exactly where and how far to take you, just as these three symbols knew to take you to Randun."

The forest changed, as if we had just stepped through a thread in time simply by walking into the shade of the trees. I glanced up at the sky, dark as night. The outline of light gray and green shadows gave me the gloomy sensation of an Edgar Allan Poe poem. A bluish-gray mist parted as we stepped into it. In front of me stood a massive arched wooden doorway with no walls adhering to it. Eldor stepped forward and, with the single click of a latch, pushed open the door, then angled his head toward the entry.

"After you." With a wave of his hand, he invited me to enter. I glanced into his face before crossing the threshold.

"How are you doing this?"

"Everything is energy, Sara. Clear the veil that covers your eyes on Earth and you will see so much more. It starts with believing more exists than what your eyes show you. You've only forgotten because it's a trait of human nature but also because the Soltari didn't want you to recall too much right away."

"Mm."

The inside reminded me of a drafty old basement with the musty scent that filled the air. A muted green light from somewhere above illuminated a small foyer and touched upon a dirt floor before being absorbed by it. Voices lifted on a current to my ear, echoing the sounds of argument. The inside was as though someone had hollowed out an enormous tree, with no ceiling and rough walls of bark that climbed upward as far as I could see. I followed Eldor down an empty corridor that opened into a large room while I scanned the walls spotted with numerous torches glowing without a flame. Instead, a white-blue haze emitted from them as if powered by a hidden LED bulb.

My eyes fell to the center of the room and the source of the voices. A large oval table consumed the space we'd entered, and around it sat a group of six individuals cloaked either in black or a deep shade of red. At our arrival, all of the members fell silent and several sets of eyes gleamed upon us. *Are there no other women who belong to this group?* They reminded me of the Professors I'd met when I'd first arrived in Ardan. A group that held the knowledge of the mission and provided our team with information about the keys of enlightenment.

"Sara, may I present the Alliance," Eldor said. "Please, be comfortable." He pulled out a chair for me.

Do I really have time for a meeting? I just need a question or two answered.

"Gentlemen, continue with the discussion," Eldor added as he selected a seat next to me. I angled my head toward him.

"Why am I here? The team is waiting for me," I whispered.

Before he could answer, one of the men in a black cloak who had been standing with palms flat against the table moved from his authoritative position at the head of the table.

"Sara, what a pleasure it is to have you at your first meeting of the Alliance since your return to Earth."

"Do you not believe it is too soon to introduce her to pertinent matters concerning the Alliance?"

"It is decided by the Soltari that she is ready. Continue, please," Eldor pressed.

"Very well," said the man standing. He stepped away from the chair and passed slowly behind the other seated members. My eyes caught the stolen glances of several members as they shifted away, one by one.

"Your arrival is quite timely, Sara. My name is Aren. You may remember some of us as the Professors you met with a few months ago." His attention turned toward another member. "As you were saying, Taros, something about the Alliance not approving?" He waved his hand in a gesture that seemed dismissive.

Taros cleared his throat. "Not *something about*, but that the Alliance does not approve of memories being restored to the Light Carrier and her past with the last warrior." Kevin's named popped into my head. "That sort of, well, for lack of a better word, interference goes against the plan." The man's fist was clenched in front of him and his body went rigid in his chair. "We simply cannot risk her knowing." The corner of his jaw clenched and his thick gray-and-black-peppered brows narrowed, forming a wrinkle between his eyes.

There was only a moment of confusion as I tried to understand the hostility. And then his words began to sink deeper into my conscience and my blood began to grow hotter through my veins. Was I absorbing his anger? I didn't think so. But I was beginning to understand my own frustration at why Kevin and I could not share in the knowledge of our past lives together.

"Agreed," said another member. Additional murmurs of the same resonated around the room.

"The warrior is a member of this order. Should his word not count as well in these meetings?" another voice called out from the end of the table. My attention shifted in that direction.

"Perhaps it should. But he has not yet been called to these meetings," Eldor replied.

And why have I?

"All in good time," Eldor whispered, hearing my thought.

My arrival was indeed timely. The fact that a decision had been made to keep certain information from me simply because I had chosen to join humanity and become Sara Forrester in this lifetime was beginning to fray at my nerves. Each carved groove of the chair back pressed through my clothing to my skin. My blood pulsed heavier with the realization it had been these individuals, not the Soltari, who had selected to omit certain memories from my recall. With the change in my emotion, all eyes fell upon me.

"Who are you to decide what memories can be shared between two who have loved?" I asked, hearing the bite in my words. "What right have you to do this?"

"Sara, it was agreed upon during the creation of the plan for the mission." A man sitting to the right of Taros leaned forward. "Because of your human tendency to become distracted, it was decided a tool to aid you in keeping your emotions contained and to hide your bond with the Last Great Warrior would be useful in keeping you headstrong. It's what is believed to be best."

"As Arwyn, you agreed," Taros added. "It is the warrior who thinks you can handle both the memories and your task, but it is a decision not agreed upon by the Alliance."

Headstrong. I paused, contemplating why Kevin believed the way that he did. *He knows me best, after all, doesn't he? He knows of my spiritual side and my human side. My strengths and weaknesses.*

"Maybe the warrior is right," I said.

"It was not part of the plan!" Taros shot back. "You must not deviate and risk your world."

"We have loved this far, without my recall of those memories, and have obtained the power of one key," I argued. "Does this not prove it is possible to have both? While I'm human, do I not also carry elements of my higher self, the entity that I am that participates with you now and in this mission?"

"It only proves that without being distracted you have been successful," Taros replied.

"It proves I can love as a human without being distracted from the mission."

"If your awareness is restored and by chance he dies, you risk a greater chance of failing the mission."

"Sara, we understand it is his desire for you to know," said Aren. "But do you wish to recall every memory you share with him?" He stopped his slow pace around the others, steepled his fingers under his chin, and lifted his eyes to me. "Do you believe in your strength on the mission, to not lose your focus? No matter the stakes?"

I waited. Answering too quickly would have been a mistake. "Of course. I have a job to do and that won't change."

"Very well," said Aren.

"Do you understand the magnitude of risk should your human tendencies override your duty?" Taros asked. "It is known that females of that species are weaker than their male counterparts."

Weaker? In what regard?

It was all I could do not to roll my eyes. Instead, I glared at him. "If that were the least bit true, the Soltari would not have agreed to me assuming this responsibility as a female on Earth. As it is, I remain the only one who can rectify the destructive path Tarsamon has placed at the feet of the humans. If being a female and suggesting I'm 'weaker' is the only basis for your argument, I'm finished giving any more time to it. It's a weak argument and you know it." I paused, daring anyone to counter. The hall was as silent as the calm of an early-morning sunrise. I stood. "And while we are discussing the subject, know that I take offense to the agreement made with Kevin, Cerys, whatever you will call him, after I accepted this mission. There will be no punishment toward him or me in the unlikely event I fail." I glanced at the other members of the Alliance. "I can't say there aren't weaknesses and benefits of flesh in being human. But I and the team carry a stronger desire to see the mission to its end than any weakness you are considering."

I was well into defending my position before I realized it wasn't

I who had asked to remember all that Kevin did. I would have liked to know and didn't like being in the dark about our past. But I also understood why Taros fought so hard against the memories to be returned—for the emotions they could evoke. What he was forgetting, I suspected, was that I wasn't an ordinary human. I had come to terms with my role in this mission soon after having been introduced to my abilities as a fighter and the knowledge that I was an immortal spiritual entity.

"We'll take the issue of restoring your memories of the last warrior to the Soltari," said Aren. "But the agreement you speak of was made between the Soltari and the warrior. We don't have the power to revoke it."

But did I want to remember all that Kevin did or was this Kevin's wish? I couldn't remember. Damn if I didn't just argue for it. It drove me mad not to know my history with Kevin and to suggest that I'd agreed to having the past kept from me. But I also didn't need to be burdened by emotions, not when my focus needed to be on the second key.

"Now, on to other matters involving Tarsamon." Aren continued his path around the table, stopping at his chair.

"Sara, the battle is at hand upon your entrance through the gateway. It is the path you must follow to retrieve Elise."

"Back to Doune? The river?"

"A passage has been created to move your team through to the next key. Allies from Ardan will stand with you. Eldor?"

"Our forces are in place upon their entrance," Eldor confirmed.

"Very well. I believe you have people waiting and we won't keep you any longer."

Eldor glanced at me, and, taking the hint, I followed him out of the room.

I waited until we passed through the doorway into the forest again, heading back to Randun before I spoke.

"Tell me about the Alliance and why I was invited to that meeting."

"You weren't invited. I happen to believe in you knowing the full truth that exists between you and the last warrior."

"I didn't ask to know."

"But yet you desire it just the same."

I nodded. "But my desires on the matter should not be considered. They could be dangerous to our mission. And if it had only been my choice not to remember, instead of a vote, to which I take some offense, I might not have argued to know." I shook my head and turned my gaze to the ground. "What have I done? If they take the matter to the Soltari..."

"My dear, if you desire to remember what is shared between you and Kevin, and you both understand the importance of succeeding in the quest, it cannot hurt you to remember all that Kevin does. The bond of that knowing may give you additional strength.

"The Alliance is a group of enlightened spirits, selected by the Soltari, a powerful collective and all-knowing entity, to administer their directive. Those at the meeting travel between worlds as you do. They've been alive longer than you can conceive."

"And why am I part of that group, a group that decides the fate of its members?"

He stopped and turned to me, taking my hands in his. "Sara, you are selected as an integral part of this order, as is Kevin. He knows this." He paused and met my eyes. "The Alliance aims to protect you and ensure the success of this quest. It is not intended to hurt you or to keep you apart."

"Maybe. I might have been wrong to choose to block the memories. I can't be sure. I do know there is pain in that decision. I can feel it." I took in a deep breath. "I couldn't have known the effects of blocking the memories, and yet somehow still retain the ability to feel so close to him. That alone is too distracting."

Eldor smiled, looked down at our hands, and released them. "You are unique. More than the Soltari could have imagined you would be as a human. I'm sure you will be granted the knowledge you seek."

"We shall see," I said. "Having this issue between us is beginning to complicate the mission. Perhaps it's best that nothing is hidden.

"What about the gateway to the second key?" I asked, shifting gears to the immediate issue at hand. "Do we need to follow each gateway back to get to the next location?"

He nodded in reply. "But you must enter first. If in the rare instance a gateway is closed to you, it is for protection. In that case, you would need to find another way, usually by going to another gateway site."

"You mean to the Yucatan or Egypt? Those sites?"

"Yes. When you attempt to open a gateway, the energy is sensed as though it were a key to a lock, and where one door may be forbidden to enter, another will grant you access. Always."

The tall grass of Randun brushed against my knees as I stepped from the arched doorway into the brisk air and beaming sunlight.

"Won't I be leading the team into an ambush at the river?"

"You have no choice but to return. This is the battle your allies have prepared for. Since you opened the primary gateway, Tarsamon and his forces have been swarming the portal. The protection you found in Randun was because the Druids wanted peace for the Light Carrier. You may or may not be granted such gifts in the next locations. However, each key provides a different level of protection for you and your team as each is obtained."

I slid a hand over the top of my head and through my hair in frustration at not knowing the full power I carried.

"With the expectation your mission would be filled with increasing danger, the Soltari included an additional gift of protection." I waited patiently for him to say what it was. He only smiled. "Only the Light Carrier is granted the knowledge when the defense is warranted."

Since the beginning of this quest, I'd wondered why all of the answers couldn't be provided. Everything seemed to be a riddle. It was damned annoying having so many unknowns. And yet I understood the reason was likely that the evil that chased us carried supernatural abilities just as I and my team did. What those were, exactly, was another riddle I didn't care to solve.

"Is it true that the dark forces cannot take the key once it has been given to me?"

"Yes. It cannot forcefully be taken. And yes, if they end your life, the power of it is released into the world," he replied, anticipating my second question. "Do not ask me about the manner of the release of all keys. I am not able to convey this information to you."

Well, that figures. I suppose I was in no hurry to know if I had to die to release the keys to save my world.

The sun was holding in the middle of the sky, suggesting late afternoon. *How long have we been gone?* Eldor stared out across the great landscape before returning his piercing gaze upon me, reading every thought.

"You've done well, Sara. You've been chosen for the emotional strength you carry in your heart as much as for your ability to lead. You will be called to use that strength many times over." He placed a hand over mine. I glanced up into the wise, quiet strength found in his face. "The battle has begun. Remember your allies at the gateway." He began to turn to leave. "Oh, and that weapon, the dagger, it's more powerful than any knife. It will always find its way back to you. Keep it close and use your abilities to manipulate energy."

With all that had been happening in Randun, I had nearly forgotten my practiced abilities to alter energy—to create a shield of light from a spark or draw upon the energy I carried to form a flaming sphere to hurl in defense against the darkness, similar to those Mac and I utilized with the angels. The dagger had been a second gift to me, after the sword.

"Thank you," I said.

He smiled and nodded once, turning back in the direction from which we had come. I watched as his image disappeared into the tall blades of dry grass that shifted direction now under the breeze. I took a few steps toward where I'd last seen my team. A rhythmic swishing sound caught my attention and I turned my head to see the source and stopped. Kevin's unshaven face hid a shadow of concern that could not be concealed. His brows furrowed slightly and his lips pressed together.

"You'll stay beside me, whatever happens," he said. A warm sensation washed over me at the sight of him.

"Did you forget I'm an avid fighter?" I asked as I walked a step past him. He caught my wrist and pulled me to him.

"No, I didn't. But I'd like for you to live. And you have a better chance of that if you are near me."

I laughed lightly, shaking my head. "Then you'd better keep up with me," I said, inches from his face. "I don't hide behind anyone." His gaze penetrated my playful yet focused attention.

"This isn't up for discussion and certainly not anything to take lightly. I won't lose you, Sara. I have too much invested." He pressed his lips to mine. Rough at first, then softening. The message in that kiss said he loved my strength, he'd tame my stubborn side, but he also knew what was best. For a moment, it was as though we were alone among the maples and rowans, whose leaves whispered a delicate song in the crisp breeze that blew between us.

You've just got to remember. The words entered as my thoughts but they weren't mine. He pulled back slowly. I opened my eyes to see him watching me. A tingling sensation rushed from my shoulder and chased a path down the length of my body. His calling card.

I couldn't know how much he'd invested, entirely. He risked his life being part of this mission, but so did the other members of the team. How long had I really known this soul? How much was invested beyond the mission? As I looked deeper into his eyes, I felt Kevin wanted to break the vow to the Soltari if only for a moment to remind me.

"Is there some—" I began.

"Ahem," came a voice from behind Kevin. I lifted my gaze over his shoulder to see Juno approaching. "I'm sorry to interrupt. I'm sure you two could spend the rest of this lifetime stuck in that position, and it is quite the picture. But we really must be moving on. Time's a tickin'." He tapped an index finger to his wrist.

I glanced back at Kevin to see his eyes still resting on my face. *Later, love. Just stay close.* I heard his thought a moment before he released the wrist he had been holding and turned toward Juno.

I took a deep breath to shake off the emotional exchange and refocus. I needed every step back to the team to regain it, too.

"We'll need to be prepared to fight when we arrive," I said to the others as Kevin and I joined them. "Reinforcements have gathered to meet us. Where is Mac?"

"He left through the passage back to Doune, feeling it safer to get to Elise without you," Aria replied. "He said he'd meet up with us at the next location through the gateway at the River Teith, after you pass through."

"Jesus. He must know that the dark forces are swarming the gateway," I said.

"There's always the chance they won't fight him," Matt said. "After all, if you aren't there…" His words trailed off.

"Did you forget that he is to lead us to the second guardian?" asked Juno. "And the evil that waits does have an interest in delaying that aspect of our mission."

"Mac left only a couple of minutes ago. The passage to the Yucatan might be open from here. And if not, we'll fight," Aria said. Her blue eyes were alight with excitement. Matt, standing beside her, brushed a hand at her hair and whispered in her ear.

"Maybe we should go through first, clear a path, and you and Aria can enter after a few minutes," suggested Matt.

"We fight together," I said. Aria gave a smile of satisfaction. "If this passage leads back to Doune and we are met with Tarsamon's forces, I'll try to open the passage to the Yucatan. If that doesn't work, or we end up splitting up, we'll meet up on the tip of the peninsula, Rio Lagartos. Mac can direct us from there."

We stepped into the shadows of the cluster of rowans that Mac had gone through. The spinning in my brain signaled the magnetic pull coming to lift us from this world and take us to the next location of the key or, God help us, back to Doune.

19

I rolled over after being tossed like a toothpick from the water at River Teith. Small currents lapped at my face and I forced myself awake. My head was throbbing either from the trip through the gateway or the sound of screaming around me. Perhaps both. "Holy Christ," I said, standing. The splitting pain running down the center of my head felt as though the two halves of my brain were dividing. As I forced myself up and drew my sword, I caught sight of Matt and Aria a few feet ahead fighting what appeared to be empty air at the bank of the river. *What the hell?* My skin prickled at the sensation of something ominous in the air, though I could see nothing. *Where are the screams coming from?*

Before I could find the answer, a heavy hand grabbed at my shoulder and tried to pull me down, leaving a trail of blood as it scraped up my left arm. I dipped my shoulder and whirled from the grip that had held me, to see nothing. A sudden clamp around my throat convinced me I wasn't imagining a presence. I dropped my sword and grabbed at it with one hand while reaching with my other for the dagger at my back. If only I could get enough space between my throat and the hidden hand trying to choke off my airway. I dropped to the ground and pushed a knee into the invisible aggressor. Whipping around my other arm that held the dagger, I sunk it into the weight above me.

A black demonic figure with long claws appeared sprawled over me, revealing itself in death. I moved forcefully to push it off me, pulling my dagger out and shoving the dying creature into the water with a splash. The residual energy from the demon shifted into a ball before spreading across the water like a pool of ink, until it was no longer visible. How many invisible assailants were here? Two arrows zoomed past me at the thought and landed a foot in front of Aria and Matt. I whipped around to see a man with long hair and almond-shaped eyes, sharp as a hawk, holding a bow, and knew he was one of Eldor's team of skillful elves that had come to battle with us.

Where the hell are Kevin and Juno? I shot glances in several directions, trying to spot any sign of them or Mac.

"You need to move quickly, Sara. The forces of evil have been awaiting your return," the elf said, walking with determination toward emptiness as he readied another bow.

I turned toward the forest, where more elves were standing, and as I did, Kevin and Juno appeared. Aria and Matt were heading in their direction.

"Get into the forest!" Kevin shouted and raced past me, his sword drawn. I turned in time to see a shadow coming at me from behind. Kevin threw himself into a tumble and, with the sword gripped tightly in both hands, thrust upward. The movement was so fast that if I blinked I would have missed it. Juno grabbed my arm, rushing me into the protection of the massive trees. Hidden among the shadows of tall tree trunks, where light filtered through the long branches to the ground, stood an army of elves, bows drawn and arrows fixed. A mist hung low, weaving among them and cloaking them in the shadows of the low-hanging branches.

"Juno, I've got to get to the gateway before we are overcome."

"Not yet," Kevin said from behind me.

I angled my head to face him. "What do you mean? It's our only chance to outrun the evil coming. I have to see that the gateway to the second key is open."

"If you do, the shadows will follow. We can't assume there is protection for us as there was with the Druids." I looked past him to see another group of elves had begun to move in closer, surrounding our team in protection.

"Mac mentioned you were given something, some sort of additional defense that could aid you. Do you know what he was referring to?"

The screaming just beyond the forest grew louder, nearly breaking my concentration. "I don't know. Maybe the power of the key is what he was referring to?"

My thoughts raced through each memory, trying to recall anything the Druid priests might have told me or anyone I might have spoken with, and stopped with the thought of Magdalene.

"These," I said, reaching into my pocket and pulling out a couple of the red berries I had stuffed deep down for safety. "Magdalene said these would provide additional protection. She said it would provide the power of the white witch or something like it. Mac would know of such folklore, but maybe not the form of how it would be delivered."

"I guess you have to eat it," Juno said. "It didn't do anything for you tucked in your pocket." I narrowed a glance at him and turned back to Kevin.

"Look, I'm going to race back to the gateway by the water's edge and try to open the passage to the second location."

"You're not," Kevin argued. "It's not safe. There are just too many of them waiting out there, Sara. Can't you see that by the sheer number of arrows still flying? Do I need to remind you we are here to protect you?" The team held their swords, ready to fight any attack that made it past the elves.

"You certainly do not," I shouted, half out of frustration and half to be heard over the constant screams. Damn, I didn't need anything standing in the way of me doing my job in this mission. "Besides, I think they have it covered." I glanced toward the elves. "I have to know if this is the passage to take us to the second key. There isn't any other way out of this. I know you don't like it, but it's what I have to do. We can't just continue to fight. Tarsamon's army will outnumber our forces the longer we stay here."

"It's possible this is not the gateway to the second location. Then what? You think I'm going to leave you out there? It's not going to happen that way. I don't care what you have to do."

"There isn't time to argue. Besides, there is an army of protection here," I said, gesturing with an open hand toward the elves that surrounded us. The elves began to move to the very edge of the forest, where the land broke off into a small empty field. Just a few feet beyond it was the rocky shore, where I had to go.

"Take these," I said, handing him several of the berries. "I don't know what Magdalene meant by the protection of the white witch. But if we both carry them, I don't think it can hurt. Maybe Mac knows something about them." I closed his fingers around the red berries. He shook his head and stuffed them down into his pocket.

Shrieks could still be heard growing louder with each moment that passed. The elves aimed their bows for the dark shadows, no longer in hiding, raining down from the sky. In a matter of moments, hell had eclipsed the sun and its bright, sunny blue patches.

"Stay here!" Kevin shouted to me above the noise. "We'll make a path and I'll signal to you when it's clear to pass." I opened my mouth to say something but shut it quickly. "Don't fight me on this. You have to stay alive or this is over. All of it!" He cupped a hand behind my neck and pressed a hard kiss against my lips before bolting with the elves into the battle. Aria, Matt, and Juno were following, swords drawn as they raced full force into the thick black forms clouding on the forest boundary.

He was right to keep me safe in the woods with the few elves that remained. I would have done the same if guarding someone's life. But it angered me that I couldn't help them. I glanced between the trunks of the trees at the shadows whose frightening faces searched among my team and the elves for me. I was what they wanted. These people I cared for were putting their lives out there for me. And while that might have been their job, it didn't ease the responsibility upon my shoulders. I watched for Kevin's sign. Every nerve in my body twitched to leap to what might be the gateway leading to the Yucatan. *They're already outnumbered.* The army of darkness continued to fall at no slower pace. Were more forces from Ardan coming to aid the elves and my team? There wasn't time to wait.

"Everything is all about energy," I said to myself. *From a mere thought to its transformation into matter.* It's a phrase I'd heard not only from Eldor but the Professors. And that's what these demons and shadows were. I remembered then my ability to create a shield out of the very energy I carried. It was one of the first lessons I'd learned in Ardan. I closed my eyes and pictured a blue-white light that started as a spark in my hand that grew into a rolling sphere, until it was the size and shape of a shield. As I pressed an open palm facing the team, the shield began expanding wider in my mind's eye, until it was encompassing all of them in an arc, separating them from the falling shadows. I opened my eyes to see the creation at work in front of me. *A stronger, more powerful shield? This had to be the additional protection the first key offered.*

The center of my stomach grew intensely warm in the same manner as when the Druid priests had given me the key. I glanced down to see the blue-white glow coming from the heat at my core. Kevin, Aria, Matt, and Juno glanced up and around quickly, realizing the fight was reduced to those inside the bubble. The shadows above slid around the shield, like a black fog being diverted.

"Now!" I said under my breath. I felt an arm grab me to hold me back, but I pulled away and broke through the trees, racing toward the shore. Over the pounding of my heart now in my ears, the only sound I heard was of the water gently spilling at the shoreline. All other noise was blocked out.

I raced to the water's edge that had carried us to Randun. The same familiar urge for me to continue into the water tugged at me. And as I went in, waist deep, there was nothing. *Where's the electrical current, the light? No spinning sensation. No pain. Shit. The passage is closed. We can't even escape to Randun for safety.* "Now what?" I said.

Eldor's words about another gateway site echoed in my head. *Got to get to the Yucatan.* How were we to get there with this much evil at our backs? I turned to run for the safety of the trees. Catching Kevin's eye, I shook my head and set my attention for the elves at the edge of the trees that bordered hell. I dodged one of the few remaining demons headed straight for me just before Matt sank his sword into its center. The screams grew louder, drawing my attention upward.

The shield was diminishing. I pulled my sword. *Let me make it back before it disappears.* With nothing to sustain its power, the shield was losing its energy. The onslaught of darkness cascading over it was too much. I might have been granted additional power after receiving the key, but even that powerful gift had its limits. I rushed close to Kevin's side as the shadows began to fall like a heavy black downpour, piercing the last of the shield. The arrows fired wildly through the air from the elves' bows. I jumped at the sound of a deep and menacing snarl. Karshan leaped from the woods and began tearing into a new type of beast that had arrived—the flesh-colored demons. I had seen them in the dark world only once in a life-threatening visit there. They were running on all fours. Void of eyes, their bald heads angled around the others, fighting their way through, scenting their prey through the black mist of shadows. There were not nearly as many as when I'd had to fight them in Ardan, which meant Tarsamon had not yet sent his entire force.

"Can we make it to the trees? Is there safety there?" I shouted.

"There's no time for all of us to get there! There are too many!" shouted Juno.

"Matt, get Sara out of here!" Kevin shouted.

"Not without you!" I said, narrowly missing another of the beasts that had thrust itself into me.

A fierce scream ripped through the air as something heavy slammed down from above onto my shoulders, smacking me to the ground. I lifted my sword and winced at the pain as a rush of fur flew past my face and the weight was lifted. Karshan had flung himself into the beast, pushing him across me into the ground, sinking his teeth into the demon's flesh. I only had a moment to glance before Matt rushed toward me and grabbed my arm, dragging me stumbling forward in the direction of the trees.

"No! Not yet!"

"Go now, Sara!" Kevin shouted. "Get out of here!"

The white witch. The berries. But before I could reach for them, a massive cloud of black surrounded us. Matt's grip broke free of my arm. I fought desperately to conjure up any element of light to fend off the numerous shadows that had combined their forces. Kevin rushed toward me as Matt, Juno, and Aria continued to fight them off close by. A harsh light pierced the sudden darkness and thunderbolts began to strike all around. Aria, with her ability to manipulate natural energy, was trying to offset the beasts' and shadows' dark energy. But as the sky grew ever darker, my feet lifted off the ground. I kicked and twisted against the force that held me. If I could just get my arm free, my sword could penetrate the solid black forms that held me. But the harder I struggled, the tighter the grip. As I rose higher into the sky, I felt the distance between my feet and the ground growing. In a desperate attempt to free myself, I yanked my arms at once and kicked at whatever had grabbed hold of my feet. My sword slipped from my hand and plummeted toward the ground. A piercing white light shot up from the ground and I knew by the color it was some element of energy Kevin had thrown.

A blood-curdling scream ripped through the rush of air around me and I recognized it this time as mine. I was falling, faster and faster, toward the ground. Kevin had hit his target. I tried frantically to imagine a protective shield to brace my fall. Sparks flew in every direction as I tried desperately to summon protection in the form of a shield to block the energy that grabbed for my arms and snagged at my clothing. An enormous black cloud swept below me, blocking the brief glimpse of Kevin and the rest of the team as I continued to fall.

I shuddered at the last sight of the closing distance of the ground beneath me and braced for impact, slamming my eyes shut and wishing the shield would light. The rush of air from below ceased and instead began pressing down from above. I opened my eyes to a cocoon of what resembled chimney smoke. *The apparition swept below.* The black shadow was racing me again toward the sky. This time the movement upward was faster, shifting directions quicker than my eyes could follow. Spheres of white light pierced the clouds in multiple directions, missing us by inches. The shadow was too elusive to be caught.

My breath grew more shallow in my lungs. I narrowed my eyes against the rush of wind and saw the red eyes of the other demon shadows peering through a sideways stare as they raced me farther into the sky and beyond the safety of my team below.

Air. Just a little more. Don't black out, damn it. If you do, you're in their world. Hold enough air to stay awake. My lungs fought for each breath as the intake of air grew shorter and faster, ripe for hyperventilating.

The pressure in my lungs tightened as though life was being squeezed from me, followed by pain, and I began losing sight of the shadows flying past. I blinked them in, then out. *Impart a block. I've got to prevent the demons' dark energy from reaching me and consuming my thoughts.* And then the pain began to ease. I heard one last strangled attempt for air in my throat before the wind that blew past me ceased and my conscience grew as black as the shadows that held me.

20

I'*ve failed.* "There was only this task," Kevin said to himself. "To protect her." Releasing the tension in a throaty growl, he hurled his sword through the air with as much strength as he had fought with. The shadows and demons had deserted the riverbank upon taking the key to this mission—Sara. There was nothing to fight and he dreaded the silence that forced him to think of what he'd lost and how he'd failed her. Without a word to the others, he strode across the grassy area near the edge of the water.

Why didn't she listen when I told her to stay in the trees? After everything, could she really not understand the danger that was facing us or her? He crouched by the water's edge. That damned gateway could have been seen to later, when the dark forces had no option but to abandon the hunt. He waited, staring silently into the clear water. Would they have given up if she had stayed in the forest? Maybe she had known the shadows wouldn't have left until they got what they had come for. And, he reconsidered, she had to know if she could open the gateway for us. "But I was going to make it safe for you," he said aloud. *There's only one answer—I have to go get her. She's wearing the bracelet.* Or at least she was when they had taken her. If it hadn't been lost in the fight. With it, he might get the signal it put off, helping him locate her in a world that blocked all of their ability to sense each other. But would he be able to get to her before the dark forces sensed his presence? *If I know where Tarsamon is, I'll have—*

"We'll go there to get her together," Matt said from behind him, tuning in to Kevin's thought.

"How?" Kevin asked. "It's unlikely we'll find her before they track us."

"There's a way. We need to talk to Mac," he said, pausing. "C'mon, were not doing any good for her or the mission standing here." Matt saw the back of Kevin's head nod in agreement before he stood and turned to face Matt. "I think you'll want this." He handed Kevin his sword. Kevin took it and shoved it into its sheath. Without a word, he clamped a hand onto Matt's shoulder in a show of appreciation. "Sara's sword is just over there." Matt pointed in the direction of the water's edge. "I can't touch it." They both turned in the direction he'd indicated. Kevin's face was blank, emotion having left him to make room for planning. "There seems to be some sort of curse on it."

"Blessing," Kevin corrected. "The blade is protected by the magic used in its creation." As they approached, the glow of the sword reflected a brilliant blue-white aura. *An image of her,* Kevin thought. The colors radiated an illuminating light when not in the presence of its owner, as if calling to her. He felt the emptiness of Sara rip through the center of his being with an ache so deep it sent a sick and angry feeling chasing after the emptiness. Kevin tore off a piece off the bottom of his shirt and placed it over the hilt, just before picking it up. He proceeded in silence, a few steps ahead of the others who had joined them as they made their way toward the large house in search of Mac.

As he passed through the birch and alder trees, the wind picked up lightly through the leaves, and Kevin swore he heard a whisper on the breeze call to him. *She lives.* Of course, there was the chance Tarsamon wouldn't kill her, for fear of releasing the key of enlightenment into the world. Although Sara only had one of them, releasing it could impede the Dark Lord from his plan to obtain the energy found in humanity. In that case, they might hang on to her awhile.

She might be safer with the key, but for how long? How long could she hold out before the dark forces wore her down? *She's strong. She'll hold out. And she damn well knows I'll come for her.*

Kevin sat in one of the large stuffed leather chairs in front of the fireplace in Mac's home, scotch in hand and deep thoughts weighing heavily on his mind from the fight hours earlier. There was guilt and plenty of it. He knew Sara would never listen to him. For that reason alone, he should have gone with her to try the gateway and make sure she was safe. But he didn't expect she would defy an order to stay put, especially with the aggressiveness of the demons that greeted them on their return to Doune. He should have. The stubborn woman had always done what she thought was best. It was hard for him to fault her for that. He might've done the same. She'd underestimated the attack, the force. From behind him, the voices of the others somewhere in the kitchen were hushed. He felt they worried for what was next. They also knew he would never take them into the dark world because of the danger it would risk to their lives as much as his. He had enough to deal with and didn't need to be looking out for the others for a mistake that was all his.

"Kevin." Mac's husky voice distracted him from the dark place he was sinking into. He angled his head toward Mac. "Can I see ye in here a moment?" Kevin nodded, took a sip from the drink, and followed Mac down the hall to the library office that reminded him so much of the one he had back home.

"Ye know well enough what we have to do. I can tell it from the look on your face," Mac said after Kevin sat. Kevin didn't look at him. His expression was distant, searching deeper into another place, a much darker, evil side of Ardan.

"Either way, one of us loses," Kevin said after a moment. "I don't think I can reach her before the dark forces hunt and track me down. For Christ's sake, I don't even know how to break into Tarsamon's lair to get to her. He'll keep her close." *Closer than I did, goddamn it.*

He swallowed the last of the drink, glanced at it, and set the glass on the desk. He stood from the chair and began to pace. Mac reached for the decanter he kept on the shelf behind his desk and poured another for Kevin and one for himself.

"She was given something, was she not?" Mac asked, glancing up at Kevin as he replaced the decanter. Mac leaned against the bookcase, glass in hand.

"What?"

"The berries. I saw Magdalene give them to her."

"Aye, she did," Kevin said. "The foolish things," he said under his breath. The thought of magic berries sounded absurd to him, like it had come from a children's fairy tale. He pulled some of them from his pocket and set them on the desk.

"Get your focus back, man. We are no' dealing with ordinary things here, as ye well know." The ice clinked in the glass as he tossed the drink back and walked to the desk. "There is some truth to the tale. Did she tell ye?"

"About the white witch?" Kevin asked. Mac raised his eyebrows. "Sara didn't know what the berries could do or if they were nothing more than folklore." Kevin waved a hand in the air as though deciding for the latter.

"There is said to be a power to the rowan berry, one that gains ye the protective power of the white witch." Mac paused. "It's active once it has been consumed."

"What sort of protection?"

"I don't rightly know. That is to say I've never had to put it to the test, until now. But it's said ye must brew it and drink to draw her out."

"We don't have time to experiment with such things," Kevin said. The frustration he felt reached a level in his tone he hadn't intended.

"We also don't have much alternative at the moment, now do we?"

Kevin stood in front of the desk, rubbed a hand over his face, stopping momentarily at the longer stubble that had formed over the last few days. "Aye." He let out a long breath. As foolish as it all sounded, he couldn't ignore that there might be a possibility of getting Sara back, however slim. The alternative was to sacrifice his life for the chance to get her back. And if they both lost…

"Come, let's eat and then have a drink and experiment in such things, shall we?" Mac said, throwing an arm around Kevin's shoulder and rolling the red rowan berries in his palm.

21

Something was pressing down on my chest, making it difficult to breathe. As I lay on my back on what felt like a table, I slowly peeled my eyelids open to glimpse my surroundings. In a space no bigger than ten by ten, a single torch hung on one of the walls. Next to it was an arched window that was barred. *Some sort of prison or dungeon.* Without moving my head, I lowered my gaze to my chest to see a black cover floating inches above me, covering my own white-blue energy. Thankfully, I still had the illuminated protective shield surrounding me. I was certain the cloak of black was the source of my reduced ability to breathe and apparent immobility. My breaths were coming in short, quick gasps into my lungs. I wanted so much for the pressure above me to ease and allow the simple task of breathing to flow through me.

"Ah, you're awake," the familiar sickening voice of C-05 said. My blood began to heat. I turned my head toward the sound. "The Dark Lord thought it would be better for you to discover me first." C-05 stood a foot from me. His look was different, but only slightly. His mannerisms were the same—the way he cocked his head at me, the almost condescending tone that always made me want to take a swing at him.

"I can't say your new look improves your image much," I said. *Don't piss him off, Sara. He's got the upper hand right now. Remember? Block him.*

The blood began to pulse faster in my veins as anger surged to the surface. His expression was a simple smile and he carried a casual air about him. His spiky white hair gave him a harder edge than I remembered. I began to gasp in short breaths faster.

"Don't get too excited to see me, Sara. I wouldn't want you to hyperventilate before we've had a chance to finish our conversation."

I hated him. And I couldn't really ever remember hating another person. Not even my biological parents, who'd left me as a child. *Is my block still in place?* I might not be able to move my body but I could feel my eyes piercing him with their own daggers, seething with fury and wanting him dead.

"I think you're going about this all wrong," he said. "You should want to work with me." He moved closer into view. "Oh, I know you can't possibly think of it. But I can make it easier for you, since you will be here for a while." He strolled around the table. One hand trailed the edge as he moved. My eyes followed him until he reached my feet. I glanced up at the ceiling to see the flicker of shadows above, as the torches' firelight danced with the darkness above me. It appeared we were alone. A sudden pull at my feet caused my breath to give way and I sucked in an enormous intake of air in several deep gulps.

"Is that better?" he asked. Not only could I breathe but I could now move with the black cloak removed. I sat up and jumped off the table. Instinctively, I reached for my sword and remembered it had fallen.

"What do you want with me?" I asked. I might not have my sword, but I could feel the dagger still tucked behind me. I was still wearing the black cloak Magdalene had given me, hiding any sign of the weapon.

"We're well past that now, don't you think?" he said. "I just had to see you since our last duel. I must say, your skill in this lifetime is indeed impressive. I would've expected you to need more time to remember your role as a fighter. But in the end, you're here just as the Dark Lord foretold." He smiled. "It turns out I made the right decision to switch sides after all."

"This isn't over."

"Well, I do admire your hope, your tenacity given your circumstances." He took two steps around the heavy wooden table and leaned against it, closing the distance between us to within an arm's length. "But without you being able to leave"—his gaze lifted around the room—"and your energies being all but useless in this side of Ardan, I'm afraid I'll have to disagree. This is a realm you are not accustomed to, and you won't be calling any shots. I do wish, however, that you keep something in mind. If you turn over the key you hold, Tarsamon has agreed to spare your life."

How? I have to die to release the key, or so I think, or, God help me, willingly sleep with... Ugh. I couldn't allow the repulsiveness of the thought to complete. The action would never happen.

"And what kind of life would that be, living in hell? Is that the kind of life you've chosen? Coward?"

"It really isn't wise to upset me, Sara." His hand shot out toward my throat. But I brought my hands to my neck a fraction of a second faster and braced my throat against his choke hold, a jiu jitsu maneuver that interrupted his grasp at my airway. He dropped his hand and smiled at me, tilting his head to the side.

"You are a wonder, aren't you? I can see why he loves you," he said. "There's so much passion there." He gestured a hand in my direction. C-05 wanted to toy with my emotions, reminding me of the love Kevin and I shared. I also sensed he wanted to implant the idea that I would never see Kevin again. A thought that I allowed myself to consider. I glared back at him.

"We've been down this path and you lost then. You'll lose again," I said.

"Oh, I don't think so. The cards do appear very much in my favor this time, I'd say." He shot a look toward the window and back to me.

"Give it some thought," he said. "Perhaps after a little while, the offer will seem reasonable to you." He turned without a second glance and left the tiny room, the heavy latch and click of a lock echoing his departure.

In the dim light of two torches that hung on the wall, I contemplated the possibility of escape. Was he right that I had no abilities here? I went to the small window and gazed out into the darkness, wondering if it was always like night. Ahead in the distance, I could make out the tops of what were once living trees, the now leafless branches edged out against a shady, blue-gray horizon. *Above ground. Good.* Screams could be heard echoing in the darkness and there was some sort of movement beyond the walls that surrounded the building. *Guards?* I closed my eyes and tried to surround myself in a blanket of the healing energy found in the residual white-blue light that remained. But nothing happened. My energy was fading here, not to be replaced in an area that didn't allow light to exist. "Cerys," I whispered, resting the top of my head against the bars. I closed my eyes as my thoughts drifted to the memory of Kevin and Cerys being one entity, able to split their energy. Could Cerys get to me if Kevin couldn't? I turned at the clicking sound of the lock being opened. I remained fixed against the opposite wall.

A small, beastly-looking creature, no taller than my waist, entered. Its skin was wrinkled and gray, as if he'd been dead and left to prune in the sun. Strings of white-gray hair fell past his shoulders. He shuffled in with a tray of what looked like food and set it on the table. His eyes met mine before redirecting his gaze to the floor. They were the color and shape of yellow peas and his nose was like that which I'd seen only on a gargoyle, grossly hooked. A sensation came over me about him. I felt the painful life he led, his inability to see his life as anything other than servitude, and his acceptance of it. He shuffled out the door and slammed it hard, locking it. I might have felt sorry for him, sensing what I did, but I was sure he would try to kill me the same as any of Tarsamon's demons, given the chance.

"A few days of this and I might go mad," I said to myself. *But I'll never release the key.*

I would have to keep my will to survive strong and guard against their attempt to weaken me mentally. That would be my test, at least until I figured out how to get out of here.

I couldn't make out the contents on the tray and instead curled up in a corner under one of the torches blazing above me, resting an arm under my head as a pillow. I still had some of the rowan berries stuffed down in my pockets and I reached for one, rolling it between my fingers and eyeing it before popping it into my mouth. I didn't know what, if anything, it might do. But if I'd learned one thing from spending time with Magdalene, it was that there was a lot of mystical belief alive in her realm. True or not, I choked down the bitterness like a bad pill.

I wasn't going to touch what was on that tray. A person could live for days without food, but I would need water. In the most desperate of situations, one could drink their own urine. I pushed that thought out of my head. I wasn't going to be here long enough to have to resort to such measures. With that thought, I refocused my attention on finding a way out. But even if I got past the guard that was assuredly outside the door, where could I go without any powers to help me leave? As much as I didn't want to admit it, C-05 might be right about the cards being in his favor. And from what I remembered, I'd arrived by being carried here. Did that mean I would have to be carried out? *No, no, no. There's got to be another way.* I closed my eyes with the intent to block out the cold cell and the hope for morning, if it ever came.

Sara, do you see? came a whispered voice from deep within my conscience. A picture of the door to a cell that looked very much like the one I was in along with the internal workings and the sound of the click of the lock filled my head, followed by the tray of repulsive items that were to pass as food. I opened my eyes to see the tray still on the table and moved toward it. I shoved a finger under the bottom of the cold, mushy substance, the texture like that of mashed potatoes, and found nothing. Lifting the boxed tray, I peered underneath to find a small square cut in the bottom. I pried it open and found a miniature set of tools tucked inside. A small, flat metal pick and a tension wrench. Could there really be someone helping me? If so, could I trust them? I had few options but to trust the vision I'd received. I picked up one of the tools.

This should unhitch the mechanism of the lock.

I moved toward the door and pressed an ear against it, listening for any sound. Hearing nothing, I carefully slipped the metal pick into the lock and proceeded as shown in the vision, adjusting in precise and painfully slow movements with a click, silence, the slide of a bolt, and another click. I pressed an ear against the door again to be certain I hadn't drawn any unwanted attention. I listened for what seemed several minutes for any rustling sounds or movement.

I tucked the tools into the front pocket of my pants and, with the gentleness of a mother putting a sleeping baby to bed, carefully pulled the door ajar. I wiped damp hands across thighs as I slipped over the threshold of my cell and past one sleeping troll-like guard, wishing I had the power to shift into another form and hide my true identity. I had joined with the energy of a tree once in Ardan with Juno at my side, so maybe... I pressed myself against the wall, willing to become one with it as C-05 had done at the cave in the cathedral. To no avail. My energy would not work in this place. There was too much darkness for positive energy to thrive in any form.

Torches lined the dark stone hall. *How big is this place? Where are the exits?* I scanned the walls as far into the depths of dark as I could see, while every sensation sharpened. The strong, musty odor of mildew filled my nostrils and reminded me I was not traveling in dream state. I placed my hand against the wall and felt the rough stone of each block beneath my palms and the sandy grit of the cement that bound them together as I stepped along the hall leading away from the cell, stopping at a set of five steps that led upward. With my back pressed against the wall, I stepped sideways up each one, ready to bolt should I be spotted. The corridor broke into two paths, one straight ahead and one that veered left. There was a light on at the end of the path directly ahead and I thought it best to move in the opposite direction. Perhaps at the end of the hall I might find a doorway leading outside. *Then what? How the hell am I going to leave this darker realm? When I traveled here in the past, it was in spirit form, during a dream.*

I pushed the thought aside. *No time.* I had to get far enough away before my energy was detected. Was my human form more detectable than my spirit? I didn't know. But being out in the open, concealed by the trees and darkness, certainly had to make it easier for Kevin or the rest of my team to find me as opposed to being locked in some dungeon.

I slipped around the corner in the direction of the darkened corridor and moved quickly down the hall, ducking past a window. Two double wooden doors were closed on my left. In front of me was a dead end forcing me to turn right down yet another hall. A few feet ahead looked to be an opening. I dropped down to my stomach at the approach of another troll-like figure who went through a door. I sucked in a single deep breath and held it as I waited to see if he would come back through. My anxiety at not knowing what waited on the other side of the door rose as I crept closer to it.

Now, a voice said from inside my head.

Who is helping me? Reaching the door in a few steps, I turned the knob and was greeted by freezing temperatures and a gust of icy wind. I slipped through the small opening to the outside. My breath fell out in a white cloud that rose and vanished in the air. I wondered if my decision to escape would mean death by freezing. I pulled the cloak tighter around me as I made my way through the cold, keeping as close to the edge of the building as I could to remain out of sight.

The only visible exit was a dark alley, along the farthest length of wall. My boots splashed through the puddles of water that collected in the gutters as I ran along the path. I had to be close. *How far does this damned alley go, anyway?* The sounds of screaming I'd heard earlier from beyond the boundaries of the prison were growing louder and I knew I was close to the next step of freedom. *How long will I be safe in the dead forest?* Even with the assistance of supernatural abilities when I had traveled here twice before, I barely got out alive. Now, without any abilities... *I just need to stay alive long enough for Kevin to find me.*

Rounding another corner, I smacked into something hard. A hand grabbed my arm and twisted it while another reached for my throat. I riveted a punch into the center of whoever held me. A shadow in the size and shape of a man could be seen in the shade of gray darkness. No torches were along the path this far from the entrance. Unable to move my head, I lifted my eyes to see if anyone was coming to provide aid to the man. The punch weakened the figure long enough for me to reach behind for the dagger, while the hand at my throat held firm. Stars filled my vision despite my struggle, as I refused to give in to the grip that was trying to squeeze me unconscious. My arm flew around in a right hook and landed at what I guessed was his neck. A throaty groan came from the figure that began slumping toward the ground. I grabbed for a breath, feeling it burn as the cold air filled my lungs, and stepped over the obstruction toward my freedom at a faster pace.

I didn't have time to check to see if the object I'd met up with was dead. I couldn't care. With the dagger in hand, I continued running, until I realized I was now beyond the walls. Through limited vision, I could see I had just passed through the gate into what looked to be a courtyard. *Is there no end to this place?* I slowed my pace, watching for any movement in the shadows. Nothing. A corridor of dead trees lined the edge of the courtyard and I walked hidden beneath their long, fingerlike branches, not a soul in sight.

"Lovely idea to take a walk." I whirled at the sound of C-05's voice and hid the weapon for fear of it being taken. "But I don't think the weather is quite fitting to my taste." The feel of cool stickiness skimmed my arm as I slid the blade back between my shirt and pants.

C-05 was a tough fight on any given day with my sword and other-worldly abilities. I didn't stand much of a chance now without them. I was walking backward now, trying to keep some distance and racing to come up with a plan. *Damn him! How did he know where I am?* I moved to run, but his quick action coupled with a reach closer than I'd anticipated won out.

"I don't think so," he said, gripping my arm hard. He had evidently been gifted with the same speed as Kevin. The more I struggled, the tighter his hand closed. "Imagine my surprise at arriving to meet with Tarsamon and hearing your thoughts so close."

I didn't expect to run into anyone who would be listening.

I relaxed, took a few steps with him in the direction I had just come from, and moved to throw a left-handed punch into his center. That he blocked. In a matter of moments, the adrenaline I had upon escaping turned into hot-blooded rage boiling through my veins. It needed an escape. I sunk my knee into his groin, with the intention it would cause him to release his grip on me. He let go but quickly made another grab, lost his balance, and pushed me to the ground as he fell. We struggled, each trying to gain the upper hand, until after a couple of minutes, he pinned my legs beneath the full weight of his body and had my arms clasped together above my head. I lay gasping for breaths, realizing I'd exhausted any reserved resources without water or food, save a single rowan berry.

"Hmm," he said. An impure thought ran through his head just then before he blocked me from reading him further. "I can see you aren't going to make this captivity easy on either of us." He stared down at my face.

Any closer and I'll bite you. I felt my lip curl in response to the thought. He slapped me then, hard enough to feel the sting linger on my cheek and a bruise on my cheekbone. He must have worn a ring. Dizziness whirled in my head at the impact.

"You wouldn't want to do that. I assure you," he said, hearing my thought. I tried to block him from any further intrusion of mind but didn't know if I could, having no other visible power in the dark world.

He moved himself off me and pulled me up by my wrists, practically dragging me toward a section of the wall where a thick black vine trailed, as if on its own path of escape. "This'll have to do," he said under his breath. With his free hand, he ripped at the vine until he had a long enough piece to wrap around my wrists.

"I can't oblige." I brought my knee up and kicked hard enough to get him to free the hand that held my wrists together as he stumbled backward. Hands free, I elbowed him in the jaw with the intent of knocking him out and turned to run into the dense brush and dead trees. With his abilities in this world, hunting me might be easy for him. The dark energy countered the otherworldly gifts I carried, zapping my ability to move at incredible speed, to feel what others felt, and even to maintain a protective shield against the dark energy. But why wasn't the key I'd been given providing the additional protection the Druids said it would? Maybe it couldn't work here. Whatever the reason, all I knew was I had to escape long enough for any member of my team to arrive.

A shrill, high-pitched call that sounded like a siren rang out across the sky. I ran faster still, never caring what it meant but with the understanding that call was for me. The heaviness of this dark place was catching up with me, as the breath in my chest grew more labored. *He's coming...keep going.* The muscles in my legs began to cramp under the cold of the night air and a numbing sensation that started at my wrist moved to my palm as I hit the dead forest. I shook out my hands and kept running.

Wear yourself out. It will make my job easier.

I heard the thought and knew it belonged to C-05. I could still hear him even though all my other strengths were gone. *Jesus, is he that close or can he project a thought from a distance?* I wasn't about to stop to look. I darted around a prickly bush and smacked into what felt like a web the size of a wall. Sticky and immobile, I hung in mid-step. A light from behind me shone as the wall began to move. I peeled my chin off to see a group of three enormous shadow demons had banded together and held me locked in place. I cursed under my breath and hoped to hell Kevin could find me in this nightmare.

"Tired yet?" C-05 said from behind me. I didn't answer. "Let her go. She won't run again." The shadows backed away, dumping me in a face-plant on the ground. Still catching his breath, C-05 pressed a knee into my back, bound my wrists behind me, and yanked me up. With C-05 at my back, I stumbled toward the fortress in silence, so much weaker than I'd ever felt.

"You know, I have a great deal of respect for you, Sara," he said after a few moments.

"Then why don't you come back to the winning side and let that work for you?"

"I just don't see it. You and your team being successful at getting all of the keys, that is."

"You underestimate us."

"Not sure about that. But I admire your confidence. I certainly underestimated your strength once. But as it seems, you're in quite the predicament. And I'm free to come and go."

We walked in silence through the halls of what, from the distance in the courtyard, appeared to be a castle, until arriving at the wooden double doors I'd passed on my way out. He knocked twice before entering.

The room was oversized and lit with several torches. A large four-poster bed was placed against the opposite wall with a gold and red plush comforter covering the top. An enormous wooden desk was angled in a corner of the room. C-05 shut the door behind us and went toward the desk, lighting a cigarette.

"It seems you've made me late for my appointment." He blew out the smoke and leaned against the desk.

"Your quarters?" I asked. My eyes narrowed to study him.

"Mm, when and if I choose." He held out the cigarette, looking at it. "Haven't needed one of these in so long." He took another drag and crushed it out on the desk.

"Are you expecting Tarsamon?'

"Not any longer. Relieved?" I didn't answer. "He doesn't wait for anyone."

"Bummer for you, huh?"

"I'll arrange something for both of us tomorrow." C-05 pushed off the desk and came toward me. I hadn't moved more than a few feet inside the door since arriving. "You may as well make yourself comfortable. You'll be staying where I can keep a closer eye on you when I'm here, since it seems security is a bit lax." He dropped a hand, reaching into my jeans pocket and pulling out the tools I used to pick the lock. "Handy," he said, looking them over.

He walked the few steps past me to the door. Would he untie me? I could feel the vines cutting into my wrists as if they were fishing line wrapped tight.

He turned at the door. "I believe I'll leave those binds in place just to be certain you don't get itchy again to tour the grounds. Besides, I wouldn't want to underestimate you again." He winked, then disappeared behind the door. I heard the latch close, followed by the click of the lock.

God, I want him dead. Too damn bad he got lucky back at the cave. Really too bad.

I stood for a moment assessing the room. There was a single window with a balcony. I could break it with my feet and... I let the thought die as the alternative of jumping and breaking my own neck occurred to me. Who was I kidding? I didn't have the same powers here that I did when I traveled in my spirit form.

The bed rested on top of an intricately woven area rug and I wondered why a demon like Tarsamon would even have a room decorated with lush fabric and an ornate rug. What kind of arrangement had C-05 made with Tarsamon to have such comforts? My eyes rested on the bed and I considered how it was a better alternative than the cold stone floor. But I still wasn't sleeping there. I opted for the small space just beyond the foot of the bed, where a couple feet of rug extended. I sat down, hands behind my back and leaned into the bedpost, eyes glued to the door. There would be little rest tonight and I knew that was part of the plan to wear me down. I'd need all my strength in the next several hours. After several moments in the silence of the room, the screeches started again somewhere in the darkness outside. I closed my eyes and scanned my thoughts, considering the next possible chance for escape.

They weren't closed long as a beautiful bright light pierced my vision. I waited to see what the faint movement in that light could be. I closed my eyelids tight and opened them again to be sure I wasn't dreaming. The blurry hue of bright white began to vanish, leaving the image of a woman dressed in white. She wore black knee-high boots and a long white coat. She was familiar but I couldn't remember how or from where. I stared into the pale face and sky-blue eyes that pierced mine with a gaze so intense I felt hypnotized. And then I remembered her. *Seria.* Eldor's partner that I had met with in Ardan on my first visit.

"Seria. Are you the one known as the white witch?"

"To those in certain realms." She stepped closer.

"You've got to get me out of here."

"I don't have the power to carry you out, but I can help the one who does. Sara, do not forget who you are in the midst of your darkness." She reached a hand to my face and I felt the fingers as a tingle that touched my cheek and ran down the length of my body. "The warrior will come, but you must remain strong." She tilted her head and smiled. And like a streak of lightning across the sky, she was gone.

I jerked my head upright as though I'd been asleep. "Oh," I said, feeling soreness in my neck, evidently from my chin resting on my chest. *Did I fall asleep?* The vision had seemed so real. The binds that held my wrists taut were burning my skin as they cut into them. I shifted slowly from the pain and stopped. There were feet, standing inches from me. I started at the sight and quickly angled my head upward, forgetting the soreness, and caught a glimpse of the face. I uncrossed my legs and went immediately to try to stand but ended up stumbling and instead settled on kneeling back on my heels. I attempted to block any thoughts, with the hope it would work this time. The person standing in front of me looked like Kevin. But it wasn't, or at least it didn't feel like Kevin's energy. The white witch had said the warrior would come. Though it looked so much like him, there was something terribly wrong. My conscience was screaming, *It's not him! It's not him!*

"Darling, I've come for you," he said. I pressed a foot into the ground to stand and backed slowly away. "Do you think I would fool you?"

There's a loaded question if I ever heard one. No, Kevin wouldn't fool me, but this wasn't Kevin. So yes, I was being fooled. I knew that well enough.

"I—I don't know who you are, but you aren't the man you want me to believe you to be," I said. *God, I hope Mac is right and the dark forces won't kill me. Would the dark energy on this side of Ardan fear the release of the key? Maybe it didn't matter to Tarsamon if one key was released. Maybe if that occurred, it would only set him back a bit in time, yet still allow him to fulfill his mission.*

"I can feel your fear, so raw and vulnerable. There's no sense in pretending any longer."

I watched in horror as the picture of the man I loved transformed into a black shadow, the grim reaper I despised. *Tarsamon.* He was a shapeshifter. I stopped moving backward, but only because I'd reached the wall.

"Sara, I believe they call you," he said. His tone changed from Kevin's to a deep, malicious one. "You don't remember me in your human form, do you? But we know each other well, Arwyn. Our history goes way back with your role as leader of the Alliance."

Leader?

"And do you recall that? Has the Soltari shared that memory with you?"

No. But you could be lying.

He moved closer to me and I felt every hair on my body rise in response. A long, bony finger extended and swiped down behind me, releasing the binds and causing a new sensation of pain as the blood began to flow to the areas that had been cut off. The numbness had consumed not only my palms but my fingers, too. I rubbed my wrists but never took my eyes off the black menace. The stickiness from where the binds had cut the skin coated my hands and a slight metallic scent filled my nostrils.

"So vulnerable as a human," he said with disgust in his gravelly tone.

Only a shadowed outline of a jaw was visible beyond the hood of his cloak. I was going to look my nemesis in the face, if I couldn't look him in the eye. I was going to be strong and not cower in the presence of this demon. I had once been told I was as strong as he, but admittedly, he had the upper hand at the moment. I didn't have a clue as to what the best method would be to fight him and hoped that rote knowledge would engage if called upon to defend myself. But he didn't appear to want to fight.

"How fortunate we are that you have come to us in the flesh," he said. A chill followed by a bead of sweat ran down my spine as if that finger had just traced a line down my back. "We can ensure a more permanent stay."

22

Dinner passed in almost complete silence. Kevin wondered how hungry Sara would be by now, as another sensation of guilt pulled at him. Each member of the team made no attempt to block their thoughts from being read and Kevin heard the silent discussion shared among them, wishing he couldn't. He set his fork down, rested his elbows on the table, and brought his hands to his face. He pressed his palms to tired eyes, let them slide past his lips, and fisted a palm into an open hand under his chin. He glanced across at the eyes that waited.

"I'll be going to the dark world to get her," Kevin said, breaking the silence.

"We'll join you," said Matt.

Kevin shook his head. "It would only be a death sentence for you."

"What is it for you if you go alone?" Juno said.

"A chance." *Maybe the only one we've got.* "I've got the advantage of speed on my side," he said and glanced at Aria, remembering her movement was like that of a spinning tornado, fast but not effective at the task he had in mind. "I don't know how yet, but I'll go."

Traveling to other realms was done in dream state and Kevin was sure there was no way in hell he was sleeping tonight. He leaned back into his chair. "The last information Sara gave us is that the gateway to the next location is not down at the river. We will need to travel to the Yucatan Peninsula, where the next key is believed to be."

"You aren't suggesting we go without you or Sara?" asked Matt.

"Not yet," Kevin replied. "But if I don't return, or..."

"If you don't return with the Light Carrier, this mission is over," Aria said. "You don't have a choice. You have to take us with you."

"I'm just as fast as you," Matt said, setting his napkin beside the plate.

"Surely one of us could block the forces that will fight you, giving you a better chance to get to Sara, maybe buying you the time you need," Juno said.

"Kevin, it's what we are trained to do," Aria added. "It's what we were *asked* to do. Look, I know you want to protect us, but it's wrong for you to keep us from our responsibility in the mission."

Kevin stood from the table and planted both hands on it. "I wouldn't keep you from your responsibility. But I am asking that you consider the risks and assess the best means for getting her out of Tarsamon's realm. That's all."

"And that means we aren't letting you go alone," Aria said, "when there may be a chance that we can get you both out."

Kevin took in a deep breath, too tired to argue. "I'll need a little time to think on it. Perhaps you're right."

"Damn straight we're right," Aria said.

Kevin nodded and turned toward the living area and down the long hall toward Mac's library.

Several minutes passed before Mac entered. Kevin was seated at the desk, leaning over a book. He glanced up at the sound of Mac's footsteps in the doorway.

"There are a number of magical beliefs the Celts have for berries, trees," Kevin said, looking down at the book. "And herbs. Are any of them true?"

"I don't practice magic," Mac replied. "But some say the power contained within the natural elements is quite strong."

"What do you say about a particular rowan berry?"

Mac smiled at him through closed lips as he pushed off from his post against the door's entry. "I was about to uncover the truth behind that mystery myself. Care to join me?" he said. Aggie was a couple of steps behind Mac, carrying a tray with a teapot and two cups.

"Out o' the way, ye brute," she said, nudging him gently and flashing a quick smile. "Here ye are," she said to Kevin. "This is brewed strong. So, if ye see any other wee creatures, I'll have nothing to do with it." She winked at Kevin, giving him a quick nod and smile, then turned and hurried out. Kevin's eyes followed her through the doorway. There was something about Aggie that reminded him of Sara, but he wasn't sure what it was. Perhaps it was her strength, he thought, a certain fight that she had in her. And for a sliver of a moment, it brought a smile to him, making the tear in his heart seem a little less painful.

"Down the hatch, aye?" Mac handed a cup of the pink tea to Kevin and took one for himself.

"Aye," Kevin said, blowing on the steaming liquid. The scent of bitter and sweet rose up through his nostrils. He took one small sip, then another and downed the rest. "How much of this do you suppose we have to drink?"

"I canna say. I suppose ye drink till ye see the woman in white," he replied, pouring another cup. "At least the taste is no' too bad." He leaned a bit closer to Kevin, raised a brow, and lowered his voice. "All the times I drank more than my share of ale, ye ken I'd be looking for women, too. I just never saw one in white. And if I had, I might have run, mind ye." He laughed lightly and emptied his cup. Kevin smiled, wondered if Mac was drunk from the ale at dinner, and

poured another cup of tea for good measure.

"Now, my eyes are only for that lass in there," Mac said, referring to Aggie. He raised his nearly empty cup in the direction of the doorway.

A silence filled the room, and like a fog, it grew heavy. "Never mind me," Mac said. "I believe I've had a bit too much already." Kevin wasn't sure if he meant the ale or the tea but set his empty cup down on the tray and leaned back in the chair. He felt his vision getting cloudy and thought it was sleep he needed. If the tea did nothing more than make him sleepy, he could at least enter the dark realm that way and find Sara.

He listened as the wind blew hard enough to whistle through the windowpanes and across the eaves. Several candles lighted the room, and as he focused on their flickering light, he noticed they, too, were growing less distinct by the minute.

"Is there anything toxic in these berries we just ingested?" Kevin asked, realizing he was belated in considering. Some woman, whom he didn't really know, had told Sara of the power of a fruit off a sacred tree. Why should he have believed her? Maybe they were only wasting time with it. He leaned back into the chair and remembered he had found mention of the berries in Mac's book of Celt magic.

"Nay, they aren't toxic to ye. There's been no talk of it that I've ever heard. But now that ye mention it, I do feel a little funny."

"You might. I wouldn't guess ale pairs too well with the tea." Kevin smiled. The cloudiness began to settle in more until the room was downright blurry. Thankfully, it wasn't spinning. Though he wasn't so sure that was the case for Mac. It wasn't long before the blurriness transformed into a hazy fog, while the yellow glow of candles encircled the white mist in his vision like a dream, as though golden orbs were the backdrop for the illumination. He stared in the center at an image that appeared denser than the white mass surrounding him. "You see what I see in the cloud of white?" he whispered to Mac.

"Aye, I see it."

And then they saw, quite clearly, a woman dressed in white.

"Seria," Kevin whispered. He'd been friends with her and Eldor for as long as he could remember. Mac turned his head to glance at Kevin and then back toward the white witch.

"Kevin, brave warrior. It has been some time since our last meeting."

"I had no idea you were—uh—the white witch to the Druids," he stumbled.

"You had no reason to know until now," she said, pausing as she reached a hand into a pocket on the side of the long robe and pulled out a handful of white dust. She blew into it gently. Kevin and Mac watched as it transformed into a solid transparent sphere. Kevin had seen a similar-looking globe once when he and his buddy as teens visited Madam Curran at the local state fair, as a joke.

"This is a gift for you," she said. "It will provide you a window to get to Sara. Use the power found in the bracelet to locate her within the dark world." Seria smoothed an open palm over the transparent crystal and held the ball out to Kevin. "This will buy you time to pull her out. But it will only give you two minutes. It is all that can be spared into the dark world before the evil becomes aware of the channel that was opened. Your speed is imperative."

"But how does the crystal work?" Kevin asked, reaching for the offering. "When do the two minutes begin?" Even with his speed, he doubted if he could locate Sara and pull her out in such a short amount of time.

"Once you arrive at the location, break it and the channel opens to allow you to move her physical form away from that world." Seria angled her head toward Mac and back to Kevin. "Remember, the danger exists to the other members of your team as it always has. This crystal does not provide protection, only a passage through the dark energy."

"Do you know if Tarsamon is keeping her in the tower?" Kevin asked, recalling a time once that he'd spent practicing on that very side of Ardan to master his fighting skills and had almost lost his own life doing so.

"Yes, the largest one. In a room much like this," Seria replied, recalling and transferring telepathically to Kevin the picture of the room she had seen Sara in before she had to leave at Tarsamon's interruption. Kevin saw the barred window and expected nothing less. "There was no time to speak with her. Tarsamon had begun to tune in to Sara's thoughts as she tried to sleep. He was probably making sure she couldn't pass her spirit from his dark world into yours to communicate."

It didn't matter that there was no more detail of Sara's exact location. The brief image was enough to give him a lead to her. The thought caused the adrenaline to surge through his veins and ignite his drive to pull Sara from the hell of demons and dark shadows and God knew what else wanted to take the light and life from her.

She's still alive.

Sara might not remember all that was locked away in her memory over the thousands of years they had been together. But her body and mind remembered the strength she needed to survive. He knew that much. Still, a single being of light was no match for the strength contained in Tarsamon's dark world. He couldn't tell from the image what condition Sara was in, but knew he had to move quickly. Every moment she spent in that life-sucking place caused her light to darken.

"Your allies in Ardan cannot help you bring her back to this realm," Seria said, breaking into Kevin's thoughts. "But tools like this one will." She nodded toward the crystal Kevin now held cupped in both hands. Her blue eyes lingered on Kevin's face and then closed, as her image retreated into the faint mist of white and faded, leaving Mac and Kevin alone in the library, wide-awake and with clear vision.

"I'll go now. I don't know how much time there is to get to her."

Mac shook his head. "Though I'd like to go with ye, I cannot. If ye are successful in rescuing her, it is my duty to take Sara to the next guardian of the key."

Kevin nodded. He began formulating a plan for getting to the tower. He could use Matt, Juno, and perhaps Aria, but not Elise, not yet. She was still healing at New York Presbyterian following the recent attack by C-05.

As he stood from the desk, Matt appeared in the doorway. "Let's go."

Kevin knew they were the fastest of all the members of the team and the most experienced of the warriors who had been sent to protect Sara on the mission. And he'd heard from Juno that rescuing Sara was more personal to Matt. He felt he owed her and Kevin for not following her when they had arrived in Randun, resulting in C-05 being able to get so close to her. Kevin read the look of determination on Matt's face. He was going with him and no one was telling him otherwise.

"And Juno?" Kevin asked.

"Right here," he said, approaching Matt.

"Aria will never let me forget if we leave her here," Matt said.

"And that's why you won't." Aria pushed past Juno.

Kevin drew in a deep breath and blew it out all at once. "Matt, you and I will head straight for the castle and into the largest of the two towers. That's where Sara is being kept. Juno and Aria, you keep watch, covering our backs. We will be most vulnerable until I can smash this thing at the tower." He held the crystal in his palm and eyed it. "Once that is done, all of you get out. Don't hesitate for anything." He glanced toward the doorway at each of them. "Don't wait for me. There won't be time. This crystal only allows two minutes to escape without detection, so there is no hanging around. Got it?" Each of them nodded.

Matt turned to Juno. "Guard her with your life," he said, raising a brow in Aria's direction.

"As if she were mine," he replied.

"You two are so sweet," Aria said. "But I won't need your protection, sweetness. I'm older than both of you and stronger still."

"Take one of these, each of ye." Aggie turned up a palm with white tablets. "Just a little something to help ye get to sleep. I'm thinkin' ye'll be needin' it." All four reached for a pill and followed Aggie to a comfortable place where they could cross into other worlds as humans, through their dreams.

23

I 'd lost track of time and how long I'd been in Tarsamon's dark realm. That was dangerous to maintaining sanity. It felt like several hours had passed and yet there was still no sign of daylight, not even the mere hint at the shift of night to dawn. I knew I was absorbing the heavy energy that engulfed me in the dead silence with increasing negative thoughts that would filter through my mind. I listened as the high-pitched screams continued in the distance, ripping me from a moment of contentment in my own thoughts as I tried to shut out the noise.

Why am I not dead? There must be truth to what Mac said about the release of the key. That can only mean Tarsamon doesn't want the key I hold to be let out into the world. I shifted, feeling weaker by the moment, and leaned my shoulder against the wall. I had to stay awake, if not to try and find a way out, then to keep my thoughts from being read by the Dark Lord.

Earlier, in the corner of the dark room where I'd huddled, pretending to sleep under the window, I'd overheard C-05 and Tarsamon in hushed tones discussing keeping me away from my team. Before leaving, they'd reminded me there was no way for me to get back unless they took me, and that wasn't going to happen unless I was dead. That was the message delivered right after I'd been levitated off the floor by Tarsamon and slammed against the wall, in an effort to grow any fear of him he thought I carried deep. The fact was I didn't fear him. If I feared anything, it was the pain death caused, not death itself. Certainly not the evil that was threatened by the power I'd been given. The back of my head had left a small indentation high above the bed. The ache from it that still filled my head and traced down my neck would be sure to keep me awake. Had I been able to sense the attack, I might have braced myself, by tightening muscles to take most of the impact. And if I'd ever had any doubt this place was all a dream, it was gone now with the constant throbbing and metallic scent of blood wafting from my wrists and head. When I did have in my hands the additional power and protection that came with all three keys, Tarsamon and the traitorous C-05 would pay, and pay big.

It hadn't been too difficult a task to get to this darker side of Ardan, I thought, staring past the bars and out the window of the room into the night. If the demons could transcend my physical form to another realm, there had to be a way to get back, but not without some help. I narrowed my eyes, scanning the horizon. The orange light I'd seen when I had visited twice before in dream state and out of sheer curiosity to see what I would fight was not visible from this vantage point. All that could be seen was a tiny sliver of gray-blue that threatened to chase the blackness of the night away while highlighting the tips of the dead arms of trees that once lived. That thread of light served as a reminder that the side of Ardan I often visited would remain just out of reach.

It had been my stubbornness that had landed me in this dungeon, that coupled with my inability to trust one person to protect me. I'd practically delivered myself into the hands of the demons. If I ever did make it back, a simple apology for screwing this up would never do.

I shifted to lean against my other side. I was so overcome with weakness I could barely stand. My wrists had been bound again and the sting of the binding cut deeper with the slightest of movements. I winced. I wanted to drop to my knees and sleep, but I needed to stay awake even though my eyes had started to close in longer increments. I couldn't trust I'd be safe if I let myself sleep. With each shift of my body, a new stab of pain jolted me back to the reality of my situation and the promise I'd made to myself to be awake should Tarsamon or C-05 return. It was torture. How much longer would I be able to endure it? My eyelids grew heavier as I stared out into nothingness. As they fell to close once more, I saw a flash across the sky. I doubted it and blinked my eyes for as long as I could hold them open.

I had never seen lightning in the couple of times I had been to the dark world, only the demons and their dogs that guarded the grounds beyond the borders of Tarsamon's lair. My previous visit wasn't a kill mission. There had been no reason to search out the nemesis. And in recalling the couple of visits I had made, I'd never seen any light other than the faint orange glow from a streetlight or two below the rooftops of vacant buildings. As I looked on now, I still saw nothing.

Maybe I won't leave. It's just so dark, and the damn shrieks... I heard another followed by one more, as if they were calling to each other. *C-05. I hope he thinks moving to join Tarsamon was worth all this. Ugh. I'd rather be dead. I just need a little sleep. Just a moment to...*

Wake up, Sara! No sleep! I banged my head against the wall once with such force I felt the pain reignite the throbbing sensation at the back of my skull that had slowed in the last few minutes. Feeling pain kept me alert...and alive.

"Damn these bindings." I felt a burning sensation running from just above one of my wrists to my forearm and wanted to soothe the feeling with something cool. *Must be a nerve.* Imagery was a pretty powerful tool for overcoming many facets of the mind. I remembered a high school science teacher had given the class an exercise in making our palms sweat by imagining the heat building until she had a class of clammy-handed students. I pictured a soft, cold compress and massaging fingers working to heal the hot sensation running up my arm. But it was no use. The heat ran the full length of my arm, growing hotter by the minute. I sat down, sucking in a breath from the increased burning sensation, and leaned my head back against the wall.

Bruise me. Burn me. I'm not giving up the key. I owed my team that much, however small an offering it might be for my stupidity, my stubbornness.

I stared up at the ceiling. How the hell was I getting out of here? *What if Kevin can't get to me? No. No, no, no.* I wouldn't think of it.

I could still feel the dagger hidden behind me pressing against my back and wondered if I'd get another chance to use it. Not with my hands bound behind me. Even if I got the dagger loose, I'd have no way to saw my hands free from behind, unless I could manipulate the blade upside down or perhaps lift it up enough and wedge it against the wall and my back to begin sawing. *Yes, that should do it.* I bent my elbows and felt the binding dig in, along with fresh drops of blood that trickled to my fingers. Leaning slightly to my left, I used the index finger and thumb of my right hand to carefully lift the blade higher. I twisted it a hair to feel it cut into my back. If I lifted it out, I'd have to wedge it against something and God help me if I dropped the damn thing to have C-05 find it.

I searched the room from my seated position for something sharp that might cut through the ties. If I could get that far, I would wait until C-05 entered again, surprise him and—I tossed aside the thought of murdering him, for the time being. As much as I hated him, I needed him for the basics. And I knew I couldn't trust a demon for that. Even if Tarsamon was aware he should provide certain necessities to keep me alive, it didn't mean he would. I needed to get to the desk. Maybe there was something in the drawer that would saw through the bindings. I glanced up to the windowsill. Perhaps the inside ledge of the wall was sharp enough to cut through. I didn't think I could bear to drag my body to a standing position once more.

"Do it," I ordered under my breath.

I lifted myself up and pushed one leg up to stand. As I did, stars began to flash in the corner of my vision. *No, not now.* I'd used up what energy I had upon arriving, breaking out of the cell, and fighting C-05. It felt as though it had been nearly three days without water. Lack of water and food was getting the best of me. I was sweating and had begun to shiver, and that wasn't from lack of food or water. Sweat was the last bit of water my body had and if I didn't get up and out now, who knew if I ever would.

"You're a survivor, remember?" I said to myself. "If you can survive being abandoned by your own parents, you can survive this." I leaned my back against the wall and brought my wrists up to the ledge to begin sawing on a sharp corner of the window ledge. Tiny beads of cold sweat broke out on my forehead from the increased pain and ran a slow path down my temples. I gritted my teeth, pressed my wrists against the wall, and sawed through the pain. Another warm, wet trickle of blood dripped off my index and middle fingers, but I kept the movement even as a dizzying sensation filled my head. I welcomed it as a mild distraction from the pain. "Almost there, just hold on."

The stars grew larger, flashing like tiny light bulbs in my darkening vision. I glanced up at the sound of the lock in the door clicking.

Not yet.

Another minute, maybe two was all I needed. I felt my body slide down the wall into a crumpled heap. Footsteps slowly approached and stopped just short of my face. My cheek was pressed to the cold stone floor.

"Sara," a male voice said. His tone was low and smooth. "Give me the key. I will protect it for you."

Don't trust anything in this place.

I blinked upward. "I can't."

The man gently lifted my chin and I gasped, seeing him crouched next to me. Confusion replaced clear thought, blowing past the pain, along with searing heat on my arm. Something wasn't right. But I couldn't arrive at why. The voice sounded like Matt's. *Not Matt, C-05. C-05.* I couldn't make out the face, but it didn't matter if I could. Nothing good could last here for long. And Matt wouldn't be asking me for the key. The pure of heart wouldn't ask to carry my responsibility. Wasn't that what Mac had said? Besides, Matt wouldn't be here.

A hand gently stroked the hair from my face. I wanted to crawl inside myself and hold on to the will to live. A tear ran from the outside corner of my eye into my hair, trying for escape. I felt my body being lifted off the floor and placed gently on the bed. A broken cry slipped from my lips as my body weight crushed the wounds at my wrists. Someone leaned over and shifted me on my side and cut the bindings. Fingers stroked my cheek and trailed down my neck. My arms rested at my sides, unresponsive to the touch. I felt my stomach quiver as a soft, silent internal cry erupted. The hands belonging to a man I couldn't see slowly slid up under my shirt, over my stomach and back down again, stopping at the button at my pants. There was no energy left in my body, no ability to fight. But I still knew a truth from a lie.

"Let me hold this burden for you," the man said at my ear. His hands cupped my face and he leaned over to kiss me, stopping to stare. I blinked in longer increments through tear-filled eyes, my vision growing dimmer.

"He's in there," I thought I heard a voice say. Maybe it was just my mind scrambling for anything other than what was happening to me.

What? Where? The thought flitted through my head, but I didn't think it was mine.

Lips pressed gently against mine, then harder, trying to force a response.

"I want to consume you," he whispered. "In every way." His hand moved and his fingers were at the button on my pants, and then the zipper. He pushed off of me and began tugging at them. I moved to kick him and missed.

"So help me, I'll kill you," I said through clenched teeth.

The dagger.

"What was that?" he said.

I covered the thought with the last image I had in my mind of the room, so as not to be readable by him.

"Never mind." He stared down at me, my pants pulled to an uncomfortable and low position on my hips. "Such fire." He eased closer. "I want to uncover every ounce of the heat you carry, flame by flame."

There's nothing for you but a dark and empty hell, as cold as your soul grows.

"My, we are bitter." He shifted again and put his lips near my cheek. "And if you won't give me the key to save your life, I will still find pleasure in you as often as I desire. Maybe when enough time has passed, you'll understand you aren't going to save the humans from Tarsamon, not with one key."

He slammed a sloppy kiss against my mouth, fisting my hair in his hand. With the last bit of energy I could muster, I turned my face away from him, feeling the wrenching of hair being pulled even harder at the resistance. The pain reached across the back of my scalp, but I held firm not to look at him.

"That's okay," his breath whispered at my ear, causing a turn of my stomach. "You'll come around." A delicious vision of C-05's head lying beside his body shone in the limelight of my conscience. It was a bright blast of light that shattered the image from my mind's eye and invaded the room, while another behind my eyelids was blinking in black stars.

I closed my eyes against the blinding light and peeked through the crack in my eyelids. There was no one staring over me or lying beside me now. My eyes moved to the source of the light to see a dark shadow blocked the doorway where the light was streaming in. Another figure blew past me and slammed C-05 to the ground. I had to find the strength to run, to get out of here. Forcing my legs over the edge of the bed, I forced my weak body into a sitting position, trying to stand. I inched my pants back up and reached an arm out to grab for balance from the sudden increased dizziness. My palms lay flat against the wall as I felt my way toward the door. There was a roar of shouting, but it was too bright to see who was angry with whom. The room began spinning and I threw an arm out for balance and hit something hard. Like a rag doll, my body fell limp over the shoulder of someone.

"Go! Go! Go! Get out of here now!" someone shouted in the distance.

"I can't," I tried to call out. But the words fell as only a whisper from my lips, as the blackness I'd seen in spots earlier enclosed me in a veil of silence.

24

Faint, indistinguishable whispering flowed into my ears from all around me and grew more distinct with every minute. I had been spending a good deal of time in episodes of unconsciousness over the last several days with the travel to Randun and to Tarsamon's realm. But at this awakening, there was calm. A peaceful, loving calm. The light coming through my closed eyelids didn't seem harsh, but soft and warm. Could I just stay in this place a while longer? No evil, no darkness, no key. My eyes shot open at that. Did I still have the key? I moved to put my hand over my stomach where I'd always felt the warmth since the Druids had given me the key of light. As I did, the familiar heat in the center of my being began to radiate through my hand and I knew it was safe. My hand, though, was attached to something and I glanced down to see the tubing that was feeding liquid into my veins. Both wrists were bandaged in white gauze and all the pain that had been there while I was in the dark world was numb.

"How is she?" Aria's voice carried to my ear.

"Awake and holding strong," an unrecognizable voice answered. I lifted my gaze to the sound above my head and saw the tall, lean outline of an elf. Butterscotch-colored hair trailed behind his shoulders and he nodded once at me in acknowledgment. Hazel eyes rested delicately on my face. Someone reached for the hand unencumbered by the IV. My eyes trailed to the side. Large, strong hands gently enclosed my hand.

How can I face Kevin? I was so stupid to take the risk. You screwed up, face it. Face him.

I lifted my eyes to see Kevin gazing at me. "I'm so sorry," I said. His eyes were sunken and a shadow filled the area around them. I placed my hand on his. "I thought I could just get to the gateway and..."

"I know." He glanced down at our linked fingers. My eyes blurred as I began to realize how I'd affected him. How could I have been so blind to think I could take on such a force and put the others at such risk? I gently pulled my hand from his and brought it to his cheek, now angled downward.

"Aria," I began, but she held a hand up as she leaned against the door's frame.

"Protecting you is what all of us are expected to do."

I sighed. "Is everyone okay?" I glanced from her to Kevin.

"We're fine," Aria said. "Get better so we can finish this mission." Her face softened and she smiled before turning to leave.

"Where are we?"

"In Scotland. Mac's home, until you're well enough to travel," Kevin said. He looked as though he hadn't slept in days.

My fault, too.

"What about the shadows and demons? Can't they get to us here?"

"The house is guarded by Eldor's forces. They won't try again immediately." He stroked my hand with the backsides of his fingers. "Sara." His eyes locked on mine. "I failed us, all of us, not protecting you."

"How could you have known you would be working against my seriously stubborn nature in this world? Had you known, you might not have signed up to protect me."

His eyes lifted and his brows closed together. "Of course I would have. I wouldn't have let the Soltari make a deal with anyone else for the job," he said, pausing. "It isn't that. I don't care how hard I have to fight or to what limits I must go to get to you. But my God"—he paused—"a couple of minutes longer and he might have had the key. He might have killed you," Kevin said, referring to C-05.

"I wasn't going to give it to him. Don't you think I realized it was C-05 I was dealing with?" The level of irritation in my voice surprised me.

"You were pretty unresponsive and weren't exactly able to fight him off either," he said calmly, letting go of my hand.

Behind the pain, I sensed the anger he tried to suppress in his tone. Or was it fear? Fear sparked anger, after all, when it felt cornered with no clue as to a way out.

Kevin stood from the chair and ran a hand through his hair, facing the wall. He turned, hands on his hips as he walked toward the door and back.

"What if I had sat at the dinner table a little longer or if Mac and I hadn't drunk that damn tea when we did or had left a few minutes later?" he said. I watched him, wanting him to pour his frustration out on me and knowing I deserved it.

"Mac said I would have to give the key willingly."

"What if he was wrong?"

"None of this is your fault. It's mine," I said. I took in a deep breath. "How did you get past Tarsamon's forces to the tower to reach me, anyway?" My eyes narrowed on him, studying the feelings I could sense from him. As an empath, it was agonizing to feel his pain and to know I was the cause.

He shook his head. "This team and I are specialists, trained to fight with every ounce of supernatural ability we carry. We know what to expect when we enter Tarsamon's realm. That's all we've done. And it doesn't matter whose fault it is. That isn't the point," he said. "This mission is and will be fraught with danger, events that will risk our lives. That's expected. It's my job to keep you safe and I didn't."

"You tried. I didn't listen to you."

"Goddamn it, Sara! I knew you wouldn't and I still didn't protect you."

Helplessness filled my heart at not being able to comfort him. I wanted him to know I would somehow make it better. Only time would prove it to him. Sorry wasn't enough. He was right that this mission would risk our lives over and over. He shook his head and the frown line between his brows grew deeper. The elf returned and whispered something to Kevin. He nodded in reply, then glanced at me.

"I'm sorry. Now isn't the time to talk about this."

"Stop that. Will you let me accept responsibility?"

"No, not entirely," he said. "You'll have to accept that you can't have everything the way you want it." He dipped his chin. "And so will I," he added under his breath, leaving me to wonder what he meant. He stood next to the bed, facing me, one arm folded across his stomach while his other hand rested at his chin. His eyes were directed at the ground. I caught a glimpse of the thought that flitted through his head. He *was* trying to block me but was either having difficulty or I was getting better at breaking through the mental barrier he put in place to keep me from knowing his true thoughts. I pushed myself to a sitting position.

"Look at me and tell me what it is you think you have to do," I said.

His eyes met mine in one blink. He pressed his lips firmly together. The struggle I could feel from him was tearing him apart. This time he didn't block me from reading his thought. It was perhaps easier to share the thought than to voice what he was thinking. His feelings streamed to me. The cut of those words needed to be made for what he believed was the greater good of the mission and its success.

"I'm too close to you," he said. "It's risking your life and this mission, just as the Soltari predicted. Don't you see?"

I felt a stab of pain run through me as the bonds he'd so carefully reestablished in this life began to fray one by one. I was grateful, if only for a second, that I did not remember the many lives we had lived together. As the ache of anticipated loss began to rise up in me, I could feel his pain was infinitely greater at holding the memories that connected us over lifetimes. I wanted to tell him not to make this decision, but I couldn't. That choice was not mine to make, nor did I have any right to voice my opinion after what I had done. I just sat in the bed, frozen. Waiting.

Getting close to people was not easy for me. I never allowed it for fear that establishing close connections would give rise to the same ghost of abandonment felt when my parents left me. My biggest fear in allowing myself close to Kevin had just become a reality as he pulled away.

"God, Sara, I don't want to do this to you, to us. I knew what it meant for you to give enough to trust me. I just don't see any other way to keep what we've had for eternity alive." He ran another hand over the top of his head, clearly conflicted. "If you fail and the Soltari determine our connection and the will to keep each other alive caused the loss of the mission, I'll lose you forever." His eyes dropped from mine.

I stared at him, all words having escaped me. A single tear fell from my eye and I brushed it away before he saw it. The little voice of caution I had silenced when we bonded this relationship in the Cape echoed to me again. *I tried to protect you from this anguish.*

"Then go," I said, hearing the coolness in my tone. "Do what you must. I'll never stand between you and what you think is right again." Pain-filled eyes glanced up at me. "Don't wait for me to console you while you leave me." His eyes narrowed and he stared at me, then turned and walked through the doorway. I held it together until I knew he had left the house. Hearing a few muffled voices and the front door close, I turned into the pillow and cried silently.

Later that evening, Aggie brought a tray containing fruit, crackers, and stew. She smiled and set the tray down across the arms of the chair next to the bed.

"I ken ye may no' feel like eating, and it won't mend your heart, but it will help ye feel better."

I nodded. "You're right. I can't thank you enough for your kindness and giving all of us a place to stay."

She brushed a hand in the air, dismissing the comment. "It's no trouble. Besides, the others are stayin' at the wee cottage up the hill from here. Only the elves are still here. Outside, of course," she said, putting her hands on her hips. "And I'll no' want ye to worry. That man loves ye more than all the stars in the universe." She reached over, put a hand to my forehead, then bent to pick up a bottle of aspirin on the small table next to the bed and opened the container. "Don't be too sad, lass. He'll be back."

I forced a smile. She didn't know Kevin. He would do what he thought was best. And if it meant he needed to pull away from me for the sake of the mission, he would. I doubted he would abandon his duty to protect me. It was the bargain he made with the Soltari in order to remain with me in this life. But if having me in his life were causing him to fail, perhaps he would abandon the mission, too.

Aggie held out two aspirin and the glass of water from the tray. I took them with thanks. "Call if ye need anything," she said, patting my shoulder as she headed toward the door.

"I should be up soon and then we'll be on our way."

She stopped and turned to face me. "Ye ken well enough why I gave ye the aspirin, bein' that you're a doctor. You won't be leavin' until that fever is coming down."

"How high has it been and for how long?"

She tilted her head and looked up, as though the numbers were written on the ceiling.

"Well, let's see now, one hundred three and a full two days. Yes, that'd be about right, last I heard."

"Two days, really?" She nodded. "All right. You win, for now." I wasn't concerned. It was possible I'd contracted an infection from the bindings that had cut into my wrists. I was certain the fever wasn't anything an antibiotic couldn't remedy.

After Aggie left, I wanted the IV out of my arm. I felt better physically. Emotionally, I was empty. I pulled the IV and applied firm pressure to the area. "That's one small step closer to getting out of here and on to the next key," I said. I ate about half of the stew before I lost what little appetite I had. The broth was soothing but filled me quickly. I kicked the covers away, feeling heat begin to rise up my back and neck. Beads of sweat had broken out across my forehead and I hoped I was breaking the fever on my own. Someone had dressed me in an oversized T-shirt and long shorts. Not my clothing, but clean and soft, the attire suited me fine. I drifted to sleep with a bit of cooler air finding its way to my burning skin.

Within moments of closing my eyes, I was standing in Ardan, where I'd met with the Alliance...and Cerys. The path beneath my feet was different. It was a grassy one, scattered with paver stones that reminded me of the garden Kevin and I had walked through in Randun. The sky was black as night with only the hue of blue light from some unknown source to light the way, an occurrence I'd become familiar with. Enormous gray and green shadows of trees surrounded me, leafy and full of life. But why was I here? Had I been called to Ardan by Eldor or perhaps Karshan? My sword was gone as well as the dagger. But strangely, I felt I wouldn't need them. No challenge of strength would be presented, no practice to engage in. I'd rounded that corner at the river in Doune.

I followed the path beyond another grouping of trees and noticed the red and yellow spotted yarrow that began to appear. I had only ever seen the plant when I'd met with Cerys on my first arrival in Ardan. I stopped and stared at it for a moment before continuing. Was I to meet with him? It would be my first visit with Cerys after discovering he and Kevin were one and the same individual. What would I say?

The path dead-ended at a row of trees, preventing passage. A strange and uncomfortable feeling settled over me, causing me to want to turn and leave, to wake back to my world. I didn't ask to speak with anyone. I didn't have questions to be answered. And yet, as I looked on, the cheery yarrow was scattered all among the grass and dead leaves of the forest floor, spiking my interest. I peered through the pine needles to see an open field, one of many I'd encountered in practicing my skills. But that wasn't what caused me to look deeper. A white mist was filling the space. Someone else was already here, waiting. *Is this for my eyes?* In the past, meetings in Ardan led to a particular location for good reason, if what was occurring involved me in some way.

I took slow, quiet steps forward, easing past a few of the branches, careful to remain hidden, while peering between thick, covered limbs. My heart sank to my stomach at the sight of Kevin. I recognized the mist as the Soltari. From what he'd said, Kevin had never called upon the entity to meet. I watched as they arranged in a massive white form surrounding him and listened as the mass settled to speak. Individual ghostly faces floated in the illuminated mist that hung like thick fog, lighting the night.

Can they sense my energy? Likely. How foolish, I thought, if I were to be caught here spying. But someone had summoned me here. I declined an urge to show myself and instead decided to let what was meant to happen play out.

"I cannot continue in this manner," Kevin said. "It wasn't the Light Carrier who almost failed you. It was I."

No. No it wasn't.

"I seek to preserve our bond. If that means I'm no longer part of the mission, so be it."

What? No.

It pulled him nearly in two to break us apart. His face was streaked with shadowed lines. And for the first time, I wondered if it caused him more pain to lose someone than it did for me. I was resilient, having built a wall against rejection. I'd hardened every angle from being touched by emotion. And yet the heartbreak I felt now hit the one soft spot I'd carved out and set aside only for Kevin, like a target to a bull's-eye. For Kevin, that pain was overwhelming enough to call upon the highest governing order, equivalent to what others would consider as God.

"Everything is as it was planned, perfectly. What do you ask of us?" A single whispering voice spoke from the cloud of white. The transparent faces floated around Kevin, waiting. I could hear his contemplation. To ask that I remember all that he did would be selfish. To ask that he no longer remember the memories that bonded us would be brutal. But for him to let go would give him the additional focus he needed. He clung to those memories as if they were an irreplaceable treasure. Kevin shook his head slowly, stuck between what he so desperately wanted—to share the same connection with me that he remembered. His want was working against his desire to fulfill the task to protect me. Right now he doubted he could have both.

"I want no more pain between us over this. Sara knows there is a connection. She can feel it and it pulls at her to not remember, putting a barrier between us."

So he does know. I didn't realize he understood so well how frustrating it was to feel so close to someone, so bonded, without knowing what the connection was that had caused it. That bond was so much deeper than the intelligence, good looks, or strength he carried. It was as though we'd known each other forever, what each other liked, what we didn't, and what moved us. He knew from the very moment he touched me exactly how my body would respond and what to say to soften the wall I'd built before turning it to rubble. He knew how to get beyond the shell of protection to the very soul of my being with a few words.

A low hum emanated from the mist as the formation of a collective answer was being created. "Remember who you are." Pause. "The Last Great Warrior with one task—guard the Light Carrier. Your demand was to remember her. You were chosen as the one who could best protect her and still show her the love she deserves. She is forever joined with you. Never to be lost."

"Unless she is destroyed by the Dark Lord," he answered. "Or she fails the mission. Those were your terms for me joining with her." He raked a hand through his hair. "My mistake nearly cost her life and failed the mission. It cannot be that she remembers nothing and I remember all. Our decisions are being impacted by the dissonance of this arrangement."

"Many attempts will be made to obtain the keys and end her life. You must remain strong. The greater connection you seek begins when the mission is complete. Your request will be considered." The mist collected into a single cloud of white around him and began to spin upward, dispersing across the sky.

I waited, watching him. What would the Soltari decide to do, remove his memories of us or return them to me? And how long before we knew which it was going to be? I hadn't woken from my sleep and that meant whoever had called me to this place was still waiting to talk with me. I didn't want Kevin to see me while I waited, and so I stepped deeper under the protection of the tree nearest me, my back to the field as I considered Kevin's request. How would the Soltari's decision affect us? Any further thought on the matter was slammed shut as Kevin's voice broke the silence. I turned and lowered my head to glance between two branches.

Standing beside Kevin was a gray outline of a woman with long hair. A hint of light, white-blue in color, emanated around her. I couldn't see her face.

"I know you're here," Kevin said. "I feel your presence. Can you not convince them? Help them understand why this is not working."

Can't he see her? Is he referring to the Soltari? Is he speaking to a separate member? They never break away from their collective being, at least that I know of.

"They will see things your way and bring you closer through the memories you wish to share. I love you."

Kevin reached a hand toward where the woman stood. Why couldn't he see her, as I could? A single tear from him caught the light and hit the ground.

What the hell?

With that thought, the woman turned her head and bright jade-green eyes lifted in my direction. Her energy pierced the night into my hiding place and rested with me. The glow of my reflection, as though I was looking into a mirror, cascaded over her face just before she left. Kevin turned in my direction. My legs moved before my thoughts directed them, and before I knew what was happening, I had stumbled backward out of the cover of the trees and onto the path with little grace. I snapped my jaw shut at seeing what could only have been the spiritual equivalent of my higher self, the copy of me that I'd wondered about since discovering Cerys and Kevin were the same entity.

I turned off the path and began picking my way through the taller saplings. I wanted to wake up, to leave this place. Instead, my feet defied my desire, slowing and finally stopping to wait beneath the limbs of a long-hanging willow.

"Sara," Kevin said from behind me.

I let out a breath and turned to face him. "I didn't follow you."

"I know." He closed the gap between us in a few short strides and reached a hand to my cheek. "If you're here, it's because the Soltari wanted you to be." His thumb stroked the corner of my mouth. "It would also explain why I was able to meet with them so easily." The dim light of the forest showed every line of his face. The softness found in his eyes and mouth had been replaced with distress and indecision.

"I wasn't trying to spy on you, either," I said.

He cocked his head to the side and raised a brow. "What other explanation would you have for standing in a grouping of trees?"

"I didn't intend, I mean, I don't know why I was called here," I stumbled. "Who was that you were speaking with?"

"Her name is Arwyn. You know the spirit with whom I speak." His hand trailed down the side of my hair and his eyes roamed my faced.

Yes. I know of that name, but not the spirit.

"We exist as immortal souls before we ever become human. Why do you think I fight so hard for you to remember? There is so much between us, my love. Let me show you something."

He took my head between both palms, each hand at my temple, and placed his forehead to mine with the intent of sharing a vision.

"Wait. Can you do this without retaliation from the Soltari?"

"I think this one will be acceptable."

A vision of a couple in their early twenties, I guessed, and who didn't resemble either me or Kevin formed in my mind's eye. A rush of feelings surged through me as though the wire connecting that woman's life had been plugged into mine. I felt all the sensations as though they belonged to me.

"Us?" I asked to be certain.

"Yes. Long ago," he whispered, still holding my head between his hands.

The man presented a single white calla lily to her as he captured her free hand and brought it to his lips. I felt the tenderness as though Kevin had just kissed my hand. He then released the fingertips, scooped her up in his arms, and carried her to their bed.

Candlelight flickered warm, glowing light across their faces as the flower lay at the tableside. My stomach quivered at the expectation of what they both knew was to come—the first of countless romantic encounters together. The visual display of memory that played was as though I'd fallen into a storyteller's dream.

The woman's silky, caramel-colored hair spilled across the ivory pillows. The man leaned close, watching her, wanting her.

"You are a such a beauty in any light," he said.

Her mouth curved into a gentle smile and her hand slipped across his neck and into his hair to bring him to her. "It's you that makes me so."

He pressed his lips against hers, holding every sensation between them with the aim to etch her into his memory to return to at his leisure. His fingers glided to her shoulder and slipped under the delicate white fabric, easing it over the curve and pulling farther still until she was naked beneath him. As he peeled his own clothing away, she pulled a knee slightly upward, hiding what he sought and revealing a lean, sexy curved hip. He lay beside her and smoothed a hand along her side, gently guiding her leg down as he moved over her. His lips grazed her ear. The heat of his breath sent a stream of tingles racing along her side. She gasped. He felt her body stiffen and relax in response to his touch. He halted his approach, enveloped in the feel of his effect on her, and locked his gaze with hers.

"My love," she whispered. "Forever." With that, he eased into her, swallowed her moans with his mouth, as he learned every movement of her body and what it desired from him.

For him, her touch was a spark, lighting a fire in his core and turning it into an uncontrollable blaze that burned every inch of him. It was a heat he would keep only for her, to use for her desires, their pleasure.

His every movement soft and strong. With the glide of his hand and the gentle urge to investigate the places that would lead to her undoing, at his pace and under his command, she knew she wouldn't last long. The contrast of him, his sensitivity and eagerness to consume, collided with her yearning to feed his passion. The intensity was too much to deny.

As she rose to a sweet climax he built with every stroke of his tongue over hers and every thrust, he slowed his rhythm, never stopping, and watched the passion crossing over her face.

"Open your eyes, love," he said. With breathless gasps, she did. "I want to remember you like this for eternity." Her eyes glazed, and he felt himself rising to meet her at that highest peak. Behind his loving gaze and past the fire, she saw the soul she'd bonded with long ago.

Kevin's touch brought me back from the vision as his hands slid from my temples to cup my jaw.

"I remember," I said. "I remember those feelings. They were… more than beautiful." My eyes searched his. "With all that you know, the memories, the feelings between us that you carry, can you pull away from me now?"

"God knows I don't want to," he said. His eyes reflected the truth of his words and the pain of his indecision. "I always thought it a curse that the Soltari hid those memories from you when you chose this life, this mission. I didn't believe you would agree to them doing so. But I understand now, the strength you need. Having the memories of us that I do would make you weaker by blinding you with emotion and making you vulnerable to Tarsamon."

"I don't know that they will. Tarsamon used them already, my feelings for you. He or C-05, it's still a blur, pretended to be you so that I would be mistaken and give up the key. They wouldn't try again because the attempt to trick me didn't work."

"Perhaps." His eyes shifted downward in reflection and returned to mine. "I would never take from you something so—"

"I know," I interrupted. Even in a mild state of incoherence with C-05 and Tarsamon weaving deception, Kevin would never want the key to hold, and not because Mac had said as much. Kevin understood the immense responsibility I carried was mine alone. "Tell me, do you think I haven't bonded with you in this world?"

"Have you?"

"Of course I have." I paused and shifted closer to him, our thighs touching. "I may not have the memories of the many pasts that we've shared, but I sense the strong connection that has lived as long. And I know the Alliance chose you for your strength, knowing you would protect me at all costs."

He pulled me close to him, pressing a palm to the back of my head, and held me. "And I will," he whispered into my hair. "I only need to know you are there at the end of it all. That is why I chose to follow you into this world and be part of the mission to save humanity with you."

I pulled back to meet his eyes and saw into the depths of his soul, realizing his true fear. "You have always had me, lifetimes over. Why would you not in this one or the next?" I paused, watching his expression in a gaze that locked with mine. "I won't leave you. You are my love. If you need to pull away to do what you must, know that I understand the reason. But I will be there for you at the end of this mission and any other."

His eyes searched mine before he dipped his head and closed his lips around mine in a slow, deep kiss. I opened my eyes as he eased back and glanced above my head.

"What?" I said, turning in the direction of his stare. A bright blurred image was approaching from beyond the trees. As the figure came into full view, Kevin wrapped an arm around my waist and pulled me against him.

"Seria," he said.

Her white hair glowed against the backdrop of night with blue eyes that beamed as clear as a starlit evening. She dismounted from a white horse that appeared as though painted by brush strokes that had leaped off a canvas.

"You will need to leave come morning," she said to Kevin. "The dark forces are developing their plan to regain what they have lost," she said, glancing at me. I felt Kevin stiffen beside me.

"Sara, come with me." Seria held out a hand for me to take. "We must heal you from the fever that is overcoming you."

"I... No. Not now." I didn't want to leave my comfortable place against Kevin's strong frame. Despite my feet remaining planted like roots into the ground, I placed my hand in Seria's, betraying the words.

In addition to being experienced in developing precision weaponry and experts in the elements of battle, the elves were masterful healers. I hadn't felt the heat of the fever since I'd arrived in Ardan. And clearly, whoever watched over me while I lay asleep in Mac's home was doing a fine job of it, as I remembered the elf that had been tending to the IV behind me when I first woke and the same one I had pulled.

"I'm sure it's nothing a course of antibiotics can't cure," I said.

"Not this time. This is no ordinary infection you are battling, but a harmful element implanted by the evil you escaped under Tarsamon. Too much time was spent in the dark realm. Quickly, we must hurry."

Seria grasped my elbow in the crook of her arm, turned toward the horse, and we climbed into the saddle. "Leave upon sunrise. She'll be taken care of and returned by the elves."

"Seria," Kevin said. She shook her head slowly.

She clutched the reins with one hand and opened the palm of her other. In it she held a fine white dust that sparkled a million tiny lights. I watched as she turned her hand over and the fine powder fell like a ghostly shadow toward the ground. My eyes locked with Kevin's.

"I love you," I mouthed, as a blinding light consumed us and spread across the forest floor, illuminating the dead foliage and brush in shades of silver and white.

The wind began to whip past us as we rode faster and faster, pulling my hair and all that had been still into a blur. It was as though I was rushing at top speed through a winter wonderland toward some forbidden place and leaving behind a wilderness blanketed in snow. My heart raced and my breath quickened as massive trees blew past us at an alarming rate. I slammed my eyes shut at the rush of white and gray-green. The bite of icy wind remained a stinging kiss at my cheeks and eyelids. The air grew colder, penetrating the layers of clothing and causing me to shiver. As my body trembled more violently with each moment, the quick pace at which we were traveling slowed, and with it, so did my heartbeat, until all was silenced and once again peaceful in a beautiful light. The place was unfamiliar but that didn't matter. Only one thought played over again in my mind—*I told him I loved him.* At last, he could be certain.

And look for the next installment of the Three Keys Series...
Dana Alexander's
Flight Of The Feathered Serpent

1

T he top of my head slammed into the wall of the ship, jolting
me awake. The wooden bed I was lying on creaked in defiance at the sudden halt in movement. Rubbing the spot that
took the hardest blow, I glanced to the ornate carvings on the ceiling
and lowered my gaze to the only porthole. The same intricate detail
encircled the window. The colors of the sky were a brush stroke of
gray and pale orange. *Land.* We'd arrived on the Yucatan Peninsula.

I rose from my semi-comfortable nest, straightened my clothing,
and strapped my sword in place. Shouts of orders being given, followed by the sounds of running footsteps, fell below deck. A slight
tingling sensation warmed at my left shoulder and ran the length of
my arm.

"I feel you," I whispered, angling my head to the side. "Will you
show yourself?" I reached a hand toward the man I'd come to know as
Cerys but felt nothing as my fingers penetrated his image. The dream
I'd awoken from so abruptly was one with detail of my bonding to the
spirit in front of me. "Are you responsible for that vision of us?"

"Not this time. Your dreams are memories of other experiences,
other places you have been. I wanted to be here when it was returned
to you."

"How could you be sure it would?"

"Having a direct connection with the entity guiding your course,
I'm privy to information released to you."

My gaze floated around the tiny quarters in search of my boots.

I was still getting accustomed to the recent knowledge that Cerys had all the information required to guide Kevin, the human form of his spirit and my love. For each human, there existed a higher level of being to guide them. The closest science had to proving such a theory was that of a parallel universe. It would take more years than I had on Earth to see the formula connecting spirits to the human experience come to light. While Cerys aided Kevin, I had yet to encounter my equal or even the memory of her. The only information I had was that her name, Arwyn, also belonged to me in realms far from Earth.

My memories had been withheld by the Alliance, a governing order that handed down the direction of the Soltari—an entity that set the rule of law for creation and its progression in the realms. They did this by voting on certain factors pertaining to the immortals and their ability to complete a mission. The Alliance believed my memories would give rise to emotions that might interfere with recovering the keys, risking the future of the humans who had opened the path for Tarsamon's consuming shadows. Kevin was sworn to secrecy to be able to join me in this life. The problem was the emotional connection existed, anyway, between Cerys, Kevin, and myself without any history to anchor it to.

I glanced up at Cerys. "I don't agree with the Alliance's decision. I fought for them to give me those memories, our history together." A seed of resentment had been planted when I'd learned it had been a vote that would alter my life. I wanted more than anything to understand the deep connection I shared with a man I'd only known a few short months. All I had were flash images revealing a life from long ago, and the need to know felt like a relentless itch I couldn't scratch.

"They've seen the clarity in your argument to not deny you, us, of what was shared."

I nodded. *Maybe.*

"And you've proven your ability by obtaining the first key."

"I hope you're right."

ABOUT THE AUTHOR

Dana Alexander is a summa cum laude graduate of Arizona State University who spent her career in Medicare policy, education and audit before being compelled to write the story of two souls connected across countless millennia and held together by their duty to the Alliance. When she isn't creating scenes, dialogue, and realms for the series, her time is spent with family keeping cool in the ridiculously hot desert with their two huge, swim loving Labs, Ryley and Brodie.

Connect with Dana at her website:
www.danaalexander.net